D1128487

DEATH RIDES A PONY

Also by Carol Miller

Moonshine mysteries

MURDER AND MOONSHINE
A NIP OF MURDER
AN OLD-FASHIONED MURDER

The Fortune Telling mysteries

THE FOOL DIES LAST *

* *available from Severn House*

DEATH RIDES A PONY

Carol Miller

EMMA S. CLARK MEMORIAL LIBRARY
Setauket, L.I., New York 11733

SEVERN
HOUSE

First world edition published in Great Britain and the USA in 2022
by Severn House, an imprint of Canongate Books Ltd,
14 High Street, Edinburgh EH1 1TE.

Trade paperback edition first published in Great Britain and the USA in 2023
by Severn House, an imprint of Canongate Books Ltd.

severnhouse.com

Copyright © Carol Miller, 2022

All rights reserved including the right of
reproduction in whole or in part in any form.
The right of Carol Miller to be identified
as the author of this work has been asserted
in accordance with the Copyright,
Designs & Patents Act 1988.

British Library Cataloguing-in-Publication Data
A CIP catalogue record for this title is available from the British Library.

ISBN-13: 978-0-7278-5095-9 (cased)
ISBN-13: 978-1-4483-0819-4 (trade paper)
ISBN-13: 978-1-4483-0818-7 (e-book)

This is a work of fiction. Names, characters, places and incidents
are either the product of the author's imagination or are used fictitiously.
Except where actual historical events and characters are being described
for the storyline of this novel, all situations in this publication are
fictitious and any resemblance to actual persons, living or dead,
business establishments, events or locales is purely coincidental.

All Severn House titles are printed on acid-free paper.

Typeset by Palimpsest Book Production Ltd.,
Falkirk, Stirlingshire, Scotland.
Printed and bound in Great Britain by
TJ Books, Padstow, Cornwall.

For my sister Susanne

ACKNOWLEDGMENTS

I am grateful to the wonderful team at Severn House: Joanne Grant, Martin Brown, Jem Butcher, Katherine Laidler, Sara Porter, and Carl Smith.

I am also grateful to my marvelous agent Kari Stuart at ICM, along with Tia Ikemoto and Jenny Simpson.

And as always, I am grateful to my dearest family and friends. Thank you.

ONE

'No,' Hope Bailey said. 'Absolutely not.'

'Not the slightest chance,' concurred her sister, Summer. 'No possibility whatsoever.'

'But, my dears,' Olivia, their maternal grandmother, reminded them, 'the festival is for charity.'

'We are aware of that, Gram.' Summer drew a wide-mouthed mason jar from the long row of tins, crocks, and pots that held her precious collection of dried flowers, herbs, and teas along the back wall of Bailey's Boutique, the little mystic shop owned by the two sisters in Asheville, North Carolina. 'Hope and I have been participating in the event the second weekend in August for the past twenty years.'

'Twenty years?' Hope glanced up from the box of brightly patterned silk scarves that she was unpacking. 'Has it been that long?'

'Just about.' Summer unscrewed the lid of the jar and carefully measured out a quantity of a pale herb that had the appearance of shredded sawdust. 'I was twelve, which would have made you eleven. I remember being terribly excited about starting the seventh grade that September, although for the life of me I can't tell you why I thought the seventh grade would be such a thrill. Anyway, that first year we helped out at the festival by filling red-striped paper cones with popcorn.'

'You're right.' Hope smiled at the memory. 'Except I'm not sure that what we did could really be considered *helping out*. As I recall, we stuffed twice as much popcorn into our mouths as we did into those cones.'

'Lord, yes!' Summer laughed, then added a moan. 'I had a stomachache for a week afterward.'

'Me, too. And as I further recall, the next year we were *not* invited back to the popcorn stand – or any other food booth, either.'

Summer laughed harder, almost spilling the sawdust-looking herb as she poured it into a small brown paper bag that already contained several other herbs. 'Instead, we were asked to sit in the information tent and hand out stacks of tourist brochures and walking maps of the historic district. A wise decision on the part of the festival organizers, I must admit. After all, what good is a charity event if your volunteers eat all the profits?' She folded the top of the bag closed and shook it gently to blend the contents. 'Speaking of eating, how is Morris's appetite of late, Gram?'

The question seemed to catch Gram by surprise. Up until that point, she had been tapping the tip of her cane against the leg of her chair with evident impatience at the direction of the conversation, but at the mention of her long-time gentleman friend, she halted the motion. 'Morris's appetite? It couldn't be better. We went out to dinner with the Palmers yesterday evening – to that new restaurant in the square, the Green Goat – and Morris cleared his plate. Don't stand in the way of the man and a fried oyster, I tell you.'

'I'm glad to hear it.' Summer walked over to Gram and set down the paper bag on the table in front of her. 'Here is a fresh batch of Morris's tea. He should prepare it the same way as previously. But remind him that it shouldn't be allowed to steep for longer than fifteen minutes, and he must limit himself to two servings a day. Although the willow bark may be excellent in helping to alleviate the residual back spasms following his surgery, Morris has been using it for quite a few weeks now, and, over time, it has the potential to irritate his digestive tract. As wonderful as herbal remedies can be, they shouldn't be overused any more than conventional pharmaceuticals.'

'Very true,' Gram agreed, this time tapping her cane against the leg of her chair in agreement. Her left hip had been giving her trouble for the past several years, and she always had the cane with her, but she tended to use it more as a stage prop than for actual support. 'Amelia Palmer was talking about that just last night. Too much of some medications can make them less effective. She's been having the most awful headaches, and the more painkillers she takes, the more she seems to need. She thinks it's from all the stress surrounding the sale.

You know that she and Stanley have been trying to sell their house, and they've had considerable problems with . . .'

Hope saw her sister stiffen. Summer's shoulders tensed, and she gripped the edge of the table with white knuckles. The sale of a house – or, more accurately, the attempted sale of a house – was an infuriating subject for her. After catching her husband (aka Shifty Gary) having an affair earlier that year, Summer had promptly filed for a divorce. Sinking to even lower depths, Shifty Gary had responded by both fighting the separation and making the ensuing division of assets as difficult as possible. After countless arguments and increasing legal threats, he had finally agreed – on the condition that he have the exclusive right to choose the real estate agent for the listing – to put their house in the Asheville suburbs on the market. Except then he did everything in his power to keep the house from actually selling. While Summer moved back downtown to the old three-story brownstone in which she and Hope had been raised and in which the boutique was located on the ground floor, Shifty Gary remained in the marital abode, turning it into a party palace filled with the proverbial wine, women, and song. The resultant chaos and heaps of trash made it impossible to show the property to any reasonable prospective purchasers.

In the beginning, Summer had done her best to be patient, figuring that her soon-to-be ex's behavior was the equivalent of screaming for attention and throwing a temper tantrum like a petulant toddler. She tried sweetness and gentle cajolery, which Shifty Gary only interpreted as an attempt at reconciliation. Firmly rebuffing that possibility, Summer turned to a more practical argument: money. Wine, women, and song might be fun for a while, but, at the same time, the outstanding mortgage and property taxes weren't being paid. Shifty Gary's reply was that he didn't care. He had no intention of shelling out an unnecessary dime, and he was going to stay in the house until somebody with the requisite authority threw him out. So Summer was forced to proceed with even more legal threats and a painful, protracted court battle, which promised relief in the long term but helped her not one whit in the interim. Without the sale of the house, the divorce couldn't be finalized, leaving her miserably married, with ever-increasing attorney's bills and a multiplying mountain of debt.

'The Palmers have a terrible real estate agent,' Gram informed them. 'Of dubious ethics, apparently. Stanley thinks the man is deliberately holding back legitimate offers, hoping to weary them into eventually accepting some lowball proposal from one of his friends or associates. Amelia calls him a slippery fish.'

At the reference to slippery-fish real estate agents, Summer's grip on the table tightened further, the skin stretching so tautly across her knuckles that it looked ready to split. Hope knew that Shifty Gary's agent of choice was also of questionable repute, and she was about to interrupt Gram to change the topic before Summer damaged either a hand or the table, but Gram ended up deftly switching subjects herself.

'With her horrible headaches and all the trouble with the sale of their house, poor Amelia could really use some good news right now,' Gram said. 'So when she told me what she and the other festival organizers had discussed – regarding your booth at the event this year – I simply didn't have the heart to decline. Amelia thinks that it's a wonderful idea. The whole festival committee thinks that it's a wonderful idea—'

This time, Hope didn't hesitate to interrupt. 'And the answer is the same as it was a few minutes ago. No. Absolutely not.'

'Not the slightest chance,' Summer echoed, releasing her grip on the table to fold her arms across her chest.

Undeterred, Gram continued, 'The booth would raise a good deal of money, my dears. The committee is sure of it. I'm sure of it also. When the two of you did that marvelous presentation in the main tent last year – explaining the meanings and showing examples of the different types of semi-precious stones and crystals – it was tremendously popular. All the ladies talked about it for months afterward. This would be even better, because instead of having just one large group with the attendance limited to the number of chairs that can be squeezed inside the tent, there would be individual readings in your own booth. Just think how many more tickets could be sold. It's a fantastic opportunity!'

'Yes, indeed,' Hope replied dryly. 'A fantastic opportunity to offend the spiritual world.'

Gram clucked her tongue. 'I'm not suggesting that. I'm not suggesting anything of the kind. No one would expect your readings at the festival to be genuine or serious as they are here at the boutique. These would be intended solely for entertainment purposes.'

'That sounds like some sort of disclaimer Summer's lawyer would make.'

'While he's charging me for an extra hour of his time to say it,' Summer groused. 'Not that there is anything remotely entertaining about my divorce from Gary.' Arms still folded, she turned to Gram. 'And there is nothing entertaining about the committee's idea, either. Wanting Hope and me to dress up like a pair of medieval soothsayers in sequined gypsy costumes and pretend to use a crystal ball is absurd. Plus, it's insulting to gypsies.'

Hope shook her head. 'No true gypsy would be insulted. They'd be laughing too hard.'

'You're probably right about that,' Summer agreed. 'In any case, we are *not* swaddling ourselves in giant velvet robes in a sweltering booth in the middle of August. It doesn't matter how many tickets we've sold for charity if we keel over dead due to dehydration and heat exhaustion.'

Gram clucked her tongue again. 'So don't wear the robes. Nobody said velvet was mandatory. It was merely a suggestion to set the tone. Why don't you drape one of those lovely scarves that Hope is unpacking over your shoulders instead? That would be just as nice – and with the silk, much cooler. Some pretty gold bangles would be effective, too. The point is to create a mood. That's what I mean by entertainment. That's why people will buy a ticket for a reading with you. They know it's an act, and that is exactly what they want. Dark curtains and flickering candles and a spooky atmosphere. Hope moving her hands ethereally over a swirling crystal ball . . .'

Summer gave a little snort. 'Where does the committee propose that we get this crystal ball? We certainly don't have junk like that here.'

Gram ignored the remark. '. . . as she appears to magically see all the pleasant things that are destined to occur in a person's future.'

Hope and Summer exchanged a glance.

'Between the two of you,' Gram went on briskly, sensing a slight wavering on the part of her granddaughters, 'you'll probably know at least half of the people who come into the booth, so you'll easily know what to say that's applicable to them. An imminent engagement perhaps, or a possible promotion at work, or maybe an unexpected windfall—'

There was another snort from Summer. 'And the other half of the people? The ones we don't know and who aren't fated to strike it rich. What do you want Hope to tell them?'

'Oh, good gracious! Hope has been reading palms and working with the Tarot for enough years that she can surely gauge a stranger with sufficient quickness and accuracy to offer some general cheerful remark. Just give them a sign of positive things to come.'

'Forget about what some stranger at the festival wants to hear,' Summer grumbled. '*I* could use a sign of positive things to come.'

Hope gave her sister a sympathetic look, then she addressed Gram. 'The issue isn't what to say to people. I can always come up with something light and optimistic, especially at an event such as this where folks are mostly just interested in having fun. What I don't understand is the abrupt about-face from you. You have *never* encouraged me to give trivial readings before or do anything remotely resembling divination at the festival. Last year, it was the semi-precious stones and crystals. The year before that, we gave a presentation on herbs. And this year, we were slated to take tickets at the carousel. Summer and I have never even had our own booth. So why the sudden change – two days before the event is scheduled to begin, I might add – to this crystal-ball baloney?'

A pair of pink spots appeared on Gram's cheeks. 'I've already explained. The booth would raise a good deal of money. And it's an extremely worthwhile charity that the committee has selected as beneficiary.'

'Wait a minute,' Summer interjected. 'It just occurred to me. Isn't Morris on the festival committee?'

The pink spots grew larger. 'Well – now that you mention

it – yes. Morris and Amelia are co-chairs of the committee this year.'

Hope and Summer exchanged another glance, and this time they added a smile. It was no secret that Morris Henshaw – earnest, soft-spoken, and aged sixty-nine – was sweet on Gram. It was also no secret that Gram – full of pep and vinegar and aged seventy-four – was equally sweet on him.

'So that's what this whole thing is about?' Hope asked, restraining a laugh. 'The reason you want us to have the booth is to help Morris?'

'Well, yes,' Gram admitted once more, the pink darkening to a deep rosy hue. 'I would like Morris to do well. He's worked so hard organizing everything – even with all of his back problems – and it would be nice if the festival turned out to be extra successful this year.'

Hope's smile grew. 'Then of course we'll do the booth, Gram. But instead of beating about the bush, you should have just come clean from the outset. You know that Summer and I are both very fond of Morris, and we'll do our best to get lots of people to buy tickets.'

'But no sequins!' Summer insisted. 'I hate sequins.'

'No sequins,' Gram agreed. She tapped her cane on the floor excitedly. 'Oh, this is splendid. Simply splendid. Morris will be so pleased. And Amelia also. As I told you before, she could really use some good news right now.'

'I could really use some good news, too,' Summer echoed in a wistful tone. 'A sign of positive things to come.'

Her repetition of the words she had used only a minute or two earlier – and with increasing plaintiveness – was not lost on Hope. She turned to her sister. Summer's hazel eyes blinked at her with a winsome expression. This time, Hope didn't restrain her laugh.

'All right. I get the hint. You want me to draw a Tarot card.'

The plaintiveness instantly vanished, and Summer nodded eagerly.

'As long as you understand,' Hope was quick to caution her, 'that there is no guarantee the card will be a positive one.'

Summer shrugged. 'It doesn't matter.'

Hope didn't agree. She knew that it mattered plenty. But

she also knew that once Summer had made up her mind for a Tarot consultation, any further warnings or arguments would be a fruitless endeavor.

Still tapping her cane with excitement, Gram paid no attention to their Tarot discussion. 'Don't worry for one moment about the set-up of the booth, my dears. You won't have a bit of work. I'll take care of everything.' Gathering her handbag and rising from her chair, she began to muse aloud. 'Now, what will we need to create the proper atmosphere? The dark curtains, certainly. I'll speak to Jocelyn Frost about those. She's an absolute whizz with a needle and thread. And then the candles. Real candles might be a problem. Too much of a fire hazard, I'm afraid, especially with the curtains. We could use those flameless candles instead. Or maybe a couple of oil lanterns would look more attractive. Amelia would be a good person to consult on that point. She has an excellent eye for lighting and decor. The most important thing is the crystal ball, of course. I wonder if Morris . . .'

Gram continued chatting to herself as she headed toward the front door of the boutique, making lists and debating various options. Watching her depart, Hope couldn't help being both amused and impressed. Although she had some doubts about the number of tickets she and Summer would be able to sell for their booth, she had no doubt whatsoever that, thanks to Gram, the booth itself would look fabulous.

'Hope?' Summer prodded her, more interested in the Tarot than the upcoming festival. 'The card?'

Hope rose from the partially unpacked box of silk scarves on the floor and walked over to the table that had been vacated by Gram. It was an aged, coffee-brown pine table set in the corner of the boutique near the large row of windows that faced the street, providing plenty of natural light for Hope's palm and Tarot readings. She seated herself on one of the simple, straight-backed chairs that matched the table and motioned for her sister to take a seat also, which Summer promptly did.

'What question would you like to have answered?' Hope asked, opening the small drawer on her side of the table and removing her well-worn deck of Tarot cards from their protective cocoon.

'The house. Whether the house will ever sell? Will I finally be free of it – and free of Gary?'

'Just the house,' Hope interjected. 'Don't think about Gary. He'll cloud the picture. Take a deep breath, clear your mind, and concentrate only on the house.'

Summer nodded. 'Only the house.' As instructed, she took a breath, closed her eyes, and attempted to focus her thoughts.

Hope began to shuffle the deck. Her fingers moved slowly, hesitantly. She didn't have a good feeling about the reading, and she wasn't sure why. Drawing a single card from the Tarot was usually harmless. A card could be interpreted in many different ways.

She stopped shuffling and placed the deck on the table. 'When you're ready, Summer, go ahead and cut the deck.'

Unless she was well acquainted with a person, Hope never let them touch her cards. It was simply too dangerous. She didn't know what kind of energy might be transferred from the person to the deck, rearing its ugly head later. But with her sister, that wasn't a concern.

There was another deep breath from Summer, then she opened her eyes, stretched out a slightly shaky hand, and cut the deck. Hope turned over the top card. She winced when she saw it. Her instinct hadn't been wrong. It was not a positive card. Even with extreme interpretative contortions, it was nigh impossible to read the Five of Coins as anything but negative.

'My god,' Summer whispered, staring at the card before her. 'It can't get much worse than that.'

The Five of Coins depicted a destitute woman in rags and a bandaged man on crutches struggling through a snowstorm in the dark of night, passing by a towering stone structure with warmth and light radiating inside. No one came out to greet them and offer assistance. No door opened to provide sustenance and shelter. They were poor and ill and alone.

Summer dropped her head into her hands and groaned. 'I'm going to be homeless. That's what this means. The house will never sell, and I'll end up on the streets.'

'You won't end up on the streets,' Hope corrected her. 'And you aren't going to be homeless. You can always live here – in the brownstone – with me and Gram, although these days Gram spends most of her time at Morris's. In any event, Gram owns this building. She certainly isn't going to evict you.'

'It still means that the house won't sell,' Summer replied morosely. 'And then I'll be crushed under an avalanche of debt, get seriously ill, and be stuck with Gary forever. Oh, he'd love that. He'd think that was absolutely fantastic.'

Hope didn't respond. She sat in silence, pondering the card.

'There is no other interpretation,' Summer went on, her voice rising with the beginnings of hysteria. 'I can see it in your face. It's bad. Very, very bad.'

'It's true the card isn't a happy one,' Hope admitted. 'There's no sugar-coating that fact. The Five of Coins indicates loss and despair. But I think, in this case, there's more to it. Something about it doesn't feel right to me, as though it's pointing in another direction. We should draw a second card to help explain—'

Just as Hope reached out her hand to turn over the next card in the deck, the front door of the boutique flew open, and a gust of hot, dusty wind shot through the shop. It tossed up the loose scarves from the box on the floor and swirled the stack of empty paper bags on the herb-and-tea counter. The squall seized the card from Hope's outstretched fingers, and it soared up into the air like a fluttering bird. When it came tumbling back down to the table, the card landed face up next to the Five of Coins.

Summer gasped. It was Death.

TWO

Death was a skeleton on a pale horse at sunset.

Hope instantly snatched the card and the Five of Coins from the table. Reuniting them with the rest of the deck, she pulled the drawer in front of her open as quickly as she could and thrust everything into it. Along with the gust of wind, two people were entering the boutique. Death was far too serious and contentious a card to be left in view.

'Hurry up and come inside,' a man said to a woman. 'You're letting out all the air conditioning.'

At the voice, Summer's horrified gaze moved from the spot on the table where Death had lain only a moment earlier to the door. She gasped once more.

Her reaction startled Hope, and she looked hastily at the man. She didn't recognize him. He was in his late forties or early fifties, and he had the shape of a flaccid pickle. He didn't stand quite straight, and all of his appendages seemed limp somehow. His black hair was slicked back from his protruding forehead with a shiny pomade. His equally protruding eyes had an incongruously sharp expression.

'It's a sign,' Summer whimpered despondently. 'A terrible, terrible sign. First the cards. Now *him*.'

Hope frowned, not understanding the connection. Who was the man?

'I'm moving as fast as I can,' the woman answered him. 'The lead is tangled around my sandal and caught in the door jamb.'

It was Hope's turn to recognize a voice, and this one unequivocally belonged to Rosemarie Potter. Rosemarie was one of Hope's most loyal clients, visiting the boutique two or three times a week without fail. She was a gregarious woman in her mid-fifties who – although divorced twice already – was an incurable romantic eternally in search of her human soulmate.

Her canine soulmate was her beloved pug, Percy, an inveterate companion for all of Rosemarie's adventures.

As if on cue, there was a sharp yip.

'Oh, he's stuck. Percy's stuck!' Rosemarie wailed. 'You must help him. Help him, Davis!'

Summer gave a woeful sigh.

Hope's frown deepened. Davis? The name seemed familiar to her, but she couldn't quite place it. She opened the drawer in the table again, this time not for the deck of Tarot cards but to retrieve the bag of doggie cookies that was also stashed inside.

'Wait. Hold on. Stop tugging,' Davis instructed either Rosemarie or Percy – or possibly both of them. He leaned down out of view, presumably to detangle the difficulty with the sandal and the door jamb.

When Davis reappeared, Rosemarie appeared with him, smiling widely and bobbing her blazing red-dyed mop animatedly. 'Thank you, Davis.' She gave him a smacking kiss. 'You've saved the day. Say thank you to Davis, Percy.'

Percy responded with a grunt. It didn't sound particularly appreciative. Nor did he look appreciative. There were no happy wags in Davis's direction, let alone smacking kisses. But Percy also didn't look traumatized by the incident. He gave an exploratory sniff, promptly recognized his surroundings, and turned an expectant eye toward Hope.

'Hello, Rosemarie. Hello, Percy,' Hope greeted them cheerfully. She reached into her bag to get a cookie for Percy, who was already approaching her in eager anticipation.

'No.' Davis took possession of the lead from Rosemarie and pulled back the pug unceremoniously. 'No treat for you, old man. That's how you've been putting on so much weight.'

Hope laughed. 'That's not true, is it, Percy? You might be a bit stout around the middle, but certainly not too stout for a cookie.'

Again, she was about to offer him the treat, but Davis held Percy firm.

'No,' he repeated, now directing the command at Hope.

She bristled at his tone, one which seemed to imply that she was also on a lead and could be ordered about. Based on the smacking kiss and the imperious manner in which he had put himself in charge of Percy, Davis was evidently Rosemarie's newest beau. From her first impressions of the man, Hope couldn't congratulate Rosemarie on her fine choice.

'He's too heavy for his size,' Davis went on. 'The old man needs toning and tightening – and a restricted diet.'

Hope almost laughed once more, this time at the irony. With his spongy figure and sagging posture, Davis was far from toned and tightened himself. As for Rosemarie, it was tricky to tell whether her weight ever fluctuated in either direction, because she had a penchant for billowy, flowered dresses, and today was no exception. She wore a wide, ankle-length wrap in a vivid indigo iris pattern.

'We've been trying to add a little more exercise to our daily routine,' Rosemarie explained, fanning herself with her hand. 'But it's so difficult in this stifling weather. Half a block – even at the most leisurely pace – and Percy and I are both panting like polar bears in the desert.'

'I'll get Percy some water,' Summer volunteered in a barely audible voice. She rose from her chair at the table and moved with swift steps toward the rear of the shop, her eyes steadfastly avoiding all contact with the group.

Hope's frown resurfaced. Summer was not a shy person, and she was ordinarily extremely affable with customers, particularly long-standing ones such as Rosemarie.

For her part, Rosemarie didn't seem to notice Summer's uncharacteristic reticence. Instead, she continued fanning herself and complaining to Hope about the weather. 'It's been terribly warm all week – all of August, so far – but today feels especially beastly. When Percy and I walked out of the house this morning, we might as well have marched straight into a blast furnace. But it's wonderfully cool in here.'

'The air-conditioning bill will be a nightmare,' Hope said, more to herself than to Rosemarie. Money was always tight at the boutique, and the skyrocketing temperatures over the past month had brought fewer tourists than usual to the city and the shop. Hope wondered if the booth at the festival would be of any help. Maybe she and Summer could get some new customers out of it.

Rosemarie nodded. 'The bill at my house is going to be astronomical, too . . . Oh, that's awfully kind of you, Summer. I'm sure Percy will be grateful.'

Summer had returned with the promised water, but instead of placing the bowl directly in front of Percy, she set it on the floor next to the table and Hope, forcing Davis to release some of the lead for Percy to reach it. As the pug came for his drink, Hope reached down to give him a pat and a soothing scratch under his harness, surreptitiously slipping him his long-awaited treat in the process.

Percy merrily crunched his cookie and lapped his water, and Hope glanced at Summer to give her a clandestine smile. Summer, however, kept her gaze glued to the ground. Her brow was furrowed, and her normally peaches-and-cream complexion had turned splotchy white.

'Did these just come in?' Rosemarie exclaimed, her attention shifting to the partially unpacked box of scarves that Percy's lead was rubbing against. She took one of the scarves from the stack and pressed it against her cheek. 'The silk is so soft. And the colors are gorgeous! That's the reason I enjoy shopping in person. It's much better to see things directly in front of you. I ordered a scarf from a catalog a few months ago, and it looked beautiful in the picture, but when it arrived, there wasn't the least resemblance. It was all washed out and faded.'

'We have the same problem here,' Hope commiserated. 'With photo-editing software, every company can make their products appear attractive digitally. Then you get the item in your hands, and it turns out to be junk. That's why when Summer and I find a quality source for the boutique, we stick with it. We've purchased from that manufacturer before.' She gestured toward the scarves. 'Their silk is soft *and* strong. It won't tear or snag as a lot of cheaper silks will after only a wearing or two. Although these scarves cost a bit more, they're worth it, because they'll last and look good not just this season but also the next and the next.'

Davis gave a dubious snort. 'It's pretty stupid of you to be hawking scarves in the summer season.'

Hope turned to him, taken aback. She had certainly dealt

with her share of difficult and discourteous customers over the years; even so, the rudeness of Davis's remark was unexpected. 'The scarves are new for autumn,' she responded defensively, 'which should be obvious from the fact they're still in the shipping box. And we don't *hawk* anything.'

Summer muttered something under her breath. Although Hope couldn't hear it, there was no doubt that it was not complimentary toward Davis.

Rosemarie giggled nervously. 'I think there's been a misunderstanding. These aren't winter scarves to bundle up in, Davis. They're year-round scarves. They're accessories, the same as a pair of earrings or a cute handbag.'

To demonstrate, she gave the scarf in her hand a deft twist and wrapped it decoratively around her neck. The rich gold tones in the silk balanced the indigo in her dress. Together, they did an excellent job of ameliorating the startling crimson of her hair.

'That looks lovely on you,' Hope complimented her.

Rosemarie inspected herself in the mirror next to the jewelry display case. 'It's nice, isn't it? I'll take it! And one for Percy, too, of course.' She bent down to search through the remaining scarves in the box.

There was another snort from Davis. 'That's ridiculous. Get the old man a cotton bandana, not an overpriced silk scarf.'

Although Rosemarie continued to work her way through the pile, Hope saw that there was now some crimson in her cheeks to match her hair. She was clearly embarrassed by Davis's behavior.

Hope made an effort to soothe the situation. 'While we're on the subject of scarves, Summer and I were thinking of wearing two of the new ones ourselves this weekend at the festival. Are you planning on going to the festival this year, Rosemarie?'

'Oh, yes! Percy and I always go. I like the hustle and bustle of the crowd, and he likes the smells and samples from the food booths.' She popped up holding a chevron-patterned scarf in classic black and white. 'Last year, we really enjoyed your talk on semi-precious stones. I have several quartzes at home, but I never understood the differences between them until you and Summer explained it all. I hope you're doing another talk this year. We'll be in the front row to listen, won't we, Percy? And Davis will be there with us. He's promised to escort us on Friday evening.'

Davis's mouth opened, and from his smirking expression, it wasn't difficult to guess that he was about to say something deprecating, either about Percy and food booths or talks on quartzes and semi-precious stones. Hope didn't give him the chance.

'Instead of a presentation,' she told Rosemarie, 'Summer and I were slated to take tickets at the carousel this year. But that changed earlier today. Now – for the first time – we're going to have our own booth.'

'Your own booth!' Rosemarie gave a cry of delight. 'Will there be palm readings? I love your palm readings!'

'Actually, I'm going to use a crystal ball.'

'A crystal ball!'

Hope found herself wincing slightly as she explained, 'The booth is intended to be more fun fortune telling than serious readings.'

Rosemarie nodded so vigorously that the gold scarf loosened and slid to her shoulder. 'How fun! Fortune telling!'

'For criminy sake,' Davis snapped. 'Stop parroting everything she says!'

There was a momentary silence. Unsure whether to respond to his outburst, Hope looked at Rosemarie. She blinked once or twice, straightened her scarf, and then let out another cry of delight, as if Davis hadn't spoken at all.

'This is so exciting! Is there a list? A waiting list to get into your booth?'

Her confidence that their booth would reach such tremendous heights of popularity made Hope smile. 'No. There isn't a waiting list. At this point, Summer and I are just keeping our fingers crossed that we manage to sell enough tickets to not embarrass ourselves. So if you run into anybody over the next day or two who you think might be interested, please tell them about the booth.'

Rosemarie nodded some more. 'I'll tell everyone I know! But only if you promise that I'll get my turn. I don't want to be stuck at the back of the line. When the list starts, you must put me at the top. And Davis, too!'

'You can't be serious.' Davis rolled his protruding eyes. 'You want me to have my fortune told?'

'But you'll love it! It's marvelous. Hope can see so much. She'll tell you all sorts of wonderful things.'

'I don't doubt it. A wonderful bunch of baloney.'

The man was obviously a skeptic – and an unpleasant one to boot. Under different circumstances, Hope might have replied more sharply, but she didn't want to hurt Rosemarie's feelings, so she kept her words light.

'It's meant to be fun,' she reiterated. 'And all the proceeds from the booth and the festival go to charity.'

Davis rolled his eyes a second time. Whether he intended to add any further derisive commentary wasn't clear, because Summer started muttering again. Although still not comprehensible, it was now loud enough for Davis to take notice of it. He turned toward her, and for the first time since entering the boutique, he seemed to really look at her.

'Hold on a minute,' he said. 'I've seen you somewhere before. Where do I know you from?'

There was a brief hesitation, then Summer's head snapped up. Her face was heavily flushed, but she met Davis's gaze straight on. 'You know me from Gary. Gary Fletcher is my husband, soon-to-be ex-husband. You're supposed to be selling our house.'

Both Hope and Rosemarie gave a little start.

'Davis is your realtor?' Rosemarie exclaimed.

'He is,' Summer confirmed crossly.

At last, Hope understood why the name had seemed familiar to her. Davis Scott. Shifty Gary's disreputable choice in real estate agents. A slippery fish just like Amelia and Stanley Palmer's realtor. Perhaps they were even one and the same. In any case, Summer's odd behavior now made complete sense. Davis coming into the boutique would have been agitating at the best of times, but his arrival just after she had drawn the Five of Coins in a Tarot reading – with all its implications of loss and despair and potential homelessness – was a miserable coincidence. Hopefully, it was no more than a coincidence.

'You're lucky, Summer,' Rosemarie went on, singing her beau's praises. 'Davis is a terrific realtor. He's got dozens of property listings.'

'A listing doesn't mean much,' Summer returned, 'if you don't actually sell the property. Or if you sell it for less than its true value to some buddy of yours so that you don't have to split the commission.'

Rosemarie's cheery expression clouded. Summer's words seemed to confuse her. They did not, however, confuse Davis. He shot Summer a vicious look.

'Don't offer opinions on things that you have no clue about. Let the professionals handle their business without interference from amateurs. Just stick to what you know.' He gave a desultory wave around the boutique. 'Your scarves and crystals and whatnot.'

Hope's gaze narrowed. Summer was on the verge of a biting retort, but Davis continued before she could get out more than a syllable.

'This place is the perfect example of what I mean.' He gave another desultory wave. 'If you knew even the slightest bit about real estate, you wouldn't be running some ludicrous little shop out of this old brownstone. You'd sell the building – lock, stock, and barrel – and make a killing.'

There was a rumble. It sounded like a train off in the distance, only instead of coming from the left or the right, it was emanating from directly above them. It grew louder and increasingly thunderous until it became an almost deafening roar. The ceiling started to shake, followed by the walls, and finally the floor. The whole brownstone was creaking and groaning. It shuddered so violently that the tea and herb containers tumbled from the shelves and the bottles of tinctures rattled in the drawers. A minute later, as abruptly as it had begun, it all stopped. Nothing moved. Stillness prevailed.

Hope was the first to react. 'Is everyone OK?'

Her hazel eyes stretched wide, Summer nodded.

Rosemarie checked each of her limbs to make sure that they were all still attached. Then she gave a sudden shout. 'Percy!'

In unison, the group whirled toward the pug. He was fine. After his cookie and his drink, Percy had curled up against one of the table legs for a contented snooze. The ruckus hadn't caused him to budge an inch.

Exhaling with relief, Rosemarie asked, 'What in heaven's name was that?'

'An earthquake,' Davis answered.

'That was no earthquake,' Summer informed him.

'Of course it was,' he rejoined. 'What else could it possibly have been?'

Hope's mind searched hurriedly for a reasonable explanation. 'Next door,' she said. 'They're working on the brownstone next door. It has foundation issues. They must have been drilling, or digging, or something similar.'

It was close enough to the truth. The neighbors were experiencing water seepage in their cellar; for the last week, a contractor and his crew had been on the premises trying to remedy the problem. Except Hope was painfully aware that what she and the others had just experienced in the boutique had no connection whatsoever to the brownstone next door.

'Earthquake,' Davis repeated with conviction.

The sisters exchanged a look. It hadn't been an earthquake – or, for that matter, any other natural phenomenon. It had been the attic. The attic didn't like Davis Scott.

THREE

As it had been every year since its inception, the festival was located in the large city park just off the square. Even though the event didn't officially open to the public for another hour, the grounds were thronged with people, the majority of whom were frantically trying to finish the necessary preparations. Extra nails were being hammered into plywood supports. Folding chairs were being carried from carts into tents. Mammoth coolers of water and mountains of paper cups were being assembled in every spare corner in an effort to cool the oncoming masses. The soaring temperatures hadn't abated, and the heat was oppressive, the more so as the throbbing orange sun began its slow descent in the west.

Hope and Summer weaved their way through the bedlam, heading in the direction of their assigned booth. Occasionally, an acquaintance would shout a greeting, and they responded with a distracted wave. The crowd was too thick and they were too engrossed in their conversation to do much more.

'We must – absolutely *must* – keep Davis away from the brownstone,' Summer said fervently.

'I agree, but what are we supposed to do if Rosemarie decides to drag him along on her next visit?' Hope considered a moment. 'No, I doubt that Rosemarie will bring him to the boutique again. She was too embarrassed the last time. When she purchased that pair of scarves for her and Percy, and Davis made those unkind remarks about people wasting perfectly good money on useless trinkets for their pets, she turned about as purple as an eggplant. And there's no chance that Davis – as dismissive of the shop as he was – would come of his own volition.'

'Yes, he would! Not for a reading or a tincture, of course, but for the building itself. I'd wager that Davis has spent the last two days practicing his slippery-fish salesman routine so that he can try to convince us to put the building up for sale.'

Hope swerved around a woman hauling a humongous basket of scented soaps, each handsomely wrapped with a Scottish plaid ribbon.

'And it doesn't matter one jot,' Summer continued, 'that the brownstone technically belongs to Gram. In fact, if Davis learns that she's the legal owner, he might become even more aggressive with his salesmanship. He'll assume because of her age and her cane, Gram is some befuddled old lady whom he can smooth-talk into anything.'

'Then he will be in for a big surprise, because there is nothing befuddled about Gram.' Hope laughed. 'Imagine having Gram *and* the attic turn on you at the same time!'

Summer laughed, too, but it quickly faded. 'You shouldn't joke about that. Considering what happened the other day, if Davis comes near the boutique again, there could be a horrible repeat.'

'Not necessarily. The attic might feel that it has already made its point.'

This time, Summer's laugh was sarcastic. 'That's some wishful thinking. But then there's no question that the attic likes you a lot better than it does me.'

'The attic likes you fine. There are just a few hard feelings.'

'A few hard feelings?' Summer exclaimed. 'I can't go beyond the third-floor landing, and even that is pushing it depending on the hour and the day!'

'True,' Hope conceded. 'They're still holding a grudge, I'm afraid, from the time you suggested that selling the brownstone would be smarter and more cost-effective than having the ancient wiring fixed.'

'It wasn't *my* suggestion. It was *Gary's* suggestion.'

'True, again. But you were the one who unfortunately made the mistake of saying it aloud in the brownstone. And they got a little testy.'

'A little testy? They locked me in and wouldn't let me out, and very nearly scared me to death with their antics! And don't forget about what happened to the poor electrician who went up there after that to work on the wiring.'

'Lord, yes. The poor electrician.'

They paused, shared a sigh, and then went onward, dodging a wheelbarrow packed with pots of wilting geraniums.

'While we're on the subject of being scared to death—' Summer began after a minute.

'No, no, no,' Hope cut her off. 'We are not going to discuss it any further. We've reviewed and debated and analyzed it ad infinitum already. You are *not* going to be homeless. And you are *not* going to die. Not for many, many years, at least. Yes, the Death card is disturbing. Yes, the Death card can indicate actual, imminent death – but not usually. As I've already explained, there are several other cards in the Tarot that are more closely associated with physically dying and funerals and mourning. In most instances, Death means change. Big change. Often difficult change. And you *are* going through big, difficult changes. The separation from Gary, moving back to the brownstone, the divorce proceedings, the ongoing sale of your house—'

It was Summer's turn to cut her off. 'The Death card is numbered thirteen.'

'Well, yes, but that's because at the time the Tarot was created, people were genuinely, seriously superstitious. Black cats and cracked mirrors and the like. You've never worried about being on the thirteenth floor of a building or waking up on the thirteenth day of a month before.'

'Maybe not before, but perhaps I am now,' Summer returned stubbornly.

'Then you're being silly – and you know it.' Hope was thoughtful. 'I still believe that there's more to it, just as I said when the Five of Coins first came up. Something about it didn't feel right to me then, as though it was pointing in another direction. And I still feel the same way. If we could have drawn more cards at the time, we would have been able to get clarification, but that wasn't possible because Rosemarie and Davis came in.'

'So it's Davis's fault. Everything is Davis's fault. I wish the festival had one of those old-fashioned dunking booths that carnivals used to have years ago. The kind where people could throw a ball at a target, and if they hit it, the person sitting on a stool would fall into the tank of water below. I'd like to dunk Davis a couple of times. That would wipe the annoying smirk off his face.'

Hope laughed. 'Sadly, there is no dunking booth here. I'm not even sure if those are allowed anymore. They might be considered too dangerous these days. But you're right about Davis having an annoying smirk. Honestly, I don't know how Rosemarie ever got involved with him. She's so good-natured, and he clearly isn't.'

'She's *too* good-natured. That's the problem. Davis is taking advantage of her. Maybe he's trying to talk her into selling her house, too! In any case, the man is a slippery fish, and I hope that Rosemarie comes to her senses soon and dumps him at the curb. She'd be much better off on her own with just Percy—' Both the sentence and Summer's feet abruptly halted. 'Oh, Hope, look at that!'

The mass of people parted to one side, and the antique carousel rose in front of them like a gleaming edifice. It was majestically beautiful, with a fabulous assortment of animals. Giraffes, elephants, and tigers. Zebras, camels, and horses. Each one carved in exquisite detail and intricately painted in brilliant colors. There were more carvings along the base and on the cornice. Cherubs and celestial bodies, all luminously gilded.

'It's marvelous,' Hope said in wonder. 'As though you've stepped back in time.'

Summer nodded. 'There probably aren't many woodworkers with the talent and the training who can put together a piece of art like that anymore.'

As they stood admiring the carousel, its lights were turned on. The display was dazzling, and they gazed at it, mesmerized.

'Enchanting, isn't it? As you know, I'm about as far from a starry-eyed dreamer as they come, but even I have to admit that it's so lovely it takes one's breath away.'

The voice was unexpected, and the sisters turned in surprise to find Megan Steele standing beside them. Aside from Summer, Megan was Hope's closest friend. They had gone to school together and saw each other on a nearly daily basis. Megan was the Director of Activities at Amethyst, the luxury hotel and spa also located in the historic district of downtown Asheville, only a few blocks from the boutique.

'I would hug you, but as you can see' – Megan gestured toward her apparel – 'it's nearly impossible for me to move in this get-up, so an air kiss will have to suffice.'

A pair of air kisses followed, but neither Hope nor Summer could immediately respond. They were too startled by Megan's ensemble. She was dressed in a petal-pink, floor-length ball gown. The satin, sequined bodice was so tight that it might as well have been lacquered on to her skin. Although it showed Megan's excellent figure to great advantage, it also looked as though it might split in half if she were to twist one millimeter too far or inhale one oxygen molecule too many. Below the bodice were layers upon layers of crinkly tulle decorated with more sparkling sequins. An equally sparkling tiara decorated Megan's blond bob.

Summer wheezed with amusement. 'What on earth are you wearing? You look like a fairy godmother that popped out of a storybook.'

'I'm supposed to be a queen,' Megan corrected her.

'Good or evil?' Hope inquired.

Megan grinned.

As she had with Gram, Summer gave vent to her dislike of sequins. 'With all those hideous sequins, definitely an evil queen.'

'They are pretty hideous,' Megan agreed. 'So is the tulle. It's beyond uncomfortable. I can barely walk, and I can't sit down. And don't get me started on how horrifically hot I am. Sean and I have a bet as to which one of us will collapse and get hauled off to the medical tent first.'

'Sean?' Hope said. 'From the spa?'

'Yup. He's supposed to be the king to my queen. His costume is made of thick corduroy, and he has this enormous cape and crown. He has to stay seated, because it's too heavy for him to stand while wearing it. And you know that he gives massages for a living, so he's strong. Also, he's sweating buckets.'

'But why?' Summer demanded. 'Why a king and queen?'

'It's the not-so-genius plan of Amethyst's upper manage-ment,' Megan explained. 'They think the best way to advertise the hotel and spa is to send the message to potential guests that they'll be treated like royalty if they spend their money at the place. It's complete rot, of course. Nobody passing by the booth will have any idea why we're dressed in this preposterous manner, let alone book a suite of rooms or a bevy of spa treatments because of it. We were also supposed to hand out the little chocolates that housekeeping usually puts on the pillows during the nightly turndown service, but that's not happening now.'

'Did somebody forget to deliver the chocolates from the hotel to the booth?'

'No, the chocolates were delivered. But unsurprisingly in this heat, the whole lot liquefied in a matter of minutes. Sean is presently sitting between two giant glass bowls of sludgy brown goop interspersed with tiny tinfoil wrappers.'

Her deadpan description made Hope laugh.

'I'd laugh, too,' Megan told her. 'Except I can't. The bodice seams will burst, and then the queen's attire will no longer be considered family-friendly.'

'You're doing a good job keeping your sense of humor about it.'

Megan replied with a resigned shrug. 'I don't really have much choice. We're all required to take a shift during the festival. Thank heaven mine will be over and done with this evening. Then tomorrow, I can play around and hang out in your booth. At least you can wear normal clothing. I like the scarf idea, by the way. Using it to twist up your hair looks great and will help to keep your neck cooler. I've seen those velvet curtains in your booth. They aren't going to give you much airflow, I'm afraid.'

'We have velvet curtains?' Hope asked.

'Yes, dark burgundy ones. They're attractive and rather atmospheric, especially with the twinkle lights. Didn't you know? Haven't you been there?'

Hope shook her head. 'Gram organized everything – in only two days. Summer and I kept offering to help, but she was adamant about doing it herself.'

Megan smiled. 'That sounds like Olivia. She's the best organizer I've ever met. I think that she missed her calling and should have been a campaign manager. With the amazing way she can coordinate and plan, in her heyday she probably could have gotten one of the ladies in her bridge club elected to the Oval Office. When I was at the booth a little while ago looking for you, Olivia had an entire platoon under her command operating with well-oiled efficiency. Hanging the curtains, stringing the lights, adjusting the banner—'

'Banner?' Summer echoed. 'What kind of a banner?'

The smile broadened. 'A big banner. Stretched across the whole front of the booth, just above the entrance. With glittery silver lettering. *Madam Bailey, Fortune Teller*.'

Hope and Summer stared at her.

'You're joking, right?' Summer croaked after a moment. 'Please say that you're only joking.'

Megan was now grinning like the Cheshire cat. 'Nope, not joking.'

'But Gram wouldn't make a banner like that.' Hope frowned, puzzled. 'She'd never call us fortune tellers – and certainly not with glitter. She knows the spiritual world wouldn't approve.'

'Forget the spiritual world!' Summer wailed. 'What if Gary – or one of his pals – sees the banner? I have another court hearing for the divorce next week. *Madam Bailey* makes it sound as though we're running a brothel. What if Gary tells the judge?'

'Maybe the judge will want to visit the brothel,' Megan suggested drolly.

'That isn't the least bit funny,' Summer snapped, her face florid.

Megan's grin vanished, replaced by a chagrined look.

'Don't worry,' Hope told her sister soothingly. 'I doubt that Gary – or one of his pals – will see the banner. And even if they do, and Gary bellows it to all and sundry in the courtroom, no judge will seriously believe that we're running a brothel. Honestly, Summer. It's completely out of the realm of possibility.'

Summer appeared neither convinced nor comforted. Her cheeks were still ruddy, and a vein was visibly throbbing in her left temple.

'I've probably exaggerated,' Megan said, her tone apologetic. 'The banner isn't really that big. I'm sure it's a lot smaller and less noticeable than I remember it. Take a look for yourselves. I'll show you.'

Signaling for them to follow, Megan turned and started moving through the crowd, which seemed to have grown even denser than before. Hope and Summer headed after her. The booths were arranged in semi-circular rows that spread out like rolling waves from the carousel. At first glance, the sheer number was overwhelming. There were booths of all types and shapes and sizes, offering a vast array of products and services. Baked goods, handicrafts, local wine and beer tastings. The food booths suffered the most from the heat. The caramel on the taffy apples was puddling. The hard candies were sticking to their cellophane wrappers. The pottery, on the other hand, appeared to experience no ill effects. Having been kiln-fired, not even the infernal Carolina sun could touch it.

No money exchanged hands at the booths, only tickets. The tickets could be purchased at cashier stands that were dotted throughout the festival grounds. Every booth had a sign, indicating the number of tickets necessary for the redemption of its goods. Two tickets for a slice of watermelon, three for a slab of fudge, four for an ice cream cone with sprinkles, five for a ride on the carousel on the animal of your choice. It was a simple-to-understand system with no haggling or fumbling in pockets for loose coins. Parents could easily dispense a set number of tickets to children, and the booths didn't have to bother with receipts or making change.

After a short distance, on the far side of the carousel but still among the first row of booths, Megan halted. Hope's initial thought was that they were pausing because they had reached a small pocket of shade, but then she looked up and discovered that the shade was being cast by a banner. A big banner. *Madam Bailey, Fortune Teller.* Megan certainly hadn't exaggerated its size or the glittery silver lettering. On the contrary, the banner was even larger and showier than Hope had anticipated.

'Brothel,' Summer muttered tetchily.

Hope sighed, and Megan gave her arm a sympathetic squeeze.

'Always remember that it could be worse,' Megan said. 'You could be dressed as an evil queen in sparkly sequins. Speaking of which, I had better go back and check on Sean. Make sure that he hasn't won the bet and passed out in a bowl of chocolate slurry. If you get a break or need an escape, come visit us. Amethyst's booth is in this row, too, about halfway around the carousel, almost directly opposite. You can't miss it. Just keep an eye out for the regal purple. The hotel and spa love their purple.'

Blowing them another air kiss, Megan turned and departed. Almost instantly, the petal-pink ball gown and tiara disappeared among the multitude.

A moment later, as though she'd had a premonition of their arrival, Gram stepped through the gap in the burgundy velvet curtains that formed the entrance to the booth.

'Hello, my dears.' She waved her cane in greeting. 'I'm glad that you're here.'

Summer responded with an unhappy gurgling noise.

Gram had no difficulty understanding her meaning. 'Yes, I'm sorry about the banner. It wasn't my doing.' She turned to Hope with a conciliatory expression. 'I know that it's not ideal . . .'

Hope raised an eyebrow at her.

'But I don't think that it will cause any trouble,' she went on. 'Truly, I don't. It's all meant in good, clean fun. You're not swindling anyone or deceiving them in any way. And every cent goes to charity. Surely that's understood. Surely there could be no objection from the powers that be to an innocent little banner.'

The eyebrow remained raised.

Gram nodded. 'Of course I agree with you. I would have preferred something else myself. A clear reference to the boutique might have helped to attract new customers. And none of this *Madam* nonsense. A picture of a crystal ball would have been best. That couldn't have caused offense in any quarter.'

Hope sighed once more.

'On the bright side,' Gram continued cheerfully, 'the banner is extremely eye-catching, which bodes well for ticket sales. The committee liked it so much that they set the booth's ticket number at five. That's the same as the carousel! Morris is quite proud. He's inside right now. So are a few of the others. You must see what a splendid job they've all done.'

Using her cane to push the velvet curtains further apart, Gram returned the way she had come. Neither Hope nor Summer immediately followed her. They both remained on the threshold of the booth, as though waiting but not quite sure for what.

'Hope' – Summer's voice quavered as she spoke – 'you know how you said before that something about the Five of Coins didn't feel right to you? That you thought it was pointing in another direction?'

Hope looked at her sister.

'Well, I think it's pointing here. I think something terrible is about to happen.'

FOUR

I f Summer was right, and something terrible was indeed about to happen, it didn't occur when they entered the booth. The interior of the booth looked nearly twice as large as the exterior. Burgundy velvet curtains decked each side, and twinkle lights glowed like bright little stars across the makeshift ceiling. In the center of the space, there was a small round table surrounded by several chairs, all of which were also draped in lush velvet. It was exactly as Megan had described: attractive and rather atmospheric. The booth was dark but not too dark. The ambiance was a touch spooky and a touch magical, just right for pretending to see all sorts of wonderful things in a crystal ball. Except there was no crystal ball in sight.

Gram immediately began an introduction of her remaining helper elves and what their respective roles had been in the booth's decoration.

'Jocelyn' – she motioned toward a plump woman with a creased brow who was kneeling at the rear of the booth, folds of velvet spread across her lap – 'has been our drapery expert. She chose the fabric, measured and cut it, and stitched it with perfect precision. She's just finishing up the cords that will tie the back curtains to let a breath of air through. The front cords are already completed, which is how you came in.'

Jocelyn gave them a friendly nod in greeting, then immediately returned her focus to the needle and thread in her hand.

'You can thank Amelia and Stanley for the lovely lighting,' Gram continued.

Stanley was balanced on a ladder in the near corner, fastening the end of an electrical cable that had apparently come loose, with Amelia standing close by, presumably to steady the ladder if it wobbled while her husband was on it. The Palmers were a matched set. They were both in their mid-sixties, reed-thin, and wearing shirts in a similar shade of forest green, one slightly more faded than the other.

'We went through all the options,' Amelia told them. 'Candles, lanterns, hurricane lamps, standing lamps, alternately blinking bulbs . . .'

'Yes, indeed,' Stanley confirmed from his perch. '*All* the options.'

Hope restrained a chuckle. Through Gram, she had encountered the Palmers on several previous occasions, and each time Amelia had been involved in the design of some project or plan, which Stanley was then expected to execute. The booth was evidently no exception. Gram may have credited Amelia with having an excellent eye for lighting and decor, but Stanley was the one who was required to actually install said lighting and decor.

'The twinkle lights look great,' Hope complimented them. 'Really terrific—'

'And the banner?' Morris interjected eagerly.

Hope turned to him. In addition to being Gram's long-time gentleman friend and co-chair of the festival committee this year, Morris Henshaw was a trusted family doctor whose office was located in another old brownstone not far from the boutique. Morris was tall and narrow, with an equally narrow, angular face topped by wispy white hair. He had a naturally solemn demeanor, and even now, when Hope could see the animated glint in his blue eyes, his overall expression was more grave than giddy.

'Doesn't the banner at the front of the booth look terrific, too?' Morris said.

Gram shot her an entreating glance.

'It certainly grabs one's attention,' Hope answered politely – and truthfully.

'I couldn't agree more.' Morris nodded with a stiff, jerky motion. Although he was no longer wearing the back brace that he had donned immediately following his surgery, his upper body movements were still somewhat slow and awkward. 'I wish that I could take the credit for it, but I can't. The banner was entirely Larkin's idea. She deserves all the praise.'

'Larkin?' Summer inquired.

'My new receptionist. A charming girl. Bright as a button—'
Gram stopped him with a small cough.

'Is that not right?' Morris frowned. 'I know you've told me
before, but I keep forgetting. The job titles are constantly
changing. When I first started out in my practice, everybody
was either a nurse or a secretary. Now there are physician's
assistants and medical assistants and transcription assistants
and billing assistants and—'

Another cough from Gram. 'It's fine to say that Larkin is
your new receptionist, but you can't call her a girl.'

'I can't? Why not?' Morris protested. 'I'm nearly seventy,
and she's barely twenty. That makes me an old man and her
a girl.'

'Don't talk rubbish, dear. You are not an old man, and you
are employing her in a professional capacity so she is not a girl.'

'Well, yes, I see your point, but—'

Gram didn't let him finish. 'How is your back feeling today?
It's not hurting too badly, is it?'

'No more than usual. Much less than it would be if I didn't
have Summer's splendid tea. Between their tinctures and readings, the *girls* do a marvelous job at the boutique.'

The glint in Morris's eye had turned decidedly mischievous.
Hope couldn't help smiling. Neither could Gram, although she
shook her head at him in reproach.

'You're being ornery on purpose. And it won't matter how
marvelous the boutique might be if the crystal ball doesn't
arrive soon.' Gram checked her watch. 'The festival will be
opening in just a few minutes, and Summer can't take people's
tickets if Hope doesn't have anything to gaze into.'

Morris checked his watch, too. 'Larkin has the crystal ball.
She promised to bring it to the booth.'

Summer raised an eyebrow. 'So Larkin is the one responsible
for the banner *and* the crystal ball?'

'Yes. She's very helpful, isn't she?'

'She certainly is. When I meet her, I'll be sure to express
my gratitude.'

Summer's voice dripped with sarcasm, and this time Gram's
reproachful shake of the head was directed at her. Morris didn't
seem to notice.

'Larkin was supposed to confirm the patient appointments for next week and then close up the office.' Morris checked his watch again, tapping its face as though it might not be functioning correctly. 'Those tasks couldn't possibly take this long. I don't know what's keeping her.'

'It's awfully crowded out there on the grounds,' Hope told him. 'She might be having a difficult time getting through.'

'But she can't be having a difficult time finding the booth with that banner of hers,' Summer said, with only slightly less sarcasm than before.

Morris's frown resurfaced. He appeared puzzled by Summer's tone. Gram looked anxiously from one to the other. In an effort to keep the peace, Hope changed the subject.

'While we're waiting, Gram, there's something that I should mention to you. Rosemarie Potter has a new boyfriend. She brought him to the boutique two days ago, and she told us that he was also going to accompany her – and Percy – to the festival tonight.'

The anxious look faded. 'Oh, how nice. Good for Rosemarie!'

'Except it's not nice, because the man isn't nice. Nor do I think that he's good for Rosemarie. But that's beside the point. They will in all likelihood come to the booth, so I wanted to give you a heads-up in case you run into them either this evening or some other time over the weekend. The boyfriend is a real estate agent, and he may have his sights set on trying to sell the brownstone.'

'Sell the brownstone?' Gram exclaimed. 'Merciful heaven, we couldn't possibly do that!'

Hope nodded in agreement.

'Can you imagine what would happen if . . . The mere idea of . . .' Gram was aghast. 'It's absolutely out of the question. I have not the slightest intention.' She dropped her voice abruptly. 'We shouldn't even be discussing it.'

Hope nodded some more. 'That's why I'm warning you. He's a pushy sort.'

'*Very* pushy,' Summer chimed in.

'I'm not sure that a simple rejection will dissuade him,' Hope went on. 'There's a good chance that he'll get aggressive, so you need to be prepared.'

As the anxious look redoubled, Gram leaned heavily on her cane. Morris came over and wrapped a supportive arm around her waist.

'There's no reason to worry, Olivia,' he said reassuringly. 'Of course you don't want to sell the brownstone – not with the boutique there, and it being Hope and Summer's home. No one can force you to put the property on the market against your will. Should this real estate fellow decide to get pushy, then we'll get pushy right back. Some salesmen get so used to treading all over people that after a while they need a proper reminder about who's who and what's what.'

Gram gave him a grateful smile. 'Thank you, Morris.'

Summer shook her head doubtfully. 'It might not be so easy with him. He isn't your average salesman. Davis Scott is—'

'Davis Scott!' Amelia cried.

There was a cry from Jocelyn as well. Stanley also gave a shout as the ladder wobbled beneath him, and he began to tumble off it. He crashed down two steps and started to tip over the side rails, before clutching furiously at the top cap to stop his further descent.

Amelia – who had plainly lapsed in her duty to hold the ladder steady in precisely such a situation – dashed toward him, flushed and panicked. 'Stanley! Are you hurt, Stanley? Do you need help?'

'Don't fuss, Amelia. I'm fine.' Although his words were calm, his hands and feet were not. With trembling fingers and unsteady steps, Stanley climbed slowly down the remainder of the ladder until he reached the safety of firm ground. 'I just banged my knee and shin. Nothing too serious. I'll survive.' He rubbed his bruised spots with a wince.

His wife gave an audible sigh of relief.

'I lost my balance,' Stanley went on in complaint, rubbing and wincing some more. 'It was all that yelling from you and Jocelyn.'

In unison, the group turned to check on Jocelyn, who was still at the rear of the booth under folds of velvet. Similar to Amelia, Jocelyn's face was flushed. For a moment, it also appeared that her hands were trembling like Stanley's, but it was difficult to tell for certain, because she held up an index finger with a scarlet streak of blood for them to see, then quickly grabbed a spare scrap of fabric that was lying by her side and wrapped it around the wound as an impromptu bandage.

'I'm sorry if I startled you,' Jocelyn apologized. 'My attention wandered off for a second, and the needle slipped. I stitched myself instead of the cords. It happens more often than I'd like to admit. But no permanent damage done – to any of us, thankfully. I'm all right, too.'

Except she didn't look all right. Her flushed face was almost as burgundy as the velvet, and her creased brow was thickly dotted with perspiration.

'You're overheated,' Hope said with concern. 'You need to get out from under those curtains and have a cool drink and a breath of air.'

'A fan!' Morris exclaimed. 'That's what we need. I should have brought one in earlier. I'll be back in a jiffy.'

As Morris hurried out of the front of the booth, Hope hurried to the back to free Jocelyn from the mounds of fabric.

'No, no. I'm all right,' Jocelyn reiterated. 'I should finish the cords.'

Hope brooked no opposition. 'The cords can wait – or remain the way they are. The curtains are gorgeous, but you've done more than enough. No draperies are worth heat exhaustion and a trip to the emergency room.'

Jocelyn didn't object further as Hope lifted the velvet from her lap and Summer handed her a cup of water.

'It's more tepid than cool,' Summer said regretfully. 'There's no ice.'

'I'll take it regardless. Thank you.'

As Jocelyn put the cup to her mouth, Hope saw how heavily both her hand and her lips were shaking. Hope was about to ask her if she really was all right and if there was anything else they could do to help her, but Morris burst back into the booth in the same instant.

'Success!' he declared. 'And look who I found in the process!'

Under his right arm, Morris held an oscillating fan. With his left arm, he ushered two people into the booth with him.

One was a stranger to Hope. The other was not. Hope's breath caught in her throat when she saw him. It was Morris's son, Dylan.

She had first met Dylan Henshaw shortly after Morris's back surgery, when Dylan – also a doctor – had taken a temporary leave of absence from his job at a prestigious university hospital in California to assist in treating his father's patients. As Morris had gradually regained his strength and mobility, allowing him to increase his working hours, Dylan had started shuttling between his father's office and his own. For the past month, he had been exclusively in California. Hope hadn't known that he had returned to Asheville.

Based on Dylan's appearance, at least some of his time in California had been spent outdoors, and it had visibly agreed with him. There were bright streaks in his thick, sandy hair. A smattering of long-forgotten childhood freckles were detectable on his sun-kissed cheeks and nose. Set against the rosy hint of a tan, Dylan's pale blue eyes had turned to azure. He looked fit and healthy and even more self-possessed than usual.

'What a fabulous surprise!' Morris chattered excitedly. 'Dylan has come back just in time for the festival. I had no idea that you were on your way! You should have let me know about your flight. I would have gone to the airport to meet you.'

'It was a last-minute decision,' Dylan explained, in a much calmer fashion than his father. 'I landed only a few hours ago, and there was no need to meet me. I rented a car as I have in the past and checked into the hotel – Amethyst, also the same as in the past – and then I went to the office to look for you. There is a matter that I'd like to discuss.'

'But you shouldn't stay in a hotel,' Morris protested. 'You should be at the house with Olivia and me. We love having you there. Isn't that right, Olivia?'

Although Gram inclined her head and started to respond in the affirmative, Morris went on before she could get out a word.

'You were saying something about a matter that you'd like to discuss? We could discuss it now, or . . .'

'There's no rush.' Dylan gave a leisurely shrug. 'We have

plenty of time for that later on. I believe there are more pressing concerns to be dealt with. I ran into Larkin at the office.' He gestured toward the other person that Morris had ushered into the booth.

It took only one glance at Larkin for Hope to know that Gram was right and Morris was wrong. Larkin was neither barely twenty nor a girl. She was on the older side of twenty-five and in every respect carried herself as a woman. Her styled brown hair had expensive chestnut highlights. She wore full make-up that had been applied with an experienced hand. One button too many was left open on her turquoise blouse, revealing more than a hint of lace underneath. Likewise, her tissue paper-thin white pants and matching turquoise high heels were a questionable choice for a professional office. But there was no question that Larkin was a striking woman, and from the way she focused her gaze on Dylan and Morris and Stanley – and only on them – it was clear that she wanted men to be struck by her.

'I'm so glad that you've met Larkin,' Morris said to Dylan. 'We're very lucky to have her. She's popular with the patients, and in just two short weeks, she's already begun a much-needed overhaul of the old filing system.'

'Three weeks,' Larkin corrected him. 'I've been at the office for three weeks now.' She turned toward Dylan, at the same time moving a step closer to him. 'I started just after you left for California. I've heard a great deal about you, of course, and I must confess that you aren't at all what I expected.'

The leisurely shrug became a leisurely smile. 'I hope you're not too disappointed.'

'Oh, no. Not in the least.' Larkin returned the smile with sparkling white teeth. 'I think we'll work beautifully together.'

Summer made a little choking noise. Hope didn't need to look at her sister to know what she was thinking, because she was thinking it, too: Larkin was a flirt.

The sound must have been loud enough for Dylan to hear, because his attention abruptly shifted to them. His gaze flitted over Summer, then landed firmly on Hope. He didn't formally greet her. Nor did she greet him. For a long minute, they simply looked at each other.

Dylan spoke first. 'This was what I meant before when I said there were more pressing concerns to be dealt with. I heard from Larkin that a certain fortune teller was missing her crystal ball.'

There was undisguised amusement in his azure eyes, and Hope's green eyes narrowed in response.

Larkin laughed. 'Yes, the crystal ball. I had forgotten all about it.' She held up a canvas tote bag that sagged under the weight of its contents. 'Who here is the fortune teller?'

Hope didn't answer. Her gaze remained locked with Dylan's.

'I'll take that from you,' Gram volunteered.

Relinquishing custody of the bag, Larkin said, 'I don't really believe in fortune tellers. But my stepmom sure does. A fortune teller once told her that a fortune would shortly fall into her lap. That's why she spends the entire day sitting in front of the television. She's afraid that if she stands up, the fortune will fall when she doesn't have a lap to catch it.'

Larkin laughed again, evidently greatly entertained by her own wit. There was a light, polite chuckle from one or two of the others in the group, but not from Hope. Her eyes narrowed further. Dylan, in turn, appeared even more amused.

'Well, it was a pleasure to meet all of you.' Larkin directed her attention back to Dylan. She was now not so much standing next to him as leaning against him. 'I'm famished, and I remember you telling me at the office that you hadn't eaten lunch. So you can take me to dinner. I know the perfect little place . . .'

Summer made another choking noise. This time Larkin must have heard the sound, because just before she once more smiled up at Dylan, she flashed Summer a venomous look. Dylan didn't see it, but Hope did. And she knew what it meant. Larkin wasn't only a flirt. She intended to make a conquest.

FIVE

Larkin's perfect little dinner place was left unnamed, because a moment later, there was a bustle at the entrance to the booth that proved impossible to ignore. The festival had opened to the public, and eager ticketholders began arriving at the burgundy velvet curtains in droves. Whether it was due to the glitter on the banner, Rosemarie Potter's advance publicity, or the irresistible desire to glean a hint about one's future, *Madam Bailey, Fortune Teller* turned out to be an instantaneous hit.

'People are coming!' Gram cried, pulling the crystal ball from its bag and thrusting it on the table.

Morris peeped through the gap in the front curtains. 'And they're lining up faster than ants at a picnic!'

Amelia handed Summer a cardboard box that had been wrapped in crinkly gold paper with a matching ribbon on top like a fancy birthday present. 'This is for the tickets. Just push them through the slot in the side. Remember, it's five for your booth. You'll probably encounter a few penny-pinchers who'll claim they only have two tickets left and don't want to buy more. Don't let them get away with it. Remind them it's for charity.'

'Hurry,' Gram admonished the group. 'Hurry!'

With the aid of the partially completed cords, Jocelyn managed to fasten up the back curtains to make a rear exit. Stanley carried out the ladder and a tool chest. Jocelyn carried out her sewing kit and a bundle of unused fabric. Amelia carried out herself.

Morris fumbled with the electrical cable that was used by the twinkle lights, but the stiff muscles in his back wouldn't allow him to stretch sufficiently. 'Dylan, help me hook the fan into the connecting plug.'

Dylan reached up and attached the fan. Morris promptly switched it on. There was a collective sigh of relief at the welcome breeze.

'That feels good,' Morris said, positioning himself directly in front of the fan.

Dylan took a gusty spot next to his father. 'I agree. Forget dinner. I'll just stand here for the rest of the evening.' The corners of his mouth curled with a hint of a smile. 'Plus, there will be entertainment. We can watch the fortune teller in action.'

Hope, who was setting up the crystal ball, threw him an irritated glance.

'No, no.' Gram herded Morris away from the fan with her cane. 'You'll have to find another fan elsewhere.' Then she herded Dylan. 'And you can enjoy the air conditioning while sitting in a restaurant.'

'Yes, exactly,' Larkin concurred, once again sidling up to Dylan. 'You're taking me to dinner. No arguments.'

Dylan's answer was lost to Hope, because Gram succeeded in steering the stragglers out of the booth.

'Goodbye, my dears!' She turned and waved to her granddaughters. 'Good luck!'

'Fortune favors the bold!' Dylan chimed in, his voice brimming with laughter.

Hope was tempted to favor Dylan with a few choice words in response, but she didn't have the chance. He was already too far outside, and duty – in the form of a crystal ball – called. The crystal ball turned out to be a cheap plasma globe that was clear white and not the least bit mystical in appearance. When its surface was touched, violet sparks of lightning shot through the interior. It looked like a cross between a kindergarten science experiment and an inane party trick. When Hope demonstrated it to her sister, Summer rolled her eyes and muttered something about Larkin's brain being equally vacuous. Hope wasn't so sure. Although based only on a single first impression, she was of the opinion that Larkin might be rather clever, at least in a manipulative fashion. Morris seemed fully convinced of her wonderfulness. Whether Dylan would be similarly persuaded was yet to be seen.

Thankfully, Larkin's poor excuse for a crystal ball wasn't necessary for the success of the booth. Only the youngest children were interested in it, and they were the easiest to please. All Hope had to do was prophesy that a frozen treat and a ride on the carousel were in their future, and they were thrilled. She let them touch the globe to see the sparks, and after half a dozen sets of sticky fingers had coated its surface with the residue of hot dogs and potato chips, Hope stopped touching it herself.

The adults were a mixed bag. Some sought winning lottery numbers. Others sought winning sports teams. A sizable number wanted to know if their significant other was cheating on them. An even greater number wanted to know if they themselves could get away with cheating. A small percentage was interested in astrological signs. A tiny percentage was interested in auras. There were no true readings of any sort. Hope found herself functioning mostly as a sympathetic, non-judgmental ear, listening patiently to each person's litany of problems. She was used to doing that from the boutique.

All in all, as the evening wore on, the unrelenting stream of ticketholders was exhausting, especially with the oppressive warmth of the booth that was only slightly ameliorated by the breeze from the fan. When it was Rosemarie Potter's turn to enter, Hope greeted her and pug Percy with a weary smile.

'At last!' Rosemarie cried in triumph. 'We finally made it inside! I was on pins and needles the whole time. Everybody who came out looked so happy and was saying such nice things about you.'

Knowing that a visit from Rosemarie was never a brief affair, Summer announced with an apology to those still waiting in line that the booth needed to take a short refreshment break, then she drew the front curtains closed and sank into one of the velvet-draped chairs across the table from Hope. She plopped the ticket box next to the crystal ball. 'I need to sit. My feet are killing me.'

'Mine, too.' Rosemarie took a neighboring seat. True to form, she was wearing a billowy white sundress dotted with miniature sprigs of red roses. The shade of the roses was almost identical to the shade of her hair. 'I put on my fanciest sandals for the occasion, but they pinch like the dickens.' She reached down and rubbed her fingers under the matching red straps to relieve the pressure. 'I'm getting a blister along the back. I can feel it. Would you consider me terribly rude if I took them off?'

'Not at all,' Hope assured her. 'Go right ahead. A bunch of the kids were running around barefoot in here, and none of them seemed to have any troubles. The grass has been cut short for the festival, so I don't think you need to worry about stepping on anything that could bite or sting.'

Rosemarie removed the sandals with a grateful exhalation. She set them carefully next to her chair, avoiding any unnecessary contact with grass or dirt. 'Davis likes this pair. I don't want them to get stained.'

Hope hesitated, unsure whether to feign polite interest in Davis's present whereabouts or simply ignore the subject of him.

'It's my own fault,' Rosemarie went on. 'I should have known that I'd be walking and standing in line most of the time. Speaking of which, the turnout for the festival has been fantastic! And your booth is a huge hit! Only the carousel and the Popsicle wagon have more people waiting.'

Summer turned to her sister with a wry grin. 'Mark this day on the calendar, Hope. Our dreams have now officially come true, and our lives can be considered complete. We're almost as popular as the Popsicle wagon.'

Hope laughed, and Percy offered a little yip.

Summer looked at him. 'You'd probably prefer a Popsicle, too, wouldn't you?'

'Goodness, no.' Rosemarie shook her head. 'Don't tempt him by even mentioning it. If he eats or drinks one more thing, he'll get a stomachache and be howling all night. He's had at least a gallon of water and a pound of food in the last hour.'

'I can see the water,' Hope said. 'Your scarf is wet, Percy.'

Rosemarie had wrapped the black-and-white chevron-patterned scarf that she had purchased at the boutique around Percy's neck like a bandana. The bottom portion on his chest was noticeably damp, no doubt from sagging into a bowl as he had been drinking. Hope found herself a bit envious. The wet fabric was probably cooling him nicely. She wouldn't have minded a damp towel on her neck.

'Doesn't he look dapper?' Rosemarie beamed at the pug.

'Next week, when the boutique is open again, we'll get another scarf for him to have as a spare. There were several others in the new assortment that would suit him, don't you think?'

Hope smiled. 'I'm sure that we can find the perfect one.'

Summer's grin resurfaced. 'I remember Megan once saying that good bone structure was the key to carrying a scarf well. If that's the case, Percy's bone structure must be outstanding—'

She was interrupted by a movement at the front curtains.

Hope sighed. 'Well, I guess that's a sign we're supposed to get back to work.'

'Couldn't we ignore it?' Summer pleaded. 'My feet are just beginning to recover. In another couple of minutes, they'll be much better. Then we can start up again.'

Rosemarie nodded in agreement. 'My feet, too. And Percy is plumb tuckered out. It's the heat, of course. Davis promised that it would get better once the sun went down and the wind picked up. But it's nearly dark out, and there's still not a wisp of wind, and it hasn't gotten one degree cooler.'

Again, Hope debated whether to address the issue of Davis, but decided against it.

'You don't have to leave,' she told Rosemarie. 'Pull your chair over to the side and stay as long as you and Percy want.'

'That's awfully kind of you, Hope. Except we mustn't keep Davis waiting. He'll be looking for us and wondering where we—'

There was another movement at the front curtains, this time with more enthusiasm – or impatience.

'All right. All right.' Grumbling, Summer stood up. She gave the crystal ball a desultory poke, then reclaimed the ticket box.

The curtains began to part, but there was so much fabric that the person attempting to open them wasn't visible.

'For criminy sake, I'm coming. Keep your shirt on.' Summer went to the curtains, and when she drew them apart, she started in surprise. 'Oh! It's you!'

Pushing roughly past her, Davis Scott entered the booth.

Rosemarie must not have expected to see him any more than Summer had, because she also gave a little shout. 'Davis!'

Davis took a brief survey of his surroundings, and his already sour expression soured further. There was a harrumph of evident displeasure. No greeting was given to any of them, not even Rosemarie.

'I thought that we were supposed to meet next to the pretzel stand,' Rosemarie said to him in confusion.

'We were,' Davis confirmed coldly. 'I was there. You weren't.'

'Dear me. I'm sorry. Percy and I got delayed. But now that you've seen the booth, I'm sure you can understand why. Isn't it lovely in here? Don't you think the twinkle lights are magical?'

There was another harrumph. Davis was apparently not a fan of twinkle lights, magical or otherwise.

Enough time had now elapsed for Summer to have regained her composure. 'Five tickets, please,' she informed Davis.

He ignored her.

'Five tickets,' she repeated, stepping toward him and holding out the gold-wrapped ticket box.

'Preposterous,' he spat.

Summer stiffened and assumed a prim, bureaucratic bearing. 'The cost for admittance to this booth is five tickets. I have been instructed by the festival committee not to accept anything less.'

Davis glowered at her with his protruding eyes.

Unruffled, Summer went on, 'If you do not wish to contribute five tickets, then I must ask you to leave the booth – immediately.'

The glower switched imperiously to Rosemarie, as though demanding her support.

She responded with a meek shrug. 'Those are the festival rules, Davis. And it is for charity.'

'Don't be a miser,' Summer added reproachfully. 'There is nothing less attractive than a man who takes pride in how cheap he is.'

Davis pawed the ground with the toe of his shoe like an irascible bull, then, with an angry snort, he spun on his heel and stomped furiously out of the booth, getting tangled in the burgundy velvet along the way. Hope had to bite her tongue to keep from laughing at the ungraceful exit.

'Dear me.' Rosemarie rose from her chair. 'I had better go

after him. They always accuse women of being the hysterical sex, but it seems to me that, more often than not, men are the overly sensitive ones.'

Summer nodded solemnly. Although she did an admirable job of concealing it from Rosemarie, Hope could see from the way her sister was sucking on her bottom lip that she was struggling to contain her laughter, too.

Rosemarie picked up her red sandals, but she didn't put them on. 'Come along, Percy. We need to be going.'

Percy, who had been sprawled on the comparatively cool grass, gave a yawn and reluctantly climbed to his feet.

'Yes, I know.' She straightened his scarf. 'It's been an exciting evening, and after we join Davis, it will be nearly time for us to head home.'

There was another yawn from the pug, which caused Rosemarie to yawn in contagion.

'Goodnight, Hope. Goodnight, Summer.' Percy's lead in one hand and her sandals in the other, Rosemarie began hobbling toward the curtains. 'I'd like to come back tomorrow, but I'm not sure whether he . . .' With an elbow, she motioned outside, indicating Davis.

'We understand,' Hope replied gently. 'Visit us whenever you have the chance. There's no need to wait in line, if there is one. Just come straight in. We'll be here all weekend.'

Rosemarie and Percy moved slowly out of the booth, the former limping noticeably. The back of her ankle was smeared with blood. It was a bad blister. Just as they were disappearing from view, Megan arrived.

'Hey there, Rosemarie. That's a nifty scarf you've got, Percy.'

'Megan, you look beautiful in that dress! It's gorgeous, and I love the sequins. I've always found sequins to be so cheery.'

'Sequins aren't *cheery*,' Summer objected indignantly. 'Sequins are—'

Hope hurriedly shushed her. Fortunately, it didn't seem that Rosemarie had heard, because she kept on talking to Megan.

'I saw you at Amethyst's booth earlier. That man sitting next to you looked so dashing in his cape and crown! I was going to come over to say hello, but Davis didn't want to. He said that . . . Oh, gosh, I think that's him there, just turning the corner by the maple syrup stand. It is Davis, isn't it? I have to rush to catch him, Megan. Goodbye! Goodbye!'

A moment later, Megan popped through the burgundy velvet. She immediately saw the oscillating fan, and as fast as her petal-pink bodice allowed, she hustled toward it.

'Bless you for having a fan,' she said, sticking her face directly in front of it. Her blond hair blew crazily. 'Without it, collapse and death were imminent. By the way, who is Davis?'

'Rosemarie's new boyfriend,' Hope told her.

'And soon-to-be third husband?'

'I sincerely hope not. He doesn't deserve her. He's—'

'A slippery fish,' Summer concluded for her sister. She started to launch into a lengthy account of Davis Scott being Shifty Gary's disreputable choice in real estate agents, but Hope stopped her.

'Are there a lot of people waiting outside, Megan?'

She didn't turn from the fan. 'No people.'

'No people?' Summer echoed in surprise. 'Really? Because when Rosemarie first came in, there were a whole bunch.' She looked at Hope, a bit chagrined. 'I guess we took too long of a break. Oops.'

'There are no people,' Megan clarified, 'because the festival has officially concluded for the evening. All the booths are closed.'

A unified shout of hurrah followed. Summer once more deposited the ticket box on the table. Hope covered the crystal ball with a surplus piece of velvet. Then they joined Megan in front of the fan.

'Now, if we only had a bottle of wine . . .'

'White, not red. Heavily, heavily chilled.'

'And a change of clothes. I *need* to get out of this gown.'

'Here's an idea. First, we pop by the brownstone so that Megan can borrow something more comfortable to wear. Then we head over to the Green Goat – that new place in the square where Gram and Morris went the other night with the Palmers – for a late dinner and some drinks and—'

The proposed plan was abruptly cut short by Rosemarie.

She burst back into the booth, breathing heavily, the hem of her dress flapping wildly around her legs.

'I can't find him!' she cried. 'I can't find him anywhere! He's disappeared!'

SIX

There was a collective moment of panic, and the group whirled around from the fan ready to spring into investigative action.

'Poor Percy! Where did you lose him?'

'Did he break free from his lead – or did somebody take his lead?'

'He's got his tags on? Does he also have a microchip?'

'No, no! Not Percy,' Rosemarie corrected them. 'Percy is right here.'

She motioned toward the ground next to her bare feet. Percy – looking hale and hearty – was once more sprawled on the grass. The collective panic turned into a collective sigh of relief. It was not shared by Rosemarie.

'Davis!' she exclaimed. 'I'm talking about Davis. He's disappeared!'

This time the response from the group was more subdued.

'Disappeared?' Megan asked her.

'Disappeared!' Rosemarie confirmed. 'Vanished. Missing. Poof!'

There was no immediate reply.

'You have to help me find him!' Rosemarie cried. 'Where can he be? Where could he have gone?'

Her face was turning as red as the sprigs of roses on her dress, and she was beginning to hyperventilate. Hope grew concerned for her health.

'It's all right,' she said as soothingly as she could. 'Don't worry. Everything is going to be fine, Rosemarie. Why don't you rest for a minute? Then we'll put our heads together and come up with a solution.'

'That's an excellent idea.' Summer followed her sister's lead and pulled out a chair for Rosemarie. 'Sit down, take a deep breath, have a drink of water—'

'I can't. There isn't time,' Rosemarie protested. But she

took a seat anyway, and when Megan handed her a full cup, she gulped down every drop.

'Good. Much better.' Hope sat down across from her. 'We've all had a chance to get our bearings. Now tell us exactly what happened.'

'I can't find Davis! He's gone! He—'

Hope reached out and put a quieting hand on Rosemarie's arm. 'We understand that. But we want to figure out where he went. To do that, you need to start at the beginning. When did you last see him?'

Rosemarie inhaled shakily. 'I was here. I was talking to Megan just outside the booth when I spotted Davis turning the corner by the maple syrup stand. That was the last time I saw him.'

'And you went after him?' Hope asked.

'Yes. I tried to catch up, but I couldn't go very fast.' She pointed at her sore heel. 'When I turned the same corner that Davis had, he was no longer there. I went up and down the row of booths, but there wasn't any sign of him. He had vanished into thin air!'

'But you're sure that it was Davis you saw at the maple syrup stand?' Summer said.

'Oh, definitely! Without question.' There was a pause, then Rosemarie's certainty began to waver. 'At least I think it was him. The person looked like him.' She turned anxiously to Megan. 'Don't you think it was him?'

'I don't know. I've never met Davis.'

Rosemarie's brow furrowed. 'Well, I suppose it's possible it wasn't him. It is pretty dark out. There's some light from the carousel and the booths, but it's not a lot. Maybe I got confused and mistook him for someone else?'

'It happens more often than you might imagine,' Megan told her. 'I'm frequently mistaking people at the hotel. And that's especially true at night. For example, when I was coming to this booth only a little while ago, I could have sworn that I saw Sean from Amethyst's booth heading in one direction when I know for certain that he had gone in the opposite direction just five minutes earlier. The eyes can play all sorts of tricks in the shadows, particularly if we *want* to see someone.'

'I do want to see Davis,' Rosemarie admitted. 'But that still doesn't explain why I haven't been able to find him. I've looked everywhere for him.'

Megan offered a sympathetic shrug. 'You went one way, and he went the other, and never the twain shall meet.'

The furrow in Rosemarie's brow deepened.

'You could try calling him,' Hope suggested.

'I've done that. There's no answer.'

'He might have gone home,' Summer said.

'But he couldn't go home. I drove us to the festival, so he's dependent on me for a ride back.'

'Maybe he got a ride from somebody else?'

Rosemarie blinked at Summer in surprise. 'Oh, no. Davis wouldn't do that. He'd never leave without telling me. It would be so rude.'

Hope and Summer exchanged a glance. It didn't seem to them that Davis Scott had any qualms about being rude.

There was another pause, and then Rosemarie came to a decision. 'We should report Davis as missing to the police.'

Megan shook her head. 'It's far too early for such a drastic step.'

'But he's missing,' Rosemarie insisted.

'Except we aren't really sure of that,' Summer countered.

Rosemarie turned to Hope for her opinion.

'I think that Megan and Summer are correct.' Hope kept her tone mild, not wanting to upset Rosemarie further. 'We can't contact the police at this point, because there could still be an easy explanation for Davis's disappearance. He might have run into a friend and left with that person. He could have tried contacting you, but the battery on his phone was dead. He might have walked to the square to grab a drink or a meal. There are numerous possibilities. And it would be awfully embarrassing both to you and to Davis if you reported him as missing and it turned out that he was simply having a beer at the pub or was tucked up in his pajamas in bed.'

Although she couldn't argue with Hope's reasoning, Rosemarie wasn't reassured. 'I don't know. I have a bad feeling.'

Hope sighed. She and Summer exchanged another glance. Summer sighed, too.

'This is what I propose.' Hope spoke the words reluctantly. She was tired, and she knew that her sister and Megan were tired also. They wanted to cool off and have their dinner and their bottle of wine, but now, thanks to Davis Scott, that was going to have to be delayed. 'We'll do a search . . .'

Rosemarie looked at her eagerly.

'A *short* search,' Hope amended, unwilling to commit to an all-night pursuit of the man. 'The four of us will divide up the rows and make a quick perusal of the festival grounds. There's a good chance that Davis is still in the vicinity and either talking with someone or waiting somewhere for you, Rosemarie.'

'We were supposed to meet next to the pretzel stand earlier.'

'I remember you saying that. So you head in the direction of the pretzel stand. Megan can turn left toward Amethyst's booth. Summer can turn right to go the opposite way. And I'll take the row behind us.'

'Thank you!' Rosemarie cried with a mixture of elation and relief. 'Thank you so much for helping to look for him!'

'It's no trouble at all,' Megan replied amiably, even though her normally pert nose was scrunched up in horror at the prospect of having to wear the petal-pink ball gown for a while longer. 'And don't fret. I'm sure Davis will turn up. He's most likely—'

'Rosemarie,' Summer interjected abruptly, 'what happened to Percy's scarf?'

Rosemarie rose from her chair. 'His scarf?'

'Yes. The scarf that he was wearing when you were in here before is gone.'

They all turned to look at Percy. He looked back at them and yawned. Summer was right. The black-and-white chevron-patterned scarf that had been tied around Percy's neck was no longer there.

Rosemarie let out a wail. 'It's missing! Everything is missing! First Davis, now Percy's scarf. I lose everything. Everything!'

'What did I say about fretting?' Megan calmly put her arm through Rosemarie's and conducted her toward the front curtains of the booth. 'The scarf isn't lost. It probably just dropped off outside. Percy – as darling as he is – loves to sniff and scratch the same as most other pups. No doubt the scarf got caught on a nail or a rock or something similar. We'll find it. We'll also find Davis. All will be well.' She glanced back at Hope and Summer with a look that added, *And then I can finally get out of this darn dress and have my darn wine!*

'Fifteen minutes,' Hope said. 'We'll each make one round and return here in fifteen minutes. If anybody spots Percy's scarf, scoop it up. If anybody spots Davis, bring him along.'

'If he objects,' Summer chimed in, 'drag him back by his slick hair.'

'Summer!' Rosemarie protested.

Not letting Rosemarie pause to debate the matter, Megan guided her resolutely – with Percy padding affably alongside – out of the booth.

'Fifteen minutes,' Megan called behind her.

'Fifteen minutes,' Summer confirmed, also heading out and turning in the opposite direction.

Unlike the others, Hope exited through the back curtains to her assigned row behind the booth. Stepping through the velvet, she halted in surprise. It was darker outside than she had anticipated, and it took her eyes a moment to adjust to the sudden inkiness. Over one shoulder, there was a pale yellow glow, presumably from the lights of the carousel. Above her, a slender crescent moon and a sprinkling of stars flickered in the clear night sky. The air was humid and not much cooler than it had been in the afternoon, but without the searing sun, the heat wasn't nearly as paralyzing.

Hope started to move forward and immediately wished that she had a flashlight. There were wires and posts and all sorts of hazards underfoot. Although not a problem during the day or when the booths were fully illuminated, after hours it became a minefield. It occurred to Hope that if she couldn't walk through the row without difficulty, then neither could Davis, and the likelihood of running into him there was slim at best. She was about to turn around and go back to her booth when the outline of a figure appeared. She jumped, startled.

'Alone at last,' the figure said.

Recognizing the voice, Hope relaxed – but only slightly. 'Hello, Dylan.'

'That's a chilly greeting. Aren't you glad to see me?'

'I can't see you. It's too dark.'

Dylan emerged from the shadows, tall and lean. 'Is that better?'

'Yes.'

'Still chilly.'

There was a brief hesitation as Hope debated how to respond, then she simply said, 'It's been a long day.'

'It has,' he agreed. 'I've been waiting all day to see you.'

'You saw me earlier. Or were you too focused on Larkin to remember?'

Dylan's mouth twitched with a hint of a smile. 'Jealous?'

'Of course not. Did you enjoy your dinner with her? How was the *perfect little place*?'

His smile grew. 'You sound jealous.'

'Then your hearing is poor.'

'My hearing is excellent. I heard all that hullabaloo in your booth about somebody named Davis. Who is he, and why is everyone so worried about him?'

'I'm not worried in the least,' Hope replied.

'Good. You shouldn't be running after him.'

It was her turn to smile. 'Now who's jealous?'

Dylan's own smile faded as he took a step toward her. 'Didn't you miss me when I was in California, Hope?'

Her pulse quickened.

He moved closer still, and his voice softened. 'I missed you.'

The blood rushed to her cheeks. Thankfully, there wasn't enough light for him to be able to see it. She had to concentrate to keep her words steady. 'But you couldn't be bothered to tell me that you were returning to Asheville today?'

'Don't be angry about that. As I said to my dad, it was a last-minute decision.'

Hope looked at him. In the darkness, Dylan's eyes were a deep midnight blue. It was impossible to read them.

'Speaking of minutes,' he continued, 'isn't the fifteen that you agreed to already over? The others haven't returned. Forget them. Forget Davis. Come with me and—'

The sentence was cut short as the pale yellow glow over Hope's shoulder brightened dramatically. There was the accompanying sound of lively music.

'Is that the carousel?' she said in surprise. 'Why would they start it up at this late hour?'

Dylan shrugged. 'Maybe Davis and the missing scarf have been found, and everyone decided to take a victory ride.'

Hope chuckled at the idea. 'Have you seen the dress that Megan is wearing? She couldn't climb up on a carousel animal for a ride if her life depended on it . . . Wait a minute, you know about Percy's scarf?'

'As I said, I have excellent hearing.'

'But why didn't you just come into the booth with the others instead of listening outside?'

'Because I didn't want to be with all of them. I want to be with *you*.'

Her heart skipped a beat. Almost involuntarily, she started to move toward him.

'Hope—' Dylan's voice was husky.

There was a loud grinding noise, punctuated by a series of high-pitched screeches. Then came one giant metallic clank, followed by silence. The music was gone, and the yellow glow had dimmed once more.

Hope frowned. 'That didn't sound good.'

'It certainly didn't,' Dylan agreed. 'I'm no expert on the inner workings of carousels, but it's pretty clear that something broke.'

'I hope not. Or least I hope it's something that can be easily fixed. The carousel is one of the main attractions of the festival. Your dad is going to be awfully upset. He was counting on it for good ticket sales.'

'Well, I think he's going to have to start counting on something else instead.' It was Dylan's turn to chuckle. 'Luckily, *Madam Bailey, Fortune Teller* appeared to be drawing in keen ticketholders like the proverbial moths to the flame – or, in this case, crystal ball.'

Hope's frown deepened.

'How's that crystal ball working out for you, by the way? Larkin told me that she got it from—'

'And you can tell Larkin that she can take it right back,' Hope snapped. With considerable annoyance, she turned away and began walking briskly in the opposite direction.

'Wait!' Dylan called. 'Where are you going?'

'I'm going to check on the carousel. You and Larkin can make all the cute little fortune-telling jokes that you want, but *I* actually care about the success of the festival. It means a great deal to your father and Gram, so it means a great deal to me.'

She thought that her rebuke would irritate him, but to her surprise and further annoyance, when he caught up to her, Dylan was smiling.

'Has anyone ever told you that you're sweet?' he said.

Hope scowled at him.

'And sexy when you're mad.'

She spun around. 'What!'

The smile became a rakish grin. 'Yup, damn sexy.'

A tetchy response bubbled on her tongue, but in the same moment, Megan came wandering up the row toward them.

'Oh, I'm so glad that I found you, Hope. Somewhere along the way, I got turned about, and then I couldn't figure out what direction the booth was in—' She stopped abruptly when she noticed Dylan. 'This is a surprise. Since when are you back from California?'

'Since this morning. And, whoa! You weren't kidding, Hope. That is some dress you're wearing, Megan.'

'Don't you dare laugh,' Megan warned him. 'It's been a wretchedly long and hot evening, and I'm about one minute away from peeling this miserable thing off and walking around naked.'

'Naked, did you say?' The grin resurfaced. 'Go right ahead. Don't let me stop you.'

Megan rolled her eyes at him, then she turned back to Hope. 'I have nothing to report. No scarf and no Davis. I didn't run into anybody at all, so it didn't matter that I don't actually know what Davis looks like.'

'We didn't run into anybody, either,' Hope told her. 'But did you hear those noises that came from the carousel a little while ago? At least, I think they were from the carousel, based on the lights and music that went with them.'

Megan nodded. 'The carousel was my guess, too. When I couldn't find the way back to the booth, I figured that I should head toward the carousel to see what was causing all the commotion.'

Hope nodded back at her, and they once more turned in the direction of the dim yellow glow. Dylan went with them. At first, they had to tread carefully in the dark, trying to avoid stumbling over loose corners of plastic sheeting on the ground and power cables running between booths, but the closer they got to the carousel and its accompanying illumination, the easier their journey became. Although they heard an occasional voice off in the distance, they saw no one.

'How quickly things can change,' Dylan said. 'When I first came here this afternoon, the place was jammed to the gills, with barely enough space to lift an elbow, and now only a few hours later, it's as empty as a graveyard.'

'That shows how little you know,' Megan remarked.

He looked at her questioningly.

'Graveyards aren't empty,' Hope said. 'You just can't see the inhabitants.'

Dylan raised an amused eyebrow. 'Can *you* see them?'

Hope didn't answer. They had reached the carousel. It was shut down for the night. The main lights were dark. The yellow glow came from the decorative row of bulbs that lined the platform on which the animals stood. There was no sign of movement. As far as Hope could tell, they were alone.

'How odd,' she mused. 'I could have sworn that this was where those noises came from. It sounded as though the carousel was running and then malfunctioned. Shouldn't there be somebody here? Who turned it on and off?'

Dylan chortled. 'Maybe it was your graveyard ghosts.'

A tetchy response once again bubbled on Hope's tongue, but it faded almost as quickly as it had arisen. Her attention was concentrated on the carousel, and she began to circle slowly around it, looking for any indication that it might be broken. At first glance, nothing appeared to be wrong. But she was no more of an expert on the inner workings of carousels than Dylan, and if some part of the mechanism had failed – as the grinding and screeching and metallic clank suggested

– Hope realized that she probably wouldn't be able to see it. She deliberated whether to report the incident to Morris that evening or wait until the morning. She didn't like to bother him so late, but if it turned out that a repair was necessary, he would want to be aware of it as soon as possible.

'I keep asking but not getting an answer,' Dylan said, as he and Megan trailed after Hope. 'Who is Davis?'

Megan shook her head. 'I don't know much more than you do. From what I understand, he is Rosemarie's newest love interest.' She laughed lightly. 'Was that a sigh of relief, Dylan? Were you concerned that a wolf other than yourself was prowling at Hope's door?'

Hope didn't hear his reply. Her feet had stopped, and her eyes were staring in horror.

'Dylan . . .'

Although it came out as no more than a ragged whisper, Dylan was next to her in an instant.

'What is it, Hope? What's wrong?'

She struggled to speak. 'That . . . That is . . .' She pointed toward a body on the carousel. 'That is Davis.'

SEVEN

Davis was lying beside an ivory pony with a flaming orange mane and a gilded saddle. He was twisted on his back, one leg partially bent and the other stretched out straight as though he had been kicking. Both of his arms were raised, with his hands directed toward his throat. There was something wrapped around his neck that he appeared to have been clutching at. His eyes were wide and bulging, and his mouth was gaping open, leaving his distended tongue dangling. It was a gruesome sight.

In one swift movement, Dylan hurdled the short protective fence that surrounded the carousel and sprang up on to the platform. He hastened toward Davis to check for signs of life, but Hope didn't need him to confirm what was appallingly obvious: Davis was dead.

'I'll contact the police,' Dylan said.

The words he spoke into his phone were a jumble to Hope. Her ears didn't hear. Her mind didn't focus. Her eyes didn't blink. They just continued to stare in horror at the grotesque figure before her.

There was a moan and a rustle close by.

'Hope!' Dylan shouted. 'Watch out for Megan! She's about to—'

In a muddled sort of slow motion, Hope turned and found Megan in her petal-pink ball gown swooning beside her. She reached over and caught hold of Megan's shoulders just as she began tumbling to the ground.

Megan gazed at her in confusion for a moment, then her senses steadied and her feet firmed.

'Oh, thanks, Hope. Sorry for almost collapsing on you. A combination of the heat and this dress, I guess. I couldn't catch my breath. I saw that man, and . . .' Megan's hands went to her throat, the same as Davis. 'There was no air.'

'Everybody all right?' Dylan called to them.

Hope responded with a nod. She was having difficulty catching her own breath.

Still conversing with someone on his phone, Dylan knelt next to Davis for a closer examination. The person on the other end was asking questions, and Dylan was answering. Hope caught snippets of him explaining the noises they had heard earlier and how exactly they had discovered the body.

When Dylan stood back up, he turned to Hope. 'Nate wants to know what Davis's surname is.'

Startled, it took Hope a second to reply. 'It's Scott. Davis Scott. You called Nate? Detective Nate?'

'Of course. He's the only cop I know in this city.'

Apparently, Nate heard the exchange and said something humorous, because Dylan laughed heartily into the phone.

Megan was thoughtful. 'Is Detective Nate the one who used to make goo-goo eyes at Summer?'

It was Hope's turn to laugh, albeit somewhat shakily. She was still unsettled by the sight of Davis. 'Yes. When they first met, Nate seemed pretty keen on Summer.'

'What happened?'

'Nothing. That's the problem. Nate is a bit shy, I think. And Summer has had too much of Shifty Gary on her plate with the pending divorce and the sale of their house—' Hope stopped herself with a groan. 'And now it will happen all over again.'

'What will?'

'Nate was giving Summer some time and space to deal with her separation from Gary. When he finds out that Davis is connected to Gary, he'll just keep doing it. Nate will politely step back and stay out of the way when what Summer really needs is for him to step forward and get smack dab in her way.'

Nodding, Megan was about to respond, but Dylan – who had finished his phone call – spoke before she could.

'How is Davis connected to Gary?' he asked.

'Davis is supposedly our realtor,' Summer answered, walking toward them across an open stretch of grass. 'Don't be taken in by him, Dylan. If you're in the market for a property in Asheville, sign up with any agent *other* than Davis Scott. The man is a slippery fish.'

There was an awkward silence from the group, but Summer didn't seem to notice.

'I thought that we were supposed to meet back at the booth,' she said to Hope and Megan, spreading her hands questioningly. 'I was there, and I waited for an eternity, but no one else ever returned. Finally, I went in search of you. Why are you over here?'

The awkward silence continued. Hope cleared her throat, trying to figure out a delicate way of pointing out the body on the carousel.

At the sound of a twig cracking under a shoe, they all turned to find another person heading across the grass in their direction.

'Who is . . .' Summer began, squinting at the approaching figure. There was a little gasp. 'Good lord, is that Nate?'

Detective Nate Phillips recognized Summer at just about the same instant that she recognized him. His steps slowed as he rubbed his hands self-consciously over his brown hair, even though it was so closely cropped that there wasn't much to be smoothed. He also made an effort to straighten his white button-down shirt. Both the shirt and his tan slacks were heavily wrinkled from a long day's work. Nate had evidently not yet gone home that evening.

Hope and Megan exchanged a glance. Detective Nate might be keeping his distance from Summer, but he was clearly still interested in making a good impression on her.

Dylan was the first to speak, hailing Nate and remarking on the speed of his arrival.

'You caught me at my desk,' Nate explained, 'so I got here sooner than I otherwise would have. I was staying late at the station to finish up reports.'

'I do the same thing myself when I'm at the hospital,' Dylan said. 'My view has always been that it's better to work into Friday evening than having to slog through it over the weekend – or, worse yet, carry it into next week.'

'Exactly,' Nate agreed. 'And it looks as though I made the right choice, because now I'm going to have this on my hands.'

Dylan nodded. 'No question about that. If you come up here, I'll show you what we've got. I hopped the fence and then jumped up on to the platform, but there's a gate around the opposite side that opens for the public – with a set of stairs – if you prefer.'

'I'll jump. Not a problem.' As Nate approached the carousel, he genially greeted Hope, then Megan, and finally Summer, lingering on her with his warm, chocolate-brown eyes.

Hope and Megan exchanged another glance, this time adding a smile.

'I don't understand,' Summer said to Nate, her hazel eyes lingering in return. 'What are you doing here?'

'Dylan called me to report the dead man they found.' He hurdled the fence. 'Your sister said his name was Davis Scott.'

There was another gasp from Summer. This one was so loud that it nearly caused Nate to trip and fall on his way up to the platform.

Summer's gaze snapped to Hope for confirmation. 'Davis is dead? Where is he?'

Hope got no further than motioning toward the ivory pony with the flaming orange mane and gilded saddle. Summer instantly spun around and began hurrying toward it. There was no misreading her intention. She planned on joining Nate and Dylan on the carousel.

'No, no, no!' Nate shouted.

'Stop her, Hope,' Dylan enjoined.

Hope succeeded in grabbing Summer's arm just before she tried to leap over the fence. It was probably a lucky thing, too. Nate – who wasn't as tall as Dylan – hadn't cleared it all that easily. Had Summer continued, she might have ended up both injured and embarrassed by the attempt.

'You can't come up here,' Nate directed sharply.

The hazel eyes now glowered rather than lingered on him.

His tone lost some of its brusqueness. 'It's for your own safety,' he told Summer. 'And to protect the potential crime scene.'

'Crime scene?' she exclaimed.

Once more, Summer's gaze snapped to Hope, but this time her sister could offer no confirmation, because she was equally startled by Nate's remark.

'Every unexplained death is always a potential crime scene,' he expounded matter-of-factly, before turning his focus to Dylan and the body in front of them.

'I don't want to overstep,' Dylan began to Nate. 'This is your arena, not mine. But look at this spot where . . .'

As the two men bent down to examine whatever it was that Dylan had noticed, their voices fell to an inaudible level. Both Hope and Summer leaned against the fence, trying to get closer and hear the conversation, without success.

After a long minute, Megan gave a doleful sigh. 'Looking back on it, I wish that we hadn't been so dismissive of Rosemarie's concerns. She told us that she had a bad feeling; clearly, she was right.'

Hope nodded in agreement. 'Maybe we should have reported Davis as missing to the police. Maybe we could have prevented this.'

'We couldn't have prevented this,' Summer said.

She spoke with such certainty that Hope and Megan turned to her with surprise.

'We couldn't have prevented it,' she reiterated. 'It wasn't only Rosemarie who was right. You were right, too, Hope.'

'I was?'

'Yes. Remember when the Five of Coins came up in the reading at the boutique? You said that something about it didn't feel right to you, as though it was pointing in another direction. We didn't understand it at the time, but you were absolutely correct. Now it's clear. The card was pointing toward the carousel. It was pointing toward Davis.'

Hope frowned.

'It fits together perfectly,' Summer continued with vigor. 'Davis was entering the shop just as you were drawing the cards, so they easily could have been intended for him rather than me. And then there's the number. The *Five* of Coins and *five* tickets required for the carousel. They match! Don't say that it's simply a coincidence, Hope, because you know that I don't believe in coincidences.'

'All right, but allow me to point out that our booth also requires five tickets.'

Although Hope offered it as evidence against her sister's

argument, Summer took it as further proof in support of her position.

'Exactly! Three examples of five. It's no secret the spiritual world loves things in triplicate. The universal power of three and all that.'

The frown deepened.

'You told me,' Summer went on, unabated, 'that the Five of Coins indicates loss and despair, eviction and homelessness.'

'*Potential* eviction and *potential* homelessness,' Hope corrected her. 'And it's a pretty broad generalization—'

'It's not a generalization when it comes to Davis,' Summer cut her off. 'He's a real estate agent. Or *was* a real estate agent,' she amended. 'Apartments and houses were his bread and butter, and the dark side of that is eviction and homelessness. There is no better card in the Tarot to represent Davis Scott and his slippery-fish ways than the Five of Coins.'

Hope wasn't sure how to respond. She felt that she should continue to dispute her sister's conclusions, but some of what Summer was saying was beginning to sound disturbingly accurate.

'Which brings us to the second card that came up in the reading.' Summer's voice rose in triumph. 'If the Five of Coins wasn't meant for me, then neither was Death. Death was meant for Davis!'

Silence followed. Too much silence. Slowly and with some trepidation, Hope turned toward the carousel. She winced as she saw Dylan and Nate. They were no longer leaning over Davis's body, engaged in examination and earnest discussion. They were now standing upright on the platform, gazing curiously at her and Summer. How much exactly they had heard – and comprehended – of the conversation wasn't clear, but they had certainly caught enough to grab their attention.

'Death was meant for Davis?' Nate echoed after a moment.

'Are you suggesting that you knew the man was going to die?' Dylan said, his tone incredulous.

'No, we didn't have any idea—' Hope began hastily.

'But the cards did,' Summer interjected. 'The cards knew.'

Dylan raised an even more incredulous eyebrow.

'You're talking about the Tarot cards?' Nate asked.

Summer waved her hand impatiently as though it was a gratuitous question. 'Of course I'm talking about the Tarot cards. The cards knew all along what was going to happen. We didn't realize it, obviously. If we had, we would have tried to warn Davis.'

Hope shook her head. 'We couldn't have warned Davis. He never would have listened to us.'

'Exactly,' Summer concurred. 'That's why I said earlier we couldn't have prevented this. Davis would have merely brushed aside – or, more likely, laughed at – any caution that we might have given him. You saw how negative and skeptical he was toward all things mystical in the booth and the boutique. And he seriously thought that it was an earthquake in the shop!'

Dylan's eyebrow went higher. 'There was an earthquake in the shop?'

Not answering him, Summer continued to Hope, 'Speaking of earthquakes, if there is an upside to all of this, at least we don't have to worry anymore about Davis coming to the brownstone – nor will he be pestering us or Gram to put the place on the market.'

'Well, yes, that's true,' Hope agreed hesitantly. She couldn't refute the point, but she wasn't sure that Summer should be making such statements in front of Dylan and Nate, let alone talking quite so freely about Death and the Tarot. With a small cough, she tried to give her sister a hint to be more circumspect.

'It occurs to me,' Summer went on, either not noticing or not caring about the admonition, 'that there is another upside to Davis being gone. Now Gary will be forced to choose a different realtor. I can't imagine that the new one could possibly be as bad as the old one, which means there might finally be a chance that the house will sell. And if the house sells, then the divorce can be finalized.'

Hope couldn't refute that point, either. But now she was positive that Summer was saying too much – and far too cheerfully – regarding the benefits of Davis's demise. Nate and Dylan were looking at Summer with troubled expressions. Again, Hope coughed, louder this time.

Undeterred, Summer pursued her stream of thoughts. 'Once

the divorce is finalized, Gary will be permanently out of the picture, too. That should make the attic happy, because then there can be no more egregious remarks from either Davis or Gary about the advantages of selling the brownstone. Maybe the attic will be so pleased that they'll at long last consider giving up their grudge against me. That would be great! If they became even just a little less irritable, I might be able to go up to the third floor without always having to worry that . . .'

The sentence trailed away unfinished. There was an audible gulp from Summer. She turned toward Hope, her eyes stretched wide at a sudden horrifying possibility.

'My god, was it the attic? Could the attic be responsible for Davis's death?'

EIGHT

There was a moment of startled silence all around. Dylan and Nate stared at Summer with a mixture of astonishment and confusion, as though they couldn't possibly have heard her correctly. Hope also stared at her sister, but for a different reason. The idea that the attic might have somehow had a hand – so to speak – in Davis's death had never occurred to her. Even in the warmth of the night air, Hope felt herself shiver. But she answered Summer as quickly and definitively as she could, mostly in an effort to close Dylan and Nate's sagging jaws.

'Of course it wasn't the attic,' she said. 'How could the attic be responsible for Davis's death? The last time Davis was in the brownstone was two days ago, and nothing happened to him there. He died here – on the carousel. It was an accident.'

'It wasn't an accident,' Dylan corrected her.

'What?' It was Hope's turn to be confused.

'It wasn't an accident,' Dylan repeated. 'Davis's death was deliberate.'

'Are you sure?' Summer asked.

'Yes, I'm sure,' Dylan responded with annoyance. 'Not that you have to take my word for it. I'm only a board-certified physician who deals with the sick and the dying on a daily basis. I might not be able to tell the difference between misadventure and murder.'

'Murder!' Megan exclaimed, aghast. 'But why? Who would do such a thing?'

'Those are two excellent questions,' Nate said, 'both of which I intend on learning the answers to. In any event, Dylan is correct. The evidence is clear and allows for no other interpretation. Davis Scott was murdered. He was strangled to death.'

'Strangled to death?' Summer was thoughtful. 'The attic probably couldn't manage that.'

Hope's head snapped to her sister, but Dylan spoke before she could, his tone heavily deprecating.

'No, your attic probably couldn't manage that. Not unless your attic can take a piece of cloth, wrap it around a man's neck, and then ensure that the ends are caught under the edge of the carousel platform as it rotates, thereby throttling the man.'

Megan grimaced. 'How awful. Shouldn't there be some sort of a safety mechanism to prevent such a thing from happening?'

'There is a safety mechanism,' Dylan replied. 'In all likelihood, you heard it. Hope and I did.'

Hope was quizzical. 'We did?'

'It was that loud grinding noise,' he told her, 'followed by the series of high-pitched screeches. And it worked. The carousel and platform stopped. Unfortunately for Davis, however, it wasn't soon enough. The cloth had already tightened around his neck, and he couldn't get it loose.'

Nate nodded. 'Based on the position of the body, he obviously tried hard to free himself. But it was a futile effort. He needed the cloth to tear or be cut away, neither of which occurred. And even that might not have saved him. I've seen it before. The force is simply too great. It's the same with a necklace being pulled into a paper shredder or a sleeve being sucked into a wood chipper. The end result is never pretty.'

Summer frowned.

'Sorry.' Nate gave an apologetic shrug. 'Curse of the job, I'm afraid. Sometimes my descriptions can get a bit grisly.'

He had misconstrued her reaction. Summer wasn't dismayed; she was perplexed. 'But your examples with the shredder and the chipper,' she said, 'those are accidents. Isn't this an accident, too? What makes you think that it was deliberate?'

'So you're no longer blaming the attic?' Dylan remarked drolly.

As Dylan and Nate exchanged an amused glance, Hope sighed. The course of the conversation wasn't good. For starters, it was a bad idea to openly discuss the attic in such a manner. Somehow the attic always seemed to know and took a perverse pleasure in reminding you of it at the most inopportune moment. And second, if Summer wanted her

relationship with Nate to grow, then repeatedly mentioning
the quirks of the attic wasn't beneficial. The attic might be
many things, but amorous and sensual were not among them.
Ghosts and goblins had a very different effect on romance
than champagne and truffles.

'I understand,' Hope interjected swiftly, trying to move
permanently off the subject of the attic, 'that the safety mechanism is what stopped the carousel, but someone must have
started it in the first place. Is that why you consider it to be
murder? Because Davis couldn't have turned on the carousel
and throttled himself at the same time?'

'An astute – and accurate – deduction,' Nate complimented
her.

There was a brief hesitation. Dylan and Nate glanced at
each other again, this time not with amusement but questioningly, as though debating how much information to share with
the others.

'You're the detective, so it's your decision in the end, but
I'm of the opinion that you should point it out to them,' Dylan
said. 'They may recognize it from somewhere, especially with
that distinct pattern.'

'Recognize it?' Summer and Megan echoed in unison.

'What pattern?' Hope asked.

They collectively stepped toward the fence, expecting Nate
to reveal the item at issue. Nate hesitated a moment longer, and
as they waited, Hope's gaze returned to Davis. Now that the
initial shock of discovering his lifeless body had passed, she
looked at him more closely. As little as she had liked the man,
she felt great sympathy for him. His final minutes must have
been horrific, filled with a dreadful panic and fear, being aware
of what was happening but unable to stop it. The way his torso
was wrenched in one direction and his legs in another. His arms
raised, and his hands desperately clawing at his throat.

'Hope . . .' Summer's words came slowly. 'The cloth . . .'

Hope didn't have to ask her what she meant, because she
was staring straight at it. The cloth that was wrapped around
Davis's neck. She had only glanced at it before, but now
her eyes observed it fully. And as Dylan had supposed, she
recognized it.

Megan drew a sharp breath, recognizing it also. 'Good lord. Is that the missing scarf?'

It was indeed the missing scarf. Or at least it very much resembled the missing scarf. Although the material was creased and crumpled, its black-and-white chevron pattern was still clearly visible.

'Could it be a different one?' Megan began. 'What are the chances that—'

'No,' Summer cut her off emphatically. 'It can't be a different scarf. It can't be a coincidence.'

As a rule, Hope was considerably more open-minded about the possibility of coincidences than her sister, but in this instance, she was obliged to agree with Summer. 'It must be the same scarf. The odds of an identical one being found here – tonight, in this location – are infinitesimal.'

Nate looked at them, then at the cloth, and back again. 'It's a scarf?'

Summer gave an affirmative nod.

'And not just any scarf,' Dylan – proving himself quick on the uptake – informed Nate. 'If I understand correctly, this particular scarf mysteriously vanished earlier in the evening, and everyone has since been searching for it, while at the same time searching for Davis.'

The affirmative nod now came from Hope.

'How interesting,' Dylan mused, 'that the missing scarf and the missing man should be found together.'

'Very interesting,' Nate agreed. 'And from a professional perspective, also potentially very helpful. From a personal perspective, however . . .' He turned to Summer. 'I sincerely hope that the scarf doesn't belong to you or your sister?'

'It doesn't,' Summer responded cheerfully.

Nate exhaled with relief. Hope didn't want to amend Summer's answer, but she knew that she had to.

'The scarf doesn't belong to us *now*,' Hope clarified, 'because we sold it two days ago at the boutique.'

The exhalation of relief was replaced by one of frustration. There was some indistinct muttering from Dylan.

'To make it completely clear and leave no room for misinterpretation, you're telling me that this scarf' – Nate pointed

at the chevron-patterned cloth wrapped around Davis's throat
– 'was previously in your possession and under your control?'

Hope winced. When he put it that way, it really didn't
sound good. For all intents and purposes, the scarf was the
murder weapon. Admitting to having been the owner of
the murder weapon could not possibly be considered
advantageous.

The same thought must have occurred to Summer, because
she replied with deliberate vagueness, 'Maybe. Or maybe
not. It's impossible to say for certain. Although at first
glance the scarf on the carousel appears to be substantially
similar to the one that Hope and I previously had contact
with at the boutique, upon closer examination there could
be subtle but significant variations between the two. They
may, in fact, be entirely different scarves. It might be a case
of mere happenstance.'

Nate folded his arms across his chest. 'Less than a minute
ago, you made the exact opposite statement. You said that it
couldn't be a different scarf, that it couldn't be a coincidence.'

Summer folded her arms back at him. 'I was confused. I
may still be confused. It's been a long, hot, stressful day – and
evening. Poor Megan can scarcely draw a breath in that hideously sequined dress. We're all hungry and thirsty and
thoroughly worn out. We can't give you an absolute assurance
or guarantee regarding a scarf that Hope had hardly even
finished unpacking from the shipping box before it was scooped
up by an eager customer and purchased. These are extremely
trying circumstances, and we're attempting to be as helpful
and cooperative as we can.'

Megan struggled to suppress a laugh. Hope likewise restrained
a smile. All the time and money that Summer had been forced
to expend on a divorce attorney was evidently paying off – if
not in terms of actually facilitating her parting from Gary, then
at least in regard to learning nebulous legal speak to use
when dealing with difficult questions from the police.

Nate sucked on his teeth. He was patently displeased. 'Can
you manage to give me a remotely straight answer as to
who you sold the scarf to? Or is the customer's name also
subject to your alleged confusion and dehydration?'

'Of course I can give you an answer.' Summer offered a winsome, conciliatory smile. 'Rosemarie Potter.'

There was a pause. Nate turned and made some comment to Dylan. It was too quiet for Hope to hear. Summer, however, caught a portion of it, and her smile faded.

'Did I hear you right?' she said to Nate. 'You can't seriously think that Rosemarie might have been involved in Davis's death.'

Now Megan did laugh, although it was limited by the bodice of her dress to a stifled chortle. 'Rosemarie Potter a murderer? How absurd!'

'Completely absurd,' Summer agreed. 'Rosemarie is as gentle as a lamb.'

That argument didn't hold sway with Nate. 'In my experience, given the right conditions, someone as gentle as a lamb can lose control just the same as someone as ill-tempered as a grizzly – with a similarly grievous outcome.'

'Yes, certainly. There's no doubt of your expertise.' The winsome smile resurfaced. 'But with regard to Rosemarie, it's simply unimaginable. She's as far from a cold-blooded killer as they come.'

'No one claimed that she was a cold-blooded killer,' Dylan responded.

Once more, the smile faded, and Summer's brow furrowed. 'But I heard Nate say to you—'

'If you're going to eavesdrop,' Dylan cut her off sharply, 'then you should at least make sure that you've overheard the conversation correctly before tossing around your own absurd accusations.'

Nate did not disagree.

Summer's face flushed with anger – and embarrassment. 'Don't lecture me,' she snapped at Dylan. 'I'm trying to support and defend my friend Rosemarie. Go back to your own friend, Little Miss Larkin. Why are you here bothering us anyway? Shouldn't you be having dinner or whatever with her?'

Dylan's eyes narrowed dangerously, but Nate was the first to speak. While not bitter, his tone also couldn't be considered convivial.

'I asked Dylan a minute ago, and now I'll ask the three of you: what connection was there between Davis Scott and Rosemarie Potter?'

'Rosemarie and Davis were dating.' Hope made an effort to keep her own tone light. It was clear that everybody's nerves were frayed, and she didn't want to inflame the situation further. 'That's one of the reasons it seems so improbable to us that Rosemarie could have had any involvement in what happened to Davis. Although I didn't discuss it with her, I had the impression that she liked him quite a bit.'

'Do you want Nate and me to recite the statistics regarding the percentages of people who have ended up in the emergency room and the morgue because their domestic partners *liked them quite a bit*?' Dylan rejoined.

This time, it was Hope's eyes that narrowed. Although she knew what Dylan said was true, she didn't appreciate his condescending tone. 'Thank you for pointing that out to me,' she replied dryly. 'I'll keep it in mind when deciding who *not* to date in the future.'

Dylan was sufficiently perceptive to catch her inference. His frosty gaze met hers.

Making her own attempt to ease the growing tension, Megan said with a touch of humor, 'All else being equal, Rosemarie couldn't possibly have harmed Davis, because she had Percy with her. She'd never take the risk that Percy would somehow be injured in the process. She loves that dog far too much.'

Unamused by the contribution, it was Nate's turn for a dry reply. 'If being a loving dog owner automatically disqualified a person from making stupid choices, then we'd have a hell of a lot less crime in this country.'

Megan's gaze now also became frosty.

Summer's expression wasn't much warmer. She looked ready to provide her own biting remark, but suddenly she threw her head back and laughed instead. It was a shrill, almost frenzied laugh, sounding frighteningly like someone on the verge of a nervous collapse.

'I've solved the case!' she cried. 'I know who the murderer is! Yes, Rosemarie bought the scarf from us at the boutique.

But she didn't keep it. She gave it away. Do you remember
to whom?'

Hope blinked at her in speechless surprise.

'That's right!' Summer laughed harder. 'Forget the attic.
And forget Rosemarie. They weren't to blame for Davis's
death. It was Percy. The pug did it!'

NINE

I f the pug had done it, he couldn't be questioned on the matter that evening, because – his lack of conversational English aside – neither he nor Rosemarie appeared at the carousel, or, for that matter, anywhere else on the festival grounds. When Hope and Summer briefly returned to their booth to collect their belongings, they found no indication that anyone had been there in their absence. Where Rosemarie and Percy had disappeared to was a mystery, but Hope and Summer were prohibited from solving it. Before permitting them to leave the crime scene, Nate strictly forbade them from having any contact with Rosemarie until further notice. He was going to be the one to inform Rosemarie of Davis's death, so that he could gauge her initial response. Under other circumstances, Hope and Summer might have been tempted to violate the injunction, but Nate didn't mince words. He sternly informed them that any breach of his directive would be considered interference with a police investigation. Although Hope doubted that Nate would go so far as to arrest them on such a dubious charge, she also thought it best not to take the chance. Tensions were running too high for them to push their luck.

Exhausted, the sisters slept hard that night. Upon waking the next morning, the events of the previous evening seemed like nothing more than a bad dream. But when they arrived back at the festival grounds to open their booth for the day, it was impossible to pretend that the nightmare hadn't really occurred. The area surrounding the carousel was cordoned off with bright yellow police tape, and there were plenty of police in action – some uniformed, others with forensic gear, and a third group that appeared to be inspecting the inner workings of the carousel. If Nate was among them, he wasn't visible.

Summer breathed a shaky sigh of relief. 'I should want to see him. I should apologize for being so . . . so . . .'

'So tired,' Hope finished for her. 'We were all tired. Nate included. Which is why I don't think that apologies are necessary. No one said or did anything scandalous or irreparable.' She chuckled. 'Well, maybe Percy deserves an apology. You did accuse him of being a murderer.'

'That probably was a step too far,' Summer conceded with a smile.

'Thank goodness Rosemarie didn't hear it. She might never have forgiven you.'

The smile broadened. 'How true.'

'Speaking of forgiveness . . .' Hope lowered her voice discreetly. As they had the previous day, they wound their way through the general bustle toward their booth. Being morning, the crowd was thinner, mostly consisting of other booth holders. The temperature wasn't much cooler, however. It was only because the sun hadn't yet reached its full height that they weren't racing for shade. 'Did you notice the attic last night?'

Alarmed, Summer halted. 'No. I didn't hear or see anything. What happened?'

'Nothing. That's what I mean. There was nothing at all. It was completely still. Not a peep, or a bump, or a shadow out of place. When was the last time we had a whole night with perfect quiet?'

'Never. At least, not that I can remember. Even years ago, when we were kids. There was always some sort of a disturbance. Whimpering, banging, restless roaming. And now, all of a sudden, there isn't anything?'

Hope nodded. 'It has to be considered an auspicious sign, don't you think? Either the attic has decided to forgive and forget the remarks that were made yesterday or it paid them no heed to begin with.'

Summer started to agree, but then she offered a third option. 'Or it might be lulling us into a false sense of security. You know how the attic loves to play games. This could just be the calm before the storm. And if that's the case, it's going to be an almighty tempest.'

'Good lord, I hope you're wrong.'

'That makes two of us.'

They exchanged an uneasy glance and began walking again.

'I wouldn't mind a storm,' Summer said after a moment. 'I'm tired of the heat. I'm tired of the dust. I'm tired of the beastly sun. I want thunder, lightning, and a torrential downpour. That would cool things down and freshen things up, if only for an hour.'

'Sounds nice. As long as it occurs outside in the open air and not inside the brownstone.'

Summer blanched. 'I wasn't suggesting . . . I meant an actual storm, in the meteorological sense.'

'From your mouth to the elementals' ears. But let's change the subject to be on the safe side. We don't want to give the attic any ideas.'

'Heaven forbid! That's the absolute last thing we want to do. And *she*,' Summer added with a pronounced groan, 'is the absolute last person I want to see.'

Hope took a swift survey of the crowd surrounding them, but no one stood out to her. 'Who?'

'Melody. Melody Witten.'

The name didn't mean anything to Hope. 'Should I know her?'

'No. Be grateful that you don't. She's about as pleasant and appealing as a malarial mosquito. Quick!' Summer grabbed her sister's arm and started to pull her to the left. 'If we turn here, maybe we can avoid her.'

Although Hope willingly followed along, they made it only a couple of paces before Summer stopped with another groan. 'Too late. She spotted us.'

Hope was about to say that she still didn't see the person, but an instant later, a woman stepped directly in front of them, blocking their path.

'Hey there, Summer,' she cooed.

'Melody,' Summer returned curtly.

Melody Witten had heavily frosted hair and such a thick layer of mascara combined with eyeliner that she had a raccoon-like appearance. She was about the same age as the sisters, but her choice of attire was not in the least similar. While Hope and Summer had selected their breeziest blouses in anticipation of a sweltering day in their booth, Melody was dressed in a skimpy, pumpkin-orange bikini.

'Maybe we were wrong,' Summer murmured to Hope. 'Maybe there is a dunking booth at the festival, after all.'

Summer's voice rose a bit too much, and Melody looked at her quizzically.

'A dunking booth? Oh, I understand.' She inclined her head. 'You mean my bikini. It's not for swimming. It's promotional. I'm wearing it for Aaron and Gary's booth.'

Hope took a startled step backward. Gary? Shifty Gary?

Summer – to her considerable credit – barely blinked at the reference. 'Promotional?' she inquired.

'Good sales require good advertising,' Melody responded in a sing-song manner. 'That's what Aaron always says.'

'Your husband certainly is an undying salesman. He invariably has a scheme afoot.'

Although it was spoken in a neutral tone, Hope could feel the contempt lurking just below the surface. Melody, on the other hand, seemed to construe Summer's words as a compliment.

'Yes, Aaron is a fantastic salesman. Except' – she glanced around surreptitiously, as though about to reveal a highly confidential secret – 'the booth wasn't very successful yesterday. We had some visitors, but we didn't get many tickets from them. So Aaron and Gary put their heads together last night and came up with this.' With a dramatic flourish of her arm, Melody motioned toward herself.

Hope and Summer exchanged their own surreptitious glance. It was Saturday morning, in a public park, at a family-oriented festival. Under such conditions, a teeny-weeny bikini didn't seem like the wisest or most effective promotional tool. On the contrary, there would in all likelihood be a substantial number of wives and girlfriends who – upon spotting said bikini – were going to briskly steer their husbands and boyfriends *away* from the booth.

'What kind of booth is it?' Hope asked.

'Mead,' Melody answered.

'Mead?'

'Alcohol made from fermented honey mixed with water,' Summer explained to her sister.

'There's much more to it than that,' Melody said. 'There can be fruits and spices also. Aaron got the idea from you, actually.'

It was Summer's turn to take a startled step backward. '*Me?*'

Melody nodded. 'Gary is continually telling us how much money you're making from the herbs and teas you put together. So Aaron started thinking about what we could do along the same lines, and he came up with mead. He figured that if you could get rich on herbs and teas, then we could just as easily get rich on mead – and Gary, too.'

Hope and Summer glanced at each other again, and this time they burst out laughing. The boutique was in a constant financial struggle. In the best of months, Summer barely managed to break even with her herbs and teas. The idea that money was merrily pouring in was hilarious.

'There's no need to be rude.' Melody scrunched up her nose indignantly. 'Aaron says that the mead market is right on the cusp of taking off. We only have to be patient. You shouldn't begrudge us our success when it happens.'

With visible effort, Summer attempted to rein in her laughter. 'I hope that you'll be very successful. And I certainly don't begrudge you anything. We're not laughing because of the mead. We're laughing because of what you said about riches. It couldn't be any further from the truth. Believe me when I tell you that there are no riches raining down on Hope and me and our little shop.'

It was clear from the way Melody's nose remained scrunched that she didn't believe Summer one jot. 'Of course, it's none of my business how much money you have or in what ways you try to hide it. That's between you and your conscience and the government tax people.' She sniffed. 'But speaking as Gary's friend, I feel it my duty to say that it's wrong of you not to share your wealth with him.'

Summer's mouth dropped open.

Hope was likewise rendered momentarily speechless. She wasn't sure which part of Melody's claim was more staggering: that Summer was in possession of secret wealth or that she was supposed to share the purported wealth with Shifty Gary.

'It's wrong of you,' Melody repeated with another sniff. 'The money was earned during the course of your marriage, so it's only fair that Gary be given half of it. And that's especially true in this instance, because you were the one to abandon the relationship. You walked out on Gary and filed for a divorce.'

Crimson fury flooded Summer's face. 'I walked out on Gary and filed for a divorce because he was having an affair! Gary lied to my face and cheated behind my back for months on end!'

'It was a fling,' Melody responded equably. 'All men have flings.' She shrugged as though an adulterous husband was no more of a problem than a sprouting potato in the pantry. 'If I'm allowed my two cents, I think that you should try to patch things up. At his core, Gary's a great guy. You won't do any better than him.'

Summer gaped at her with a mixture of anger and disbelief. Hope, on the other hand, was beginning to feel some pity for Melody. It was partly because of the pumpkin-orange bikini and partly because it wasn't much of a stretch to assume that husband Aaron was a cheater, as well. For her part, Melody didn't appear at all upset or rattled by the conversation.

'Well, it was nice chatting with you,' she said, 'but I have to get back to our booth. And you have to get to yours. The festival will be opening soon. Good luck today!'

Summer was still gaping, so Hope replied politely, 'Good luck to you also.'

With a cheerful wave, Melody turned and started to walk away. After a step or two, she abruptly turned back.

'I'll tell Gary that I saw you,' she cooed. 'I'm sure he'll want to know, so that he can see you, too!'

'Oh, no,' Summer began. 'That's a really bad . . .'

Either Melody didn't hear her or didn't want to hear her, because she waved once more, cooed a goodbye, and disappeared into the crowd.

For a long moment, Hope and Summer stared after her in silence. Then Summer groaned just as she had at Melody's first appearance.

'Why? Why did we have to run into her? Why does she have to tell Gary?'

'Were you aware that Gary had a booth here?' Hope asked.

'No! I remember him mentioning mead once a long time ago. That's how I knew what it was. But I had no idea that he was trying to turn it into a business. Why would I?' Summer gave a derisive snort. 'I didn't have a clue about Gary's lovers, so why would I have a clue about his hobbies?'

Hope had no answer for that.

'And now' – Summer groaned again – 'thanks to Melody and her big mouth, he'll come to our booth.'

'Not necessarily. It isn't guaranteed that Melody will tell him. And even if she does, Gary might not be any more eager to see you than you are to see him. Plus, we don't know whether he's heard about what happened to Davis. As you said yesterday, with Davis gone, Gary will be forced to choose a new realtor for the house. He may not react so well to that.'

'Good point. But if Gary does come' – Summer revisited her fear from the day before – 'then he'll see Larkin's glittery brothel banner, and he'll tell the judge about it at the court hearing next week.'

'I would worry less about the banner,' Hope said, 'and more about Gary telling the judge how fabulously wealthy you supposedly are.'

'Except I'm not!' she protested.

'I know that, of course. But how would a judge know? Especially a judge who handles family matters. They must be continually dealing with people who hide assets or pretend to earn less than they really do in an effort to avoid paying maintenance or support. I would guess that most judges take those sorts of claims pretty seriously.'

Summer sighed. 'Well, Gary can make whatever claims he likes. And the judge can believe whatever he likes. I can't pay what I don't have. What's the old saying? You can't squeeze blood from a turnip.'

'That's an old saying?'

'What's an old saying?' asked an unexpected voice.

Spinning around in surprise, Hope and Summer found Morris Henshaw standing behind them. Hope's first thought was one of concern. Was Morris all right? How was he handling the shock and disappointment of losing the carousel for the remainder of the festival? To her relief, he appeared to have taken the bad news in his stride. Morris's face was calm. His eyes were alert. And in his hands was a clipboard that contained a typed to-do list, with priorities highlighted in fluorescent ink and notes neatly printed in the margins. It looked as though Morris might be challenging Gram for the title of Best Organizer.

'I didn't mean to startle you,' Morris apologized. 'I thought that you heard me approach. But I suppose in this hullabaloo it's impossible to hear much of anything.' He smiled with undisguised satisfaction. 'Isn't it marvelous? So many people – and all here so early! The ticket sales will be excellent today.'

'Speaking of ticket sales,' Hope said, 'I'm terribly sorry about the carousel.'

'It's upsetting,' he agreed. 'The most appalling part is the lack of quality.'

'Lack of quality?' Summer asked.

'Lack of quality,' Morris repeated, his voice rising to empha-size the point. 'A piece of junk. That's what the carousel is. Breaks down without any warning whatsoever. Snaps in two like a brittle twig in a mere puff of wind. And they expect us to hand over good money for such rubbish? Absolutely not! Amelia Palmer and I discussed it first thing. As co-chairs of the festival committee, we came to an immediate decision. Not only will the committee refuse to pay the remainder of the outstanding rental fee, but we intend to demand the full return of our deposit. It's a matter of principle. They sent us a faulty carousel, and they'll take it straight back without a penny from us. In my mind, that's the final word on the subject.'

'Have you spoken to the company about it?'

'Olivia has. She was on the phone with them for half of the morning. You should have heard her. The company was arguing one thing and threatening another—'

'Threatening?' Summer exclaimed.

'There's no need to worry. Olivia would never stand for any attempt to bully her. She gave them a good scolding in response.' Morris smiled again. 'Your grandmother may have the tenderness of a kitten, but if provoked, the razor-sharp claws of a tiger come out. And when she showed any sign of wavering, Dylan buoyed her up.'

'Dylan?' Hope said in surprise.

'Yes. Dylan came by the house with croissants and fresh juice for breakfast. Wasn't that kind of him?' Morris didn't pause for a reply. 'He said that he wanted to check on us after the debacle with the carousel, because he knows that the success of the festival means a great deal to Olivia and me, so it means a great deal to him.'

Hope raised an eyebrow. Funny how *she* had used those exact same words with Dylan the evening before.

'He's so thoughtful,' Morris continued to gush. 'When Olivia asked me to tell you that she might be too busy to visit your booth today – she has more calls to make concerning the carousel and the festival insurers – Dylan volunteered to drop by the booth in her place. It was very considerate of him.'

The eyebrow went higher.

'Very considerate indeed,' Summer remarked. 'Did Dylan happen to say whether he intended on having dear Larkin with him?'

A crease formed in Morris's brow. At first, Hope thought that it was because he had detected Summer's thinly veiled sarcasm, but it turned out that he was simply pondering the question.

'I don't know what Larkin's plans are for the day. The office isn't open on the weekend, of course. Dylan didn't mention their dinner last night, so I'm not sure if that went forward or not. They may have changed it to another evening – or lunch instead. If that's the case, then Dylan might bring Larkin along to the booth.'

Annoyed, Hope shifted her weight from one foot to the other.

Checking his clipboard and wristwatch simultaneously, Morris gave a shout of dismay. 'Oh, I'm running late! I'm scheduled to meet with the detective to discuss the matter of the carousel. Detective Phillips. Such a competent and congenial fellow. When we arranged the appointment, he made a comment about stopping by your booth later today also. Apparently, you spoke with him yesterday evening? I had the impression that he hadn't gotten all the answers he was looking for.'

It was Summer's turn to shift her weight with annoyance.

Morris checked his watch again. 'And I believe that you're running late, too. Shouldn't you be at your booth? Eager ticketholders must be knocking on the door – or, in this case, the draperies.'

His tone was reminiscent of a parent scolding a child who wanted to play in the yard on a sunny afternoon rather than sit quietly inside and finish a homework assignment. But it was difficult to be irritated with Morris, because he never intended any malice. He always meant well.

'We're heading straight there,' Hope told him. 'And we'll do our best to collect as many tickets as we can today.'

'Wonderful!' Morris beamed his gratitude. 'And if you encounter any problems with the booth, just give Stanley Palmer a call. He'll sort it out for you. Olivia gave you his number previously, didn't she?'

Hope nodded.

Nodding affably in return, Morris departed, studying his clipboard as he went.

'Terrific,' Summer muttered when Morris had moved out of earshot. 'I anticipate this day will be as enjoyable as a root canal. In between entertaining a horde of ticketholders with a wretched crystal ball, we will be set upon by some combination of Gary, Nate, Dylan, Larkin, and Rosemarie. With our luck, they'll all arrive at the booth at the same time. What a joyous occasion that will be! Rosemarie weeping over Davis. Gary yelling about the house. Larkin flirting as though she should have her own brothel. I don't know what exactly Nate and Dylan will do.'

'Probably flirt back at Larkin,' Hope said.

'Probably,' Summer agreed. 'In any event, it will be excruciating for us.'

Hope shrugged.

Summer frowned at her sister. 'It doesn't bother you?'

'Sure it bothers me.' She shrugged once more, this time adding a hint of a smile. 'But I have a plan. While they're all yelling, weeping, and flirting with each other, we'll slip out the back. They can have the booth, the crystal ball, and the ticketholders. You and Megan and I will retire to the Green Goat for cocktails.'

'Three cheers to that!'

TEN

Sadly, the Green Goat wasn't yet a viable option, because it was still far too early in the day for cocktails. There were also far too many ticketholders now milling around the festival grounds for the booth to be left unattended much longer. The booth itself required little preparation for the public. Hope and Summer fastened up the cords to open both the front and back curtains to allow for a modicum of airflow. Summer switched on the oscillating fan, followed by the twinkle lights. One strand of lights gave a sharp pop and then promptly went dark.

'And the troubles have officially begun,' Summer announced. 'Mark my words, this day – cocktails or not – is going to be an unholy mess.'

Although Hope didn't say it aloud, she was inclined to agree.

'I'll call Stanley to see if he can come by and fix the lights for us.' Summer rummaged through her handbag to find her phone. 'Why are you moving the crystal ball? Doesn't it have to be on the table?'

'I'm moving the crystal ball because I'm no longer going to use the crystal ball.' With an unceremonious thud, Hope deposited Larkin's plasma globe – still covered by the surplus piece of velvet from the night before – on the ground.

'There's no question that the crystal ball is ridiculous, but don't you need it as a prop?'

'Nope. Today I'm switching to palmistry. Nothing needed but a hand.'

'Oh, but that won't work.' Summer shook her head. 'I mean, in theory, it's a great idea. Everybody loves your palm readings. They're engaging. They're accurate. They're insightful. And that's the problem. Your readings are *too* good. Once you start, no one is going to leave. They'll all want to hear more and more. Five minutes with a ticketholder will become fifty minutes with a ticketholder. We'll never get them out of the booth.'

'I won't do a full reading,' Hope told her, 'or even a partial reading. No lines, or mounts, or special markings. Only the hand shape. It's simple for me. It's easy for them to understand. And it's relatively quick. Happiness all around.'

Summer shook her head again. 'You say that now, but it won't turn out that way. Palm readings are never quick at the boutique. Everybody overstays their allotted time. They always have an extra question, followed by another question. I've seen it happen a thousand times before. One word from you about a fortunate finger or a providential knuckle, and like a snake charmer with a flute, you've got the person hypnotized.'

Hope laughed. 'Don't you think you're exaggerating a bit?'

'Not in the least! How are we going to fill our ticket box' – Summer pointed at the gold-wrapped box that was sitting on the table – 'if you talk to every person for an hour apiece? Instead of a monstrous heap of tickets, we'll end up with a pathetic little pile. Then Morris will give us that tragically disappointed look of his, as though we're a pair of puppies who piddled on the Persian rug in the parlor—' She interrupted herself with a cry of excitement. 'I've got it! I have the solution!'

Once more, Summer began rummaging through her handbag. Hope watched her curiously.

'Here they are!' Summer triumphantly pulled out a stack of the boutique's business cards and slapped them down on the table. 'I had a feeling that they might come in handy, so I grabbed them this morning before we left the brownstone.'

There was no immediate response from Hope.

'You'll do the palm readings,' Summer explained to her. 'The abridged version, as you said before. Just the hand shape, nothing else. And when you've sucked the person in and whetted their appetite, you give them the business card. Then they can contact us for a follow-up appointment at the boutique. They'll have the opportunity to get your full time and attention, and we'll have the opportunity to get a new customer. Everybody wins.'

Hope gave her sister a dubious look. 'Is that really in keeping with the spirit of a charity event?'

'Of course it is! No one is obligated to make a follow-up appointment. It's simply an option for the person. And at the same time, it's a way for you to get the person out of the booth and avoid endless lingering. You're still doing the initial reading in exchange for their tickets, so it's all above board. Plus, an actual palm reading – even in the most abbreviated form – is irrefutably more honest and legitimate than spouting drivel with that inane crystal ball. There can be no complaining from the spiritual world on that score.'

Hope couldn't dispute the point.

'I think it's an excellent plan,' Summer concluded. 'If Aaron Witten, the *fantastic salesman* were here right now' – she mimicked both Melody's words and her self-righteous sniffing – 'he would be impressed with my business savvy and promotional tools, even if they don't include a minuscule bikini.'

'He probably would be,' Hope agreed with a chuckle.

'In truth, Aaron is a lousy salesman.' Summer picked up the ticket box and headed toward the front curtains. 'He and Gary have been friends for years, and in all that time, Aaron was never successful in any of his many schemes. It almost – but not quite – makes me feel sorry for Gary. I sincerely hope that Gary hasn't given up his construction job for the mead venture. He was the foreman on his last two projects, and that's a good, steady, not easily replaceable income.'

'Oh, there's no reason for Gary to worry.' Hope took her seat at the table and smoothed the velvet cloth that covered it. 'If he's given up his job and the mead venture doesn't pan out, he always has a fallback.'

Summer, who was about to admit the first ticketholder of the day, turned quizzically to her sister. 'He does?'

'Certainly. Your vast herb-and-tea wealth.'

There wasn't time for Summer to do more than purse her lips in response. A line had formed outside the curtains, and for the next several hours, Hope and Summer were too busy to focus on anything but the ceaseless flow of ticketholders. In between ushering people into the booth, collecting their tickets, answering inquiries about the boutique, and ushering people back out of the booth, Summer contacted Stanley Palmer for assistance with the dead strand of twinkle lights. Apparently, Stanley and his ladder and tool chest had several other festival repairs to attend to before theirs and would arrive as soon as possible.

Hope, meanwhile, held a lot of hands. There were conic hands, square hands, knotty hands, pointed hands, and spatulate hands. And on all counts, Summer was proven correct. The abridged palm readings were so prodigiously popular that no one wanted to leave the booth. Everybody had questions and was eager for more information. The business cards were rapidly scooped up, and some people were so anxious to obtain a follow-up appointment that instead of waiting to contact the boutique the following week, they wanted to schedule a particular day and time on the spot.

After an especially loquacious and sticky-palmed ticket-holder had departed, Hope reached down next to her chair for a drink of water and a squirt of hand sanitizer. To her astonishment, when she straightened back up, instead of a new ticketholder sitting across the table from her, she found Dylan.

'Tell me, wise woman,' he said, 'what does my future hold?'

Hope blinked at him.

Dylan's lips curled with a smile. 'Will I be handsome? Will I be rich?'

'You're already handsome,' she replied dryly. 'And you're already rich. As you're well aware.'

The smile grew. 'But I very much like hearing it from you, Hope.'

It was difficult not to smile back at him. She bit the inside of her cheek in the attempt. 'That seat is for valid ticketholders only.'

'I am a valid ticketholder. I put my five tickets in the box, as requested and required. Ask your sister. She'll confirm it.'

Hope glanced over at Summer.

She shrugged. 'Dylan is fully paid up. And I'm not complaining about his arrival, because it gives me a chance to sit down and cool off.' Summer dropped the ticket box next to the front curtains, took hold of an empty chair, and dragged it toward the oscillating fan. As she passed by the table, she frowned at Dylan. 'How do you do it?'

'Do what?' he asked her.

'It's hotter than the surface of the sun out there – and nearly so in here – but somehow you never look warm and mussed like the rest of us.'

Dylan smiled once more.

'It's the ice in his veins,' Hope said. 'Or at least the ice in his eyes.'

The pale blue eyes shifted to her. 'That isn't true at all. There's no ice in my veins – or heart – for you, Hope.'

Summer gave a snort. 'Save your silver tongue for Larkin. Hope isn't gullible enough to fall for your hooey.' Not waiting for a response and deliberately turning her back, she settled herself down comfortably in front of the fan and closed her eyes for a brief respite.

Dylan's eyes remained on Hope. She met his gaze and found considerably more fire than frost in it.

'Tonight,' he said, after a minute. 'Do you have any plans?'

'Yes,' she answered. 'Or more accurately, we have the plans from last night. Summer, Megan, and I are headed to the new place in the square – the Green Goat – and hopefully this time there won't be a dead body to interrupt us.'

'The Green Goat? I think I've heard of it.'

'Probably from your dad. He and Gram had dinner there earlier this week with the Palmers. If I recall correctly, Morris greatly enjoyed the fried oysters.'

'Good to know. I'll keep that in mind.'

There was a pause.

'And do you have any plans for tonight?' Hope inquired politely.

'I had intended to spend the evening with you, but now it appears that I'll be forced to make alternative arrangements.'

Hope didn't reply, mostly because she couldn't tell if he meant it seriously. Fire or frost, the man's gaze was inscrutable.

There was another pause.

'I'm waiting patiently,' Dylan said.

She shook her head, not understanding. 'Waiting for what?'

'Waiting for you to read my palm.'

A distinct gleam of amusement was now visible in the pale blue eyes. Hope rolled her own eyes in response.

'It's too late,' she informed him. 'Your session is nearly up.'

Dylan reached into his pocket, pulled out a mass of tickets, and pushed them toward her on the table. 'Here's another ten or twenty. Now you can't kick me out under the guise of time limits.'

'That's not how it works. You can't purchase extra slots. Other people are waiting for their turn. And there are plenty of booths that would appreciate your patronage. The mead booth, for example. Summer and I were told just this morning that the mead booth isn't getting as much business as they would like. I'm sure that they'd love to have your tickets.'

'As it happens, I was at the mead booth earlier.'

'Were you? What a funny coincidence that of all the booths at the festival you could visit, you would choose the one—' Hope broke off abruptly as it occurred to her that coincidence probably had very little to do with it. More likely, it was a skimpy, pumpkin-orange bikini.

'The one . . .?' Dylan prompted her after a moment.

'I was going to say the one run by Summer's shifty husband, but then I realized' – Hope rolled her eyes again – 'that Gary and Aaron's promotional idea actually worked.'

It was Dylan's turn to shake his head, not understanding. 'I didn't see Gary at the mead booth.'

'But you no doubt saw Melody.'

'Melody?'

'Pumpkin-orange bikini.'

'Oh, yes, her . . .'

He nodded, and Hope anticipated a grin, a chortle, or some other sign of bikini appreciation to follow. To her surprise, Dylan's expression grew stern instead, and his medical training jumped to the fore.

'Melody is a foolish woman. Running around outdoors in the midday sun without proper clothing on this far south in August! Hasn't she ever heard of melanoma? And even if she's fortunate enough to avoid that, along with the other typically less dangerous forms of skin cancer, no amount of skilled surgery or cutting-edge dermatological treatments can correct leathery skin that's lost its elasticity and collagen. The damage will be permanent, and I can assure you that, in another few years, Melody won't like how she looks one bit.'

'So, then, you're a fan of us all wearing wide-brimmed hats?' Although Hope said it jokingly, Dylan didn't laugh.

'Without question,' he replied. 'You have beautiful skin, Hope, and you should do everything you can to protect it.'

She felt her cheeks flush. Thankfully, with the one strand of twinkle lights still dark, the booth was too dusky for Dylan to notice – or at least she hoped so.

'Now can we stop talking about Melody and mead and Summer's ex?' Dylan said. 'I've purchased a palm reading, and I would like my palm reading.'

Hope hesitated. Dylan was an avowed skeptic, and as a result, she was wary of his intentions. But at the same time, he had just paid her an awfully nice compliment.

'You haven't denied anyone else a palm reading today, have you?' he asked her.

'No, but—'

'Then I'm entitled to mine. And I'm on the edge of my seat with curiosity. The woman who came out of the booth just before I entered was in the throes of rapture because you had called her hand *artistic.*'

The wariness grew, and the compliment began to recede. 'Yes, I remember. She had a conic hand,' Hope explained, 'which is cone-like or triangular in shape, broad at the base and tapering at the tip, both in the palm and the fingers.'

'And that somehow makes it artistic?'

'That shape is often referred to as artistic, because it's considered – generally speaking – to be a hand of feeling and emotion. People with conic hands tend to be more instinctive and impulsive. They are inclined to enjoy the physical pleasures of life.'

'Hmm.' Dylan cocked his head at her. 'I thought that perhaps you had seen all those buttons and stickers on the woman's bag regarding funding the local theater and supporting the school music program.'

Hope's gaze narrowed, and the compliment was now entirely forgotten. 'What exactly are you suggesting?'

'I am suggesting,' Dylan said, his voice droll, 'that you are using external cues to guide your supposed readings. In this instance, the buttons and stickers told you that the woman felt strongly about the arts, and she would, therefore, relish receiving recognition of that fact from you.'

A hush descended over the booth. There was not a sound from the previously bustling area outside the front curtains. Summer sat perfectly still. Even the fan barely seemed to hum. Hope's steely expression met Dylan's mocking one.

'Take this as an external cue.' Hope pointed a stiff finger at the curtains. 'Get out. And stay out.'

If she had expected Dylan to promptly stand up and stomp off in a huff, she was sorely disappointed. Instead, he leaned back in his chair, his head still cocked and his expression still mocking.

'Darling,' he drawled, 'I have no intention of going anywhere.'

ELEVEN

There was an instant – the briefest of moments – when Hope's emerald-green eyes went coal-black. Dylan must have seen it, because his own eyes flickered in surprise. And although her back was turned, Summer must have somehow felt it, because she sprang up from her seat in front of the fan and spun toward her sister.

'No, no!' she cried. 'Don't do it, Hope! You mustn't do it.'

Hope was silent.

'There will be a price.' Summer hurried to the table. 'There is *always* a price. You've said so yourself many times. Karma is sticky, and curses are messy. They turn out differently than expected.'

She still didn't speak.

'I'm usually the rash, impetuous one. You're usually the calm, level-headed one,' Summer reminded her. 'Stop and think about it, Hope. Think about what could go wrong. Especially here, in this place. We don't know how thin the veil might be in the surrounding area – particularly so close in time to Davis's death – and what could be let through in the process. Plus, we don't know where Gram is right now, so we can't be sure whether she might be affected.'

Hope's eyes closed, and when they fluttered open again a second later, the darkness in them had vanished. Only clear bright green remained.

'Oh, thank heaven.' Summer breathed a weighty sigh of relief. 'You had me worried there for a minute. The last time that happened – well, you know how it turned out . . .' She shuddered.

'The cost was very high,' Hope agreed somberly.

Dylan looked back and forth between them with a mixture of fascination and incredulity. They paid no attention to him.

'You're right,' Hope continued to her sister. 'There are too many variables to take such a risk. It's not worth it. *He's* not worth it.'

'He certainly isn't,' Summer concurred. Then, with a smug air, she turned to Dylan. 'You should thank me. I just saved your bacon.'

'You can't be serious.' There was no gratitude in Dylan's tone. On the contrary, there was a good deal of derision. 'You can't seriously be implying that without your intervention, Hope would have placed a ghastly curse on me—'

'Not only you,' Summer interjected. 'You and all of your descendants. A curse includes them, too.'

'It doesn't always include them,' Hope corrected her. 'There are some exceptions. But in most cases, yes, the curse attaches to the descendants also.'

'I have no descendants,' Dylan said.

'You don't now, but you may have in the future,' Summer pointed out.

'Some consider that to be unfair,' Hope remarked. 'The sins of the parent passing to the child.'

Summer shrugged. 'Fairness has nothing to do with it. If a person doesn't want to bear the consequences for themselves or their progeny, then they should take care not to get cursed in the first place. Or, in the alternative, they can get the curse lifted.'

Hope shook her head. 'You know that's much easier said than done. Lifting curses is quite tricky. It requires a significant amount of preparation and knowledge. There aren't many who have the necessary skill to achieve a positive outcome.'

'How about this for a simpler solution?' Dylan proposed. 'Just as they did in the olden days, kill the witch that's responsible for the curse.'

If he was hoping to provoke their outrage or indignation with the remark, he didn't succeed. The sisters looked at each other and laughed.

'It won't work,' Summer told Dylan in between guffaws. 'In fact, that's the worst possible thing anyone could do. Then the curse can never be lifted. It's made permanent for the entire bloodline.'

They were left to guess how Dylan might have responded,

because in the next moment – without warning – Detective Nate stepped through the front curtains of the booth. Both Hope and Summer jumped slightly in surprise. Dylan, on the other hand, showed not the least sign of astonishment. It made Hope wonder whether he had been expecting the detective's arrival. Was that the reason Dylan had said he had no intention of leaving?

Nate greeted them as a group, but just as he had upon his appearance at the carousel the night before, his eyes lingered on Summer, making it amply clear that he held no grudge regarding the prior evening's course of events or conversation. Any residual embarrassment or awkward feelings on Summer's part also seemed to have been forgotten, because she gave Nate a warm welcome.

'Busy day so far?' Dylan asked him.

'Horrible. Absolutely horrible. I haven't been able to stop for even a second to catch my breath.' Nate sank wearily into an empty chair next to Dylan. 'Not that there's any air to catch in this miserable weather.'

'You can take that chair instead,' Summer offered, motioning toward the one that she had recently vacated in front of the fan. 'It'll give you a little breeze, at least.'

'Thanks' – Nate gave her an appreciative nod – 'but I'm fine here. To be honest, I just don't want to get up again. And I apologize for being late.'

'Late?' she inquired.

Nate glanced at his watch. 'Dylan and I agreed to an earlier time.'

That answered one of Hope's questions. Dylan had indeed been expecting the detective's arrival at the booth.

'It's not a problem,' Dylan told him. 'Although you did miss an extremely interesting dialogue. Just before you came in, the sisters were instructing me that a curse can't be lifted by killing the witch that's responsible for it.'

Nate appeared momentarily startled. Then he exchanged a look with Dylan. It gave Hope the distinct impression that the two men had previously discussed – at least once and possibly more often – her and Summer's connection with the mystical world.

'That's a helpful piece of information,' Nate remarked, betraying a hint of a smile. 'I'll be sure to remember it the next time I encounter a witch's hex.'

Hope was keen to switch the subject as quickly as she could, but Summer – who didn't seem to have noticed either the look or the smile – spoke first.

'A hex isn't synonymous with a curse,' she said.

The hint of a smile resurfaced. 'It isn't?'

'No. A curse can be a hex,' Summer explained. 'But not all hexes are curses.'

Nate and Dylan exchanged another look.

Again, Hope tried to shift the topic, and again Summer pre-empted her.

'For example, there are plenty of harmless hexes. There are no harmless curses, however. Isn't that right, Hope?'

The three of them collectively turned toward Hope, awaiting her response. Summer was earnest. Nate was now openly smiling. Dylan was nearly grinning. Hope threw Dylan an irritated glance, and then she addressed Nate.

'So what brings you to our booth, Detective?' Although she recalled what Morris had told them earlier about Nate intending to stop by with regard to some unanswered questions from the evening before, she added politely, 'Business or pleasure?'

'You could try getting a palm reading,' Dylan suggested to him. 'But I must warn you that it's not an easy thing to attain. I paid more than my fair share' – he indicated the tickets that were still lying on the table in front of them – 'and I was summarily denied. Perhaps fortune will shine more favorably on you.'

Nate chuckled. 'I'm sorry to say that I don't have any tickets.'

'No tickets would be required for you,' Summer responded sweetly. 'Consider it complimentary in appreciation for your job as a first responder. Like a gratis cup of coffee at a restaurant.'

'Except gratis cups aren't allowed anymore,' he told her. 'There have been memos from the higher-ups declaring that the receipt of free coffee – or any other complimentary beverage – smacks of graft, bribery, and corruption.'

'That's absurd!' Summer protested. 'Obviously, you can't accept a case of wine or a keg of beer, but how on earth could receiving a bottle of water or a can of soda be viewed as crooked?'

Nate shrugged. 'I can't explain it. But I learned a long time ago that, in my line of work, I don't make the rules.'

'And the people who do make the rules,' Dylan said, 'have clearly never gotten up from behind their cushy desk or worked a shift longer than eight hours.'

'Ain't that the truth,' Nate agreed.

'Well, if Hope and I had any coffee or soda in the booth to give to you, we'd definitely violate that stupid policy—' Summer interrupted herself with an excited shout. 'Wait, I have a much better idea! You can come with us to the Green Goat this evening, and we'll treat you to a cocktail there!'

Even in the limited light, Hope could see Nate's ears grow slightly pink.

'Drinks at the Green Goat? That sounds great,' he began eagerly, only to stop with a gloomy sigh. 'But I can't make any promises. It depends on how the investigation is proceeding.'

'Of course.' Summer nodded. 'We understand. But if you can manage to find the time, we'd love for you to join us. A seat – along with a cocktail – will be reserved especially for you!'

The ears became pinker, and Nate responded suavely, 'I'd rather treat *you* to the cocktail.'

It was Summer's turn to flush.

Doing her best to suppress a smile, Hope glanced at Dylan to see if he was as entertained by the exchange as she was. She found him already looking at her, his expression expectant. It wasn't difficult for her to guess what he wanted.

'Feel free to join us tonight, too, Dylan,' Hope said.

It was a tepid offer, primarily because she was still annoyed at his comments about her palm readings. But now that the number of participants in the Green Goat expedition appeared to be growing, it seemed somehow inevitable that Dylan should be included, no matter how reluctantly on Hope's part.

'How can I refuse such an enthusiastic invitation?' Dylan remarked dryly.

Apparently, Summer hadn't forgotten his comments, either, because she replied with equal dryness, 'Consider yourself lucky that you got any invitation at all. If you want unbridled enthusiasm, have another dinner with Larkin. I'm sure that she would be thrilled to fawn and flatter your ego.'

Dylan glared at her.

'Larkin?' Nate questioned. 'I met someone named Larkin earlier today.' He pulled out a notepad and began thumbing through the pages. 'It was while I was talking to Morris. She was assisting him in some fashion.'

'That's Larkin,' Dylan confirmed.

Nate continued flipping through the notepad. 'Very nice woman. She was exceedingly friendly – and helpful.'

'I bet she was,' Summer muttered.

'Ah, yes.' Finding the page that he had been searching for, Nate studied it for a minute. Then he raised his head with a grave expression, and his tone grew formal. 'I'm afraid that it can't be put off any longer. Regardless of the consequences, the time has come to get down to business.'

A crease appeared in Summer's brow. 'All right.'

'I suggest that you take a seat,' he directed her stiffly.

The crease deepened, but Summer didn't argue. She walked to the chair in front of the fan and began to carry it back toward the table.

Hope started to rise. 'If this is going to take a while, I should do something about the ticketholders who are waiting in line—'

Nate lifted his hand, indicating for her to stop. 'There's no need. I've already taken care of them.'

'You have?' she asked in surprise.

'Yes. I cleared the line and sent everybody away as soon as I arrived. A uniformed officer has been stationed at the entrance to advise passers-by that the booth is closed for the remainder of the day.'

'What!' the sisters exclaimed in unison. Summer was so startled that she dropped the chair.

Standing up, Nate motioned for Hope to return to her seat.

With a frown, Hope slowly sat back down. That explained why the previously bustling area outside the front curtains had gone quiet earlier. But was it really necessary to shut the booth with a policeman standing guard?

'There is no question' – Nate went to pick up Summer's chair – 'that this is an unpleasant and uncomfortable situation for all involved, especially considering . . .' He paused and gave Summer an awkward glance. 'In any event, I have a duty, and the law must be obeyed.'

There was something so rigidly official in Nate's manner that it was beginning to make Hope feel rather ill at ease, as though she and Summer should contact an attorney before remaining in the booth and permitting the conversation with the detective to go any further. Almost involuntarily, she looked at Dylan.

He leaned toward her, faintly amused. 'I believe that it's you – and not me – who needs their bacon saved.'

At first blush, Hope wasn't sure how to interpret the remark, but a moment later, Dylan was proven correct.

Setting Summer's chair upright and offering it to her, Nate said, 'I regret to inform you that you and Hope have been accused of murder.'

TWELVE

'Rot,' Summer said. 'Utter rot.'

There was a brief hesitation, then Nate once more offered her the empty chair. Summer took a pronounced step away from it and from him.

'Rot,' she said again.

After another hesitation, Nate returned to his own chair next to Dylan.

Summer remained standing and put her hands angrily on her hips. 'I demand to know who had the gall to accuse—'

'Don't,' Hope stopped her. 'Don't say another word on the matter. Not before we consult with an attorney – or, at a minimum, find out precisely what the charges are.'

'Yes. Absolutely. Excellent point,' Summer concurred. Then she turned back to Nate. 'Are you going to arrest us? Charge us? Tell us right now. Is this considered an interrogation? Don't you need to read us our rights?'

Nate looked taken aback. 'Good god, I'm not going to arrest you.'

Summer squinted at him. 'You aren't?'

'No. Of course not. On what grounds would I arrest you, or charge you, or even bring you in for formal questioning?'

Although she had no immediate answer, Summer's squint remained, indicating that she wasn't fully convinced.

Hope gave an internal sigh of relief at the detective's response. Then fury bubbled out. 'If you're not going to arrest us or charge us with a crime, then don't close our booth without our consent and post a policeman as a guard! Don't make menacing statements about your supposed duty and obeying the law! Don't try to intimidate us with your bureaucratic tone and demeanor! And don't start throwing around accusations of murder!'

Summer nodded vigorously in accord.

'And you can forget about getting any free drinks here, or

at the boutique, or anywhere else ever,' Hope continued heat-edly. 'The only complimentary cocktail that you'll be receiving from us at the Green Goat this evening will be the one that we throw in your face.'

'He wouldn't dare show up there after this,' Summer growled.

Hope's eyes moved from Nate's flabbergasted expression to Dylan's, which was decidedly less solemn.

'What are you smiling at?' she snapped.

'You,' Dylan said. 'The family resemblance is remarkable. You sound just like Olivia did this morning when she was berating the carousel people. Brimstone and daggers. The purr of a kitten one second, followed by the roar of a lion the next.'

Under other circumstances, Hope would have issued a stinging retort. But a favorable comparison to her grandmother was considered high praise in the Bailey family.

'Thank you,' Hope said coolly. 'I'll take that as a compliment.'

'Trust me, it is one.' Dylan's smile grew. 'I was fully prepared to assume the role of the gallant hero and ride to the rescue on my snow-white steed by providing you with an irrefutable alibi for the time of Davis's death, but it's evident that you don't need a champion and you're capable of saving your own bacon.'

'I certainly am,' Hope replied. 'Summer and I don't allow ourselves to be bullied any more than our grandmother does. And you can stop pretending that you were about to engage in some wonderfully valiant act. By providing me with an alibi, you also happen to be conveniently providing yourself with one.'

From the way Dylan chuckled, it was clear that the idea had already occurred to him. 'That may be the case, but – unlike you – I don't need an alibi. I had no connection whatsoever with Davis Scott. I never met the man while he was alive. And the first time I ever saw him was with you when we discovered his body on the carousel.'

'We only have your word for that,' Hope countered.

'And even if your statement is accurate,' Summer chimed in, 'just because you hadn't previously seen or met Davis doesn't automatically guarantee that you weren't involved in his death. There are other potential scenarios. For instance, you could have paid someone to kill him.'

Dylan chuckled harder. 'I hired a contract killer? You really have a fantastical imagination. I suppose, in some bizarre way, I should be flattered. First, you blame your attic, then you blame a pug, and now you're blaming me.'

'I'm not blaming you,' Summer returned peevishly. 'I'm just offering it as a hypothetical. We need to consider all the possibilities, no matter how seemingly remote—'

'Then we should consider you, too,' Dylan interjected. 'Because in contrast to your sister, you don't have an alibi.'

'Yes, I do! You saw me arrive at the carousel.'

'Exactly. You arrived *after* Hope and Megan and I had already found Davis's body and I had reported it to the police.'

'Well, technically that's correct,' Summer admitted. 'But from a timing standpoint, it isn't feasible for me to have played a part in the death. I would have had to kill Davis, slip silently away without anyone noticing me, and then return moments later, perfectly calm and unruffled, pretending to be as stunned as everybody else by the discovery. I'm not that good of an actress!'

Dylan merely shrugged.

'And furthermore,' Summer went on, 'it isn't remotely logical. Why would I want to murder Davis Scott?'

'You gave us a long list of reasons on that subject yesterday,' Dylan reminded her. He enumerated: 'Davis was a slippery fish; he wasn't selling your marital home quickly enough; you wanted a new realtor so that your divorce could be finalized; Davis was pestering your family about putting the brownstone on the market; and – my personal favorite – your attic didn't like him.'

Appearing rather chagrined at the recitation, Summer shot back defensively, 'There are plenty of other people who thought that Davis was a slippery fish. Amelia and Stanley Palmer, for example. They've had terrible problems with the sale of their house. Stanley is convinced that legitimate offers have been held back in order to push them into accepting a lowball proposal. It's caused Amelia so much stress that she's been having the most horrible headaches. Gram said—'

Hope shook her head to stop her sister. 'But we don't know for sure that Davis was the Palmers' real estate agent.'

'Of course he was,' Summer rejoined. 'It's obvious. Amelia was the one who first called him a slippery fish. What more proof do you need?'

Distracted, Hope didn't respond. Ever since Dylan had mentioned Percy, her mind had been on Rosemarie. She turned to Nate.

'Have you seen Rosemarie and talked to her about Davis? How is she handling it? As you directed us, we haven't had any contact with her since yesterday, but I'm worried about her. Rosemarie is such an old-world romantic, and even though I think she deserved better than Davis, I'm afraid that she might be – or, at least, believe herself to be – dreadfully heartbroken by the loss.'

There was a short pause, then Nate replied, 'Yes, I have seen Rosemarie, and I have informed her about Davis.'

'And how did she take it?' Summer pressed him. 'Did she explain to you where she went last night after the four of us – well, five, if you include Percy – split up at the booth? Why didn't she ever come to the carousel?'

'It's probably a good thing she didn't come to the carousel,' Hope remarked. 'Can you imagine how awful it would have been for her if she had seen Davis lying there the way we did?'

Summer grimaced. 'That's true. Poor Rosemarie.'

'To answer your first question,' Nate said, 'Rosemarie took the news of her boyfriend's demise reasonably well. She wasn't nearly as shocked as you might suppose. It was almost as though she expected it.'

'Oh, poor Rosemarie.' Summer sighed. 'Her intuition was correct from the outset. She told us that she had a bad feeling when Davis went missing.'

Hope nodded.

'And to answer your second question,' Nate went on, 'according to Rosemarie, after first searching for Davis and then subsequently searching for you – both unsuccessfully, apparently

– she and her dog were tired and went home. She claims that her feet were hurting and the dog had indigestion.'

'Rosemarie had a bad blister,' Hope corroborated. 'Too much walking in strappy sandals. And Percy had a bad stomach. Too much festival food.'

'Poor Percy.' Summer sighed once more. 'Poor Rosemarie.'

Nate didn't appear to share her sympathy. 'You really should stop referring to her as *poor Rosemarie.*'

'Not this again!' Summer exclaimed. 'You're not going to contend that because Rosemarie didn't break down in wailing hysterics in front of you, it demonstrates that she was somehow involved in the death. We covered all the arguments in that regard yesterday. Rosemarie couldn't have been in any way responsible for what happened to Davis.'

'I'm not saying that she was responsible,' Nate replied. 'I'm not accusing Rosemarie of Davis's murder. You might feel less pity for the woman and be more aggrieved at her, however, when you learn that *she* is the one who accused you.'

Hope and Summer stared at him.

'R–Rosemarie?' Summer said unevenly after a moment. 'Rosemarie Potter?'

Nate inclined his head in confirmation.

'Rosemarie accused *us* – Hope and me – of murdering Davis Scott?'

He inclined his head again.

'No,' Summer declared, her hands returning to her hips. 'I don't believe it. I don't believe it for one second. Rosemarie would never do something like that. *Never.* She's loyal, and Percy's loyal—'

'Percy's loyalty lies with whomever is providing him the most treats at any given time,' Dylan interjected wryly.

Summer scowled. 'That has no bearing whatsoever! At the end of the day, Rosemarie wouldn't turn on us. She believes deeply in Hope and has great faith in her abilities. Without Hope's readings, Rosemarie would be lost. She wouldn't take the chance that, by slandering us, she could no longer come to the boutique. Isn't that right, Hope?'

Hope considered a minute. 'What exactly did Rosemarie say?' she asked Nate.

'When she learned that Davis had been strangled with one of the scarves she had purchased from your shop, she said that it was your fault. You were to blame, because the quality of your silk was too good. If the material had been cheaper and weaker, it would have ripped apart in the carousel before causing Davis any harm. Therefore – in Rosemarie's view – without your scarf, the man would still be alive.'

'I suppose in a way that's true,' Hope mused.

'It is not!' Summer disputed. 'The scarf was just the most readily available tool. The murderer probably saw it lying on the ground wherever Percy had lost it and—'

'Do you think so?' Hope said. 'I've been wondering about how the person got the scarf. Did they find it by accident and merely decide to pick it up? Or did they steal it with the deliberate intention of using it to kill Davis?'

'I've been wondering the same thing,' Nate told her.

'Does it really matter?' Summer returned. 'Either way, if it hadn't been the scarf, it would have been something else. Without the scarf, the murderer would have simply selected another method.'

'It's impossible to know for certain, of course, but I think that you're most likely correct,' Nate agreed. 'If not the scarf, then the next best thing at hand. One of those cords, for example.' He gestured toward the curtains. 'With the way they're stitched and the thickness of the fabric, they would serve the purpose much better. What's your opinion, Dylan, from a medical standpoint?'

'A silk scarf – even a strong one – is far from an optimal tourniquet,' he answered, 'so it can't be relied on as a surefire mode of strangulation. Which suggests to me that Davis's murder wasn't premeditated. All else being equal, his killer would have chosen a more dependable weapon.'

Nate nodded. 'I share your assessment. Rosemarie, on the other hand, takes the opposite position. She believes that the murder was premeditated. She is convinced Summer planned it from the very beginning.'

'I did *what*?' Summer cried, aghast.

'According to Rosemarie, you wouldn't allow Davis to

remain in the booth yesterday evening. You threw him out when he wouldn't provide the requisite number of tickets. As a result, Rosemarie was forced to separate from him. In her mind, if it wasn't for that separation and the scarf, Davis Scott would continue to roam on this earth.'

'He probably does continue to roam on this earth,' Summer grumbled. 'And in another couple of days, he'll most likely start haunting either us or his killer.'

Hope cleared her throat.

Summer glanced at her. 'I know. I'm sorry. I might have jinxed us.' She turned back to Nate. 'For your information, Rosemarie's account isn't at all accurate. She was already separated from Davis before the kerfuffle about the tickets. They were supposed to meet at the pretzel stand, but Rosemarie and Percy got delayed waiting in line to see us, so Davis came to our booth to find her.'

'Interesting,' Nate murmured, scribbling in his notepad.

'Furthermore,' Summer went on, 'if it had been premeditated on my part, I would have stolen Percy's scarf then, while he and Rosemarie were in the booth. But I didn't. Percy was still wearing his scarf when they ran after Davis.'

Nate paused his writing. 'You're sure about the scarf? It was definitely on the dog when they left?'

'Yes. I remember because as Rosemarie was going out and Megan was coming in, I noticed Rosemarie limping and saw the blood on her ankle. As Hope said earlier, it was a bad blister—'

'There was blood on Rosemarie's ankle?' Nate interrupted her. 'How much blood?' He shifted in his seat and motioned to a spot on the ground. 'That blood?'

Summer took a step toward it, and Hope leaned forward in her chair to see the place that he was indicating. There was a dark-red streak along the short tufts of grass not far from the table. Hope gave Nate a quizzical look.

'I observed it when I picked up the chair,' he explained. 'Is it Rosemarie's?'

'It might be,' Hope answered. 'Or it might not. We've had so many people in here over the last two days, including a considerable number of children who were running around barefoot. The blood could be from any of them. I don't see what difference it would make regardless . . .'

She broke off as Dylan and Nate exchanged a glance. Hope took it as a sign that she had unwittingly hit on something of significance.

'But it could make a difference,' she amended slowly, thoughtfully, 'if you had also found blood somewhere else, somewhere important.' She remembered how Dylan and Nate had bent down on the carousel platform to examine a spot near Davis's body. 'At the crime scene, perhaps?'

There was another glance between the men, and Nate more or less confirmed Hope's supposition by switching the subject.

'Returning to the scarf,' he said to Summer, 'you were telling me that Rosemarie was going out of the booth while Megan was coming in?'

There was a marked inflection in Nate's voice when he spoke Megan's name, which gave Hope the impression that his query had a specific purpose, even though she had no idea what it was.

Summer nodded. 'That's why I'm positive about Percy still having the scarf then. Rosemarie complimented Megan on her hideously sequined dress, and Megan complimented Percy on his nifty scarf.'

'And what happened after that?' Nate asked her.

'Nothing. Rosemarie – and Percy – rushed away to try to catch up with Davis, and Megan rushed over to our fan to try to cool off.'

'So when did Rosemarie and Megan discuss Sean?'

The inflection redoubled, and Hope was now certain that Nate had a particular point in mind. It put her on alert, especially when joined with the unexpected reference to Sean.

Summer must have also thought that Nate's questions were becoming increasingly odd, because there was a delay in her response. 'Sean? There was some mention of Rosemarie seeing him in the cape and crown that he was wearing for Amethyst's booth. Rosemarie found it dashing, of course, because she likes all things fairytale related.'

Hope tried to remember what exactly Rosemarie had told them. She had wanted to greet Megan at Amethyst's booth, but Davis had refused to participate. At the time, Hope had thought that Davis was simply being unpleasant as usual, but maybe there was more to it than that. Maybe Davis had recognized someone in the booth, and he didn't want to see or speak with that person. It couldn't have been Megan, because she hadn't known Davis. Could Davis and Sean have known each other?

'There might have been some other mention of Sean later on,' Summer continued hesitantly, watching her sister's contemplative expression. 'Wasn't there, Hope?'

Hope was likewise hesitant in her answer. Since she didn't know what Nate was looking for, she was concerned about further entangling Megan in the situation. And although she was only slightly acquainted with Sean, he was Megan's colleague and friend, so she didn't want to inadvertently get him into trouble, either.

'Rosemarie was quite upset,' Hope said at last, 'because she thought that she had seen Davis near the maple syrup stand, but when she got there, he had vanished. Megan tried to comfort her by explaining that it could have been a trick of her eyes in the dark. She used as an example her own experience from a short while earlier where she thought that she had seen Sean heading in one direction when she knew for certain that five minutes previous he had gone in the opposite direction.'

Hope had believed it to be a harmless, trivial anecdote, but when Nate began scribbling in his notepad again, she winced with regret. Apparently, there was something interesting about it, after all, and it might have been better if she hadn't shared the story.

'I will need to speak with both Megan and Sean,' Nate informed her. 'Are they at Amethyst's booth today?'

'I don't know.' She was deliberately vague. 'I'm not sure what their work schedule is.' Then Hope posed her own question. 'Who told you about Sean? I assume that it was Rosemarie. But I'm curious why she would mention him.'

Nate continued writing. 'Rosemarie believes that Megan and Sean might be accessories to the crime. The woman has a lot of theories.'

Hope and Summer looked at each other in surprise. Hope's first thought was that she had better talk to Megan as soon as she could and warn her – and Sean, too, if possible – about everything that was happening.

Summer gave a doleful exhalation. 'Oh, poor Rosemarie.'

It was Nate and Dylan's turn to look surprised.

'Poor Rosemarie?' Nate echoed incredulously. 'You're still calling her that after she called you a murderess?'

Summer responded with a slight shrug. 'She didn't really mean it. She's just stressed and confused right now. When Rosemarie's had a chance to properly rest and wrap her mind around things, she'll come to her senses. One day, in a week or two – when her feet are healed – she and Percy will walk through the door of the boutique. There will be an awkward moment and a few tears, and then we'll all laugh, hug, and move on.'

Hope nodded. 'And Percy will make out like a little bandit, because we'll give him a pile of extra treats.'

'You're a lot more forgiving than I would be,' Dylan said.

'And me,' Nate concurred.

'The Baileys have a very forgiving nature,' Summer replied. 'Fortunately for the two of you,' she added under her breath.

Hope smiled.

There was a commotion at the front of the booth. A woman's voice could be heard, although it was too muffled through the thick curtains to identify. A man with the distinct air of law enforcement responded gruffly. The woman argued in return.

'It sounds as though we have a visitor,' Nate said, rising from his chair. He paused and gave his own shrug. 'Maybe you're a better judge of human nature than I am. Maybe it's Rosemarie, already seeking forgiveness and redemption.'

Hope didn't think so. Although she agreed with Summer that the situation with Rosemarie would in all likelihood smooth itself out in due course, she was doubtful that the time had come so quickly.

'Although I can't legally prohibit you from having contact with her at this stage,' Nate went on, 'I would strongly advise you not to discuss the pending matter with Rosemarie. It won't be beneficial for either side.'

Summer's response was muted by the pair of voices growing steadily louder outside the curtains. The woman was evidently unwilling to take instructions from the policeman. The velvet folds began to move, but just as when Davis had arrived at the booth, there was so much fabric that the person entering wasn't immediately visible.

'My money is on Rosemarie,' Nate predicted.

'Olivia, perhaps?' Dylan proffered. 'Or maybe Megan?'

Hope and Summer shared an uneasy glance. They didn't think that it was any of the three.

Finally, the curtains parted, and the visitor appeared, followed closely by an irate uniformed policeman.

'Hello.' The woman simpered at them.

It was Larkin.

THIRTEEN

'Maybe we should have stayed,' Summer said, her voice uncertain.

'No,' Hope replied decisively. 'Staying would have only made things worse.'

Less than a minute after Larkin's arrival at their booth, they had made the decision to leave it. That was all the time they had needed to see Larkin in action. Smooth as silk, she had presented Nate with a sparkling white smile, draped herself on Dylan's shoulder, and batted apologetic eyelashes at the uniformed policeman. It had taken only another minute for the sisters to secure the opportunity for a successful departure. Larkin had promptly launched into a dramatic explanation for her appearance at the booth. According to her, Morris had been gravely anxious to find Dylan and had eagerly sent her to look for him. Hope doubted the veracity of the tale. More likely, Morris had mentioned his son in passing, and Larkin had used it as an excuse to track Dylan down with the tenacity of a bloodhound. In any event, the men had been so engrossed in Larkin's account that they hadn't noticed Hope and Summer slip out of the back curtains.

'Maybe we should have gotten permission,' Summer suggested.

Hope raised an eyebrow at her.

'Well, not permission exactly,' she amended. 'But maybe we should have told Nate where we were going.'

'Why? You heard him earlier. He has no intention of either arresting or charging us, which means that we're free to go wherever, whenever we please. And it's not as though we're racing up to the Canadian border or hopping on a transcontinental flight in a desperate attempt to evade the authorities. We're simply taking a stroll through the festival grounds to visit our friend at her booth.'

Summer made a nervous mewing sound.

Hope nodded sympathetically. 'I know. You're worried about how much Larkin will flirt with Nate in your absence. If it's any consolation, I think it's quite clear that she has her sights set on Dylan.'

'Even so, she might choose Nate as her fallback. Larkin seems like the type who always wants to keep a fallback – or two – on hand.'

'No doubt,' Hope agreed scornfully.

'And why can't she properly button her blouses? The one that she has on today is even worse than the one from yesterday. The way that she leaves them undone in such an obvious fashion is insulting to all womankind.'

That made Hope laugh.

'I told you this would be a bad day, didn't I?' Summer groused.

'You did. But keep in mind that the day isn't over yet. It could still end very nicely. There's the Green Goat this evening, remember?'

'That's too many hours away.' Summer squinted unhappily at the height of the blazing sun. 'And I can't imagine that Nate will come tonight after we threatened to pelt him with cocktails.'

Hope smiled. 'I wouldn't be so sure. I have the feeling that dear Detective Nate will use any available opportunity to enjoy your company.'

Although her face was already flushed from the heat of the day, Summer's cheeks grew a bit rosier. 'You really think that?'

'I do. We'll pick a quiet table in a darkened corner of the place, and when everybody's had a drink and gotten themselves nice and comfortable, Megan and I will inconspicuously move to a different table, leaving you and Nate alone.'

'Oh, gosh, I don't know if that's necessary.'

'Yes, it is. Obviously, at this point, you don't know where things will end up with him, but nothing can happen if you don't at least give it a chance. All things considered, the timing is pretty good. The divorce is slowly but steadily proceeding, and now the sale of the house might finally move forward. My only concern—'

'Gary,' Summer interjected. 'The concern is Gary. I was thinking about what you said this morning after we ran into Melody, and you're right. By now – with the carousel shut down and all the police on the festival grounds – Gary must have heard about what happened to Davis, but we still don't know what shape his reaction will take. Even though he's technically required to choose a new realtor, will he actually do so? Or will he drag his feet for months on end so that he can keep living and partying in the house?'

'That's a good question.' Hope hesitated a moment, deliberating whether to continue. 'Sometimes I wonder if it's not about the house at all. Maybe what Gary really wants is to hold on to you.'

Summer stopped short and gaped at her. 'He couldn't possibly want that! He's the one who's been sleeping around, not me!'

'True, but' – Hope hesitated once more – 'just because Gary can't manage to be faithful to you, it doesn't mean that he's eager for your marriage to end. He might be all right with the current separation; in his mind, it could prove temporary. A divorce, on the other hand, is irrevocably permanent and final.'

Although Summer didn't respond, Hope could see that her sister was seriously considering what she had said. After a minute, they began walking again, and Hope returned to an earlier point in the conversation.

'Going back to the Green Goat this evening, my concern is Dylan, not Gary. I fear that Dylan might be a little like the attic with its love of revenge. He may want some payback for us sneaking away just now, and it's possible that the payback could involve your rendezvous with Nate tonight.'

At the comparison of Dylan to the attic, a hint of a grin crept into Summer's otherwise pensive expression. 'It's too bad that while we're having our cocktails, we can't get Dylan to spend an hour or two alone in the attic. I can guarantee you that experience would bring an end to his skepticism once and for all.'

'The downside, however, is that we would have to start worrying again about being arrested. Leaving Dylan alone in the attic could lead to a charge against us for attempted murder, reckless endangerment, and the intentional infliction of emotional distress.'

Summer burst out laughing.

Hope's own laugh quickly faded. 'While we're on the subject of potential arrests and charges, we have to warn Megan as soon as we can. Obviously, she isn't guilty of anything, but it's not fair to let her get blindsided by Rosemarie's accusations. And the same goes for Sean. Since they work together, Megan must know how to get in touch with him.'

'Speaking of Sean' – Summer grew serious also – 'did you notice how Nate reacted to what you told him about Megan thinking she had seen Sean heading in one direction five minutes after he had gone in the opposite direction? Why would Nate consider that to be important?'

'I have no idea. Even if it actually occurred and wasn't just a trick of Megan's eyes in the dark, I don't understand how it would matter. So what if Sean switched directions? Everybody does that on occasion. You forget something and have to go back, or you change your mind about where you want to go. The only thing that makes it even a tiny bit suspicious is that it occurred after the booths had closed for the evening and Davis had disappeared. But in my mind, that's not much to get excited about, especially when we don't even know if Sean and Davis were acquainted with each other.'

'We should definitely try to find that out,' Summer said. 'And we should also ask Megan what else she can remember about Sean's movements last night. It can't hurt for all of us to have our stories straight and get our ducks in a row before Nate comes around asking more questions. Do you think that Megan will be at Amethyst's booth? I was under the impression that she had finished her obligatory shift yesterday.'

'She had finished her shift yesterday,' Hope confirmed. 'But according to her message, there was some problem with the booth today, and as Amethyst's Director of Activities, Megan is the one who's required to deal with it.'

'That's lousy. Maybe she can get Stanley to fix the problem. Although that might take a while considering that he still hasn't fixed the strand of twinkle lights in our booth.' Summer frowned. 'I hope Megan isn't forced to wear that hideous dress again. In this heat, it could be injurious to her health. And while we're on the topic of hideous outfits . . .'

Hope followed her sister's gaze and found Melody Witten and the mead booth a short distance ahead of them on the left. Melody was still clad in the pumpkin-orange bikini from that morning, except now the skimpy swimsuit didn't draw one's attention nearly as much as the fact that the woman's skin tone resembled a broiled crustacean.

'Yikes,' Hope muttered. 'Dylan wasn't kidding about the potential for serious sun damage.'

The booth had no visitors, and with a weary, languid expression, Melody's raccoon eyes circled in search of something to do or someone to chat with. Her face instantly brightened when she spotted Summer.

'Hey there!' Melody called and waved at them.

Summer's pace reflexively slowed. 'I guess we're stuck. We have to go talk to her, don't we?'

'I'm afraid so.'

'Oh lord, it just occurred to me.' Summer's own eyes started circling around but with substantially more angst than Melody's. 'Gary is probably around here somewhere. Do you see him?'

Hope did a quick visual search. 'No. Melody is definitely alone at the booth. Maybe Gary and Aaron went to run an errand.'

There was an audible sigh of relief from Summer. 'Then let's go visit her fast. But we can't linger. Sooner or later, Gary will show up, and I really don't have the energy or the patience for a confrontation with him today.'

Hope nodded. 'I'll keep an eye out, and if I spot him approaching, I'll give you a nudge with my elbow.'

'Then we'll hightail it . . .'

Summer was prohibited from saying anything more, because

they were now within earshot of the mead booth. Melody was still waving at them, and it was with such enthusiasm that her bikini kept shifting precariously.

'It's wonderful to see you,' Melody cooed when they had reached her. 'How nice of you to stop by.'

'How's the advertising going?' Summer inquired, gesturing toward the bikini.

Although Summer's mirth was barely concealed, Melody took the question seriously, and even more seriously, she shook her head.

'Not good in the least. Business hasn't improved at all from yesterday. Our ticket box is nearly empty. I told Aaron that it's the weather. It's simply too hot and sunny for people to want to eat and drink.'

A single glance at the passing crowd with its collective arms loaded full of food and beverages proved the statement false, but Melody appeared so genuinely obtuse that neither Hope nor Summer had the heart to point it out to her.

'Has your business been bad, too?' Melody asked them. 'Are you as bored as I am? It was a lot more fun when Aaron and Gary were here. But they left to go to one of the craft beer booths.'

The irony that the two men had departed their own booth offering alcoholic beverages to visit another booth with different alcoholic beverages seemed to be completely lost on Melody. Feeling the same degree of pity for her that she had on their first meeting, Hope took a page from Dylan's medical handbook.

'You're right about it being so hot and sunny,' Hope said. 'Speaking of which, I hate to overstep, but you may want to consider covering up. It's easy to get sunburned on a day like this without even realizing it.'

The possibility didn't appear to have occurred to Melody, because her brow furrowed slightly, and she poked her forearm with an index finger. The spot went bright white, then promptly returned to broiled crustacean.

'Golly,' Melody murmured. 'That'll hurt tomorrow.' She looked up at Hope. 'Thank you for mentioning it. I appreciate it.'

Hope nodded, but a moment later, she found her own brow furrowing when Melody made no move to pull on a shirt or even throw a towel over her shoulders. Hope felt a sharp nudge in her side from Summer's elbow, and she was instantly on alert to make a hasty departure. But when no sign of Gary's imminent arrival at the booth followed, Hope gave her sister a questioning glance. Summer inclined her head toward Melody's arm. There was a bandage on the underside of the woman's right wrist that Hope hadn't noticed before. It was spotted with dried blood.

'That looks like it hurts, as well,' Summer remarked to Melody, motioning toward the wound. 'Did you cut yourself?'

Melody gazed at the bandage as though pondering it intently, and then she answered, 'I was filling the jelly jars that we use for the mead. The lids have a rough edge.'

'That's too bad.' Summer's brow now also furrowed. 'By the way, did you hear about what happened on the carousel last night?'

Hope blinked at her sister in surprise. Did Summer think that it might be Melody's blood on the carousel platform?

Continuing to ponder the bandage on her wrist, Melody responded, 'It's a terrible tragedy. Davis was such a lovely man.'

It was Summer's turn to blink in surprise. 'You knew Davis Scott?'

'Of course.' Melody blinked back at her. 'You did, too, didn't you? Wasn't he handling the sale of your house?'

'Well, yes . . .'

'That's what I thought.' Melody nodded. 'Davis was our realtor the last time we moved. Aaron was the one who recommended him to Gary.'

Summer's face contorted, and she made an aggrieved choking sound. It wasn't hard for Hope to guess what her sister was thinking. If Summer could have cursed someone at that moment, it would have been Aaron Witten for his real estate agent referral.

'You will stay until Gary and Aaron come back, won't you?' Melody pleaded with Summer. 'I would love the company, and Gary will be sorry that he missed you otherwise. When I mentioned to him that I had seen you earlier, he told me that he had seen you, too. And yesterday also.'

'He did?' Summer said, puzzled. 'But I haven't seen Gary this weekend.'

Either Melody didn't hear her or didn't want to hear her, because she continued, 'I'm so glad the two of you have started talking again. It's the first step to a reunion. As I said this morning, you really should try to patch things up—'

'That isn't going to happen,' Summer cut her off crisply. 'There will be no patching of any kind.'

Again Melody took no notice and went on, 'It would be fantastic for all of us to be friends again.'

Hope was beginning to wonder if Melody's brain might have gotten a bit broiled along with her skin. Summer must have been thinking something similar, because both her tone and her answer were mild.

'You and I *are* friends, Melody. Why don't you drop by the boutique one day next week, and we'll sit down for a pot of tea? A cup of chamomile always soothes the soul.'

'That would be delightful,' Melody replied, appearing quite pleased by the invitation. 'But could there be coffee, as well? Aaron doesn't like tea, and I don't think that Gary does, either.'

Although Summer's mouth opened to respond, she closed it again a moment later without uttering so much as a syllable. Hope gave her sister a slight nod in agreement. There was no point in arguing with Melody. At best, she was only half listening to them. Hope wished that Dylan was there, because he would have been able to tell if the woman was indeed suffering from a touch of sunstroke and what the best course of action was. Thinking about the insidious effect of the sun's rays on Melody, Hope was starting to feel a little singed herself and decided that it was time for shade, particularly before Gary and Aaron returned from their sojourn to the beer booth.

'Summer and I have to go now, Melody,' she said. 'We need to give an important message to another friend. But maybe you'd like to come with us? Then you wouldn't be alone, and you could get out of the sun for a while.'

'Oh.' Melody looked crestfallen. 'You're going away already? But Gary will be so sad. And that makes me sad. I can't leave the booth unattended.'

'Yes, you can,' Summer told her. 'Nobody is visiting now anyway. And Hope is right. You really should cover up and get out of the sun.'

'The sun?' Melody echoed, perplexed. 'But I like the sun.'

There was a pause as Hope and Summer looked at each other, debating what to do. Finally, Summer shrugged.

'We'll see you later, Melody.' Although Summer gave a cheerful smile, beneath it her expression was troubled. 'Take care of yourself.'

Summer turned and began to walk away. Hope gave a quick wave to Melody and followed her sister. Melody cooed a melancholy goodbye.

'After we talk to Megan,' Hope said, as soon as they were out of earshot of the booth, 'we have to go back and check on Melody. We'll do it surreptitiously. If we see from a distance that Aaron or Gary is there, then we'll give the place a wide berth; otherwise, we really need to make sure that Melody is all right and hasn't passed out in a charred heap.'

'Good idea. We'll definitely do that,' Summer agreed absently. After a brief hesitation, she asked, 'Do you think what Melody said was true?'

'About how she got the cut on her wrist? It couldn't be Melody's blood on the carousel, could it? Could she have been involved in Davis's death?'

Summer gave an agitated snort. 'Why would Melody want to kill Davis? *Davis was such a lovely man.* No, I'm not referring to her wrist. I'm referring to what she said about Gary seeing me today. And yesterday. Was that true?'

Hope considered a moment. 'Well, there are two possibilities. First, Melody could have been fibbing to further her misguided effort of getting you and Gary back together. Has she lied about things previously?'

'Not that I'm aware of. Melody has always been an irritating combination of ditzy and officious – like when she lectured me this morning on my supposed financial obligations toward Gary – which is why I've never really warmed to her. But I can't recall her ever telling outright lies before.'

'Then the second possibility,' Hope said, 'is that Gary was fibbing.'

Summer nodded. 'Obviously, Gary has no qualms about being untruthful. He lied for months about his affair. But when we were living together, he never used to fib about little or trivial things. That's the reason I'm confused. Why would he tell Melody that he had seen me when he hadn't? What purpose does it serve?'

Hope considered again. 'Maybe Gary wasn't lying. Maybe he did see you. But maybe you didn't see him.'

'He saw me, but I didn't see him? Repeatedly?' Summer frowned. 'That can't be right. It would mean Gary was following me. Why would he follow me?'

'I can't answer that other than to reiterate what I said earlier about Gary possibly wanting to hold on to you. Don't forget that when you're at the boutique and the brownstone, you're effectively inaccessible to him. But here – with our booth and his booth and the open festival grounds – Gary can wander about and more or less check on you whenever he feels the inclination.'

'You're making it sound as though he's stalking me.'

'I didn't say that. I just worry that with the divorce proceedings and the sale of the house dragging on for so long, it might be affecting Gary in unpredictable ways. It must be hard on him.'

'Hard on him? It's hard on me!' Summer exclaimed with a touch of indignation.

'Of course it is,' Hope commiserated. 'But you have much more support than he does. You have me and Gram and Megan, the boutique and the brownstone, and lots of other friends and diversions. What does Gary have to help him through this difficult time?'

Summer's nose twitched, betraying a hint of amusement. 'He's got Aaron, Melody, and mead.'

Hope smiled. 'Exactly.'

After a pause, Summer said, 'Then it's settled. Gary wasn't following me. He just happened to see me – yesterday and today – when I didn't see him. It's nothing but a coincidence.'

Hope didn't respond, because she knew that Summer didn't believe it any more than she did.

FOURTEEN

Regardless of whether or not he had been following Summer over the last two days, Shifty Gary was forgotten the moment the sisters turned the corner and saw Amethyst's booth. To their surprise, there was no one minding the booth. Nor was anyone near it. In fact, it appeared as though passers-by were deliberately making as wide a circle as possible around the booth, which was adorned in the hotel and spa's namesake purple.

'Is it my imagination,' Summer remarked slowly, 'or does Amethyst's booth seem to be moving?'

'I'm glad you see that, too,' Hope said. 'For a second, I was afraid that I might have sunstroke like Melody.'

Summer half squinted, half frowned at it. 'Is it shaking? Why would the booth be shaking?'

'In theory, it could be an earthquake, except nothing else in the vicinity is shaking.'

'And we're too far from the attic!'

Hope laughed.

'That's strange.' The frown overtook the squint. 'The two big bowls of liquefied pillow chocolates that Megan told us about are still up on the counter. Shouldn't somebody have gotten rid of those by now?'

'They're probably too large and messy to move during the festival. My guess is that they'll stay there until the whole booth is dismantled at the end of the weekend.'

'I hope Megan doesn't get in trouble for leaving the booth unattended.' Summer gave a sudden gasp. 'Good lord, you don't think something bad has happened to her, do you? Or to whoever else was supposed to be manning the booth? That could be why it's empty.'

'No. Of course not.' Hope shook her head. 'What could have happened? It's broad daylight with a mass of people milling about. If Megan or one of her colleagues had been injured or taken ill, there would have been an enormous crowd to help.'

'Yes, but—'

'It's the stress of Davis and the carousel. We're thinking about the scarf and the blood and trying to understand why someone killed the man. It's making us unduly apprehensive about everything else.'

Summer didn't appear entirely reassured, and truth be told, Hope wasn't nearly as confident as she pretended to be. With quick steps, the pair headed toward Amethyst's booth. The closer they got, the more the booth seemed to move. Hope couldn't figure out why. At first, she thought that maybe it was a heat mirage, like shimmering water appearing on a blistering road or desert sands. Except that didn't explain why no other booth was moving. And when Hope looked at each part of the booth in turn, she realized that it was only the sides and the base that were shaking. The top of the booth was still.

'Fingers crossed that everyone is all right,' Summer murmured. 'And that we don't find something horrible—'

There was an abrupt shout from a woman. 'Oh, wait! Wait!'

Startled, Hope and Summer stopped short.

'I wouldn't go any nearer if I were you,' the woman – who popped out of the booth directly before Amethyst's – warned them. 'They're feisty critters.'

Summer's frown resurfaced. 'Huh?'

'They were all over one man's arm,' the woman said. 'At first, he tried to brush them off, and when that didn't work, he poured a bottle of water on them to wash them away. He got stung a good number of times, I'm sure. Most people don't know that they can sting. If it's just one or two, you don't really notice. But multiply it by a dozen or a couple of dozen and it can begin to get pretty painful.'

Not understanding, Hope and Summer turned from the woman to Amethyst's booth. Up close, the booth's movement was even more like a watery mirage, shifting and flowing and continuously changing. And then Hope realized it wasn't the booth that was moving. It was what was *on* the booth. Ants. There must have been thousands, probably tens or hundreds of thousands of them. Endless streaming rows of the small black creatures, all heading toward the two giant glass bowls of brown sludgy goop interspersed with tiny tinfoil wrappers. A million pavement ants marching inexorably to the hotel's complimentary chocolates.

'Egad!' Summer jumped backward.

The woman nodded. 'It's best to stay clear of them. I've been watching their various routes and courses all day. Fascinating, from a naturalist standpoint.'

After her own pronounced step away from Amethyst's booth, Hope took a better look at the woman as she spoke. Somewhere in her mid-thirties, she was dressed in an eclectic, bohemian fashion with a multicolored patchwork skirt, a leopard print smock top, and a jaunty mulberry beret set on top of shoulder-length ginger hair. Although the beret seemed to be an incomprehensible choice in the searing heat, the woman appeared comfortable and managed to carry it off with style.

She went on, 'Of course, I would be a lot less tolerant of the little beasts if I had a sugary product to peddle and they were attacking my booth, as well. But so far, they've mercifully left me alone.'

Hope directed her attention to the woman's booth, which was decorated by a modest, hand-stenciled sign: *Sorrel's Sachets*. Similar to its proprietor, the booth was a hodgepodge containing assorted baskets of potpourri, mounds of mismatched incense sticks, and piles of aromatic packets that were filled with various dried flowers and herbs. Summer was instantly intrigued.

'Pineapple sage!' she exclaimed, picking up one of the labeled packets and inhaling its scent. 'It's a marvelous salvia, Hope. Take a sniff.'

Hope took a breath of the fragrance as bidden. The sachet did indeed smell wonderfully like fresh-cut pineapple.

'Would you mind if I asked whether you purchased it commercially or grew it yourself?' Summer said. 'My sister and I have a green space at the back of our brownstone – I'm Summer, and she's Hope, by the way – where we garden, but this year all of my salvia have performed poorly. Although I don't have any pineapple, I grow anise, culinary, and several varieties of meadow sage.'

Nodding, the woman replied convivially, 'It's a pleasure to meet you both. As you've probably guessed from the sign, I'm Sorrel. Sorrel Packard. And yes, I do grow nearly everything myself. I couldn't possibly afford to sell it otherwise.'

Fully comprehending the tight economics of the herb business, Summer nodded back at her.

'In this climate,' Sorrel continued, 'pineapple sage needs some dappled shade in the afternoon. If it's in full sun for an entire August day, the leaves simply bake and fade, with no scent remaining at all. Without having seen the location of your plantings, I would wager that the trouble with your salvia is the high humidity. The night-time temperatures this summer haven't gone as low as they normally do. It's the same with lavender in this area. Plenty of heat, which they love, but too much humidity, which they hate. Several of my specimens have even started to rot at the crown recently.'

'My lavender is having that problem, too,' Summer sympathized. 'I hope you won't consider me outrageously pushy, but I would love to purchase one of your pineapple sages or a cutting from it.'

'I don't generally sell my plants,' Sorrel told her, 'but I would be more than happy to let you have a cutting. And there's no need to pay for it. Why don't you just give me a cutting of one of your plants in exchange? An unusual variety, perhaps?'

'What a delightful idea! I have an heirloom calendula that you might be interested in. It produces a better oil than most of the newer hybrids currently available. The buds . . .'

As the two women launched into a protracted calendula discussion, Hope smiled to herself. This was exactly what she had meant when she had said a short while earlier that Summer had plenty of diversions from Gary, but Gary might not be equally as fortunate. And then, all of a sudden, there he was. Gary Fletcher – with blond hair that was so light it was almost bordering on white, and a deeply dimpled chin – was standing at the far back corner of Amethyst's booth, partially concealed beneath a floppy purple awning. Hope blinked and started to lift her hand to point him out to Summer, but just as abruptly as he had appeared, the man vanished.

She blinked again, and Gary was no longer there. The space under the awning was empty. The far back corner of the booth was bare. Had it been another mirage created by the sun and the heat? She had been thinking about Shifty Gary, so Shifty Gary had materialized in front of her? Hope sincerely wished for that to be the case, because the alternative explanation – that Gary was in actuality following Summer and had raced off the moment he was spotted – wasn't good.

Hope's eyes circled, searching for some lingering indication of Summer's estranged husband and thankfully finding none, and her gaze came to rest once more on the columns of ants that were trooping relentlessly toward the bowls of melted chocolate. Megan's message hadn't been exaggerated; there was certainly a problem at Amethyst's booth. But it wasn't a problem that Stanley Palmer and his trusty ladder and tool chest could fix – not unless the tool chest contained several barrels of insecticide. Although Hope was far from an expert on pest control, she thought that what Sorrel had told them about the man with the ants all over his arm pouring a bottle of water on them to wash them off was probably the best solution on a larger scale, too. Somebody would need to hose down the entire booth. Hope wondered if the man with the ants had been Sean or a different Amethyst employee. It wasn't surprising that he and Megan were no longer at the booth. They had undoubtedly fled at the first sign of the invading hordes. But where had they gone?

'I'm sorry for interrupting,' Hope said to Sorrel, breaking into her ongoing herbal dialogue with Summer, which had progressed to the many positive attributes of thyme, 'but I'm anxious to find one of the people who was previously working at the booth now overrun with ants. Her name is Megan Steele, and you might remember seeing her because yesterday she was wearing a petal-pink ball gown with a tiara.'

'Oh, yes, of course. What we all suffer through for the sake of our jobs.' Sorrel shook her head in commiseration. 'I should have mentioned it earlier when you first introduced yourselves. Megan asked me to tell you if you came by the booth that she would be in the big tent at the end of this row.'

'The big tent at the end of this row? Thanks so much.' Hope

looked at her sister inquiringly. Did she want to stay and continue her conversation with Sorrel, or was she coming along to the big tent to meet up with Megan?

There was no indecision on Summer's part. 'We have to dash,' she told Sorrel. 'But it was great chatting with you! Pop by the boutique any day next week. Sometime in the morning or early evening would be best; otherwise, the garden will be much too hot for us to look around properly.'

'Sounds good. And I'll bring along that cutting you wanted.' With a friendly nod in parting, Sorrel turned back to her booth to assist an apparent mother-and-daughter duo who were debating what scent of sachet would be best to help freshen a stale laundry hamper.

'I like Sorrel. She's a little off the beaten path,' Summer said, as they left the army of ants at Amethyst's booth behind and headed toward the end of the row in search of Megan. 'You weren't too bored listening to us, were you?'

'Not in the least,' Hope replied somewhat distractedly. She was considering whether to tell her sister about the possible sighting of Gary beneath the purple awning, but after a minute, she decided against it. It would only cause Summer additional stress, and, after all, the sighting might have been no more than an optical illusion. Too much talk of Shifty Gary could have created visions of Gary being shifty.

The sisters recognized the big tent as they drew near to it. It was the same tent in which they had given their presentation on semi-precious stones and crystals the previous year. There were only a few people ambling around the entrance, so it didn't appear as though any event was about to commence.

Summer studied one of several posted placards that had the tent schedule printed on it. Then she checked her watch. 'The last talk was an hour ago.'

'What was the subject?' Hope asked.

'Organic and biodynamic lawn care.'

Hope smiled. 'Well, we know Megan didn't come for that, considering she doesn't have a lawn.'

Although there was no articulable reason for them to delay, they found themselves approaching the tent with halting steps. They paused in front of the flap door entrance.

'Should we go in?' Summer mused.

'I suppose so.'

Still they hesitated.

'This is ridiculous,' Summer said. 'Why are we being such scaredy-cats? It's a festival tent, not a firing squad. And for that matter, we've been in this exact tent before—'

A loud voice could be heard from inside the tent, followed by several equally loud cheers. It sounded as though someone had made a speech and was being enthusiastically applauded for it.

'How odd,' Summer murmured. 'I'm sure that there was nothing listed on the schedule. The sign specifically said the tent was free for the remainder of the day.'

'Maybe a group decided to have an impromptu meeting?'

Summer began to nod, then she laughed. 'Yes, everybody who was supposed to work at Amethyst's booth for the rest of the weekend is celebrating the ant invasion. No more capes, crowns, tiaras, or gowns!'

Hope laughed with her.

Laughter echoed from inside the tent, too. If it was a meeting, it gave the impression of being a merry one. Suddenly, the pair of flap doors opened, and a man emerged. He was swaying slightly and carrying an amber bottle of beer.

There was an audible gulp from Summer. 'Now I understand why we were dragging our feet coming here. We felt it in our bones. Somehow we sensed that this was where Gary and Aaron might be drinking.'

Hope frowned. 'But Melody told us that they went to one of the craft beer booths. This is the main tent. The main tent has never offered food or beverages before.'

'There is a first time for everything,' Summer rejoined, 'and how do you explain that man and his beer otherwise?'

'I can't,' Hope admitted, watching the man wander – his steps not quite steady – in the direction of a pizza stand.

Summer watched him also. 'If he wasn't so far away already, I would ask him if he had seen anyone in the tent who resembled Gary. Since that's not possible, I say we turn around and make a speedy departure, before somebody else comes out who might recognize us.'

'What about Megan? She wouldn't be sitting in a tent drinking with Gary. She despises Gary.'

'That's true, but maybe Gary arrived after Megan, and she was forced to leave because of him. Check your phone. There could be a message from her. In any case, we have to get away – immediately. The only thing worse than being trapped in a tent with Gary is being trapped while Gary is drinking with a buddy who will buck up his nerve. Can you imagine what Gary might say or do if there's enough alcohol in him? Thank heaven Nate isn't here to witness it, because that would probably put an end to any potential . . .'

She didn't finish the sentence. The pair of flap doors opened again, this time with enough vigor that Hope and Summer got a good look at the group inside the tent – and the group got a good look at them in return.

FIFTEEN

'Hello, hello, my darlings!' Megan called.

She waltzed toward them from the center of the group, her arms spread wide in greeting. There was no satin, sequins, or crinkly tulle for her today. Megan looked as comfortable as could be in an airy scoop-neck top and cropped chinos.

'Welcome, Bailey sisters!' a man shouted from the same direction and raised an amber bottle in salutation.

It was Sean, and there was no Amethyst regalia for him, either. On the contrary, he looked ready for a tropical vacation in his bright teal golf shirt and palm-tree print shorts.

Summer exhaled with such a monstrous sigh of relief that her body almost seemed to deflate. Then a tremendous smile spread across her face.

'If Megan is here, that means Gary isn't,' she exclaimed. 'And I see available beer!'

Without waiting another second, Summer charged into the tent and made a beeline straight for Sean and what appeared from a distance to be a large aluminum tub crowded with ice and amber bottles at his side. Megan exchanged an air kiss with Summer as they passed, but Summer didn't slow or veer from her path.

Megan laughed when she and Hope reached each other. 'I've never seen Summer so eager to get her hands on a cold beer before.'

'It's anxiety,' Hope told her. 'Shifty Gary is roaming about the festival.'

A shadow momentarily clouded Megan's cheery expression. 'He is? Well, he won't get in here. I can promise you that. As you could probably tell from his greeting, Sean is in an excellent mood today. He and his bulging masseur muscles will be more than happy to chuck out anyone we deem unworthy.'

'That's encouraging,' Hope said, and she meant it.

Now that she was inside the tent, Hope was able to take a better look around. The far half of the space contained an empty speaker's stage and many neat rows of folding chairs. The near half was filled with the beginnings of a party. About twenty-five people of varied ages were laughing, chatting, lounging on disordered folding chairs, and reaching for bottles of beer from several aluminum tubs similar to the one next to Sean.

'Where did all of this come from?' Hope asked Megan.

'Me. Morris. Olivia. And Daniel.'

Hope raised an eyebrow at the way Megan purred the last name on the list.

Megan grinned. 'Daniel Drexler is eye candy, and he makes my heart go pitter-patter. Just wait until you see him, then you'll understand.'

Hope glanced around in search of the purported eye candy. 'Is he here now?'

'No. He's gone to provision us with more food and drink. Which means that I have time to tell you the rest of the story before I must focus all of my attention on batting my baby blues at him. Let's sit down.'

Megan pulled over a pair of folding chairs and grabbed two beers from the nearest tub. Taking one of the bottles from her, Hope looked at the label.

'The Green Goat has its own beer?'

'Yup. Daniel is co-owner of the place.'

Hope's eyebrow went higher. 'So am I correct in assuming that instead of heading there tonight, we'll be staying here?'

'Indubitably. And I know that you won't mind, because you aren't any more enthusiastic about going back out in the heat than I am.' Megan sank into a chair and took a long drink. 'All things considered – with the industrial fans and chilled beverages – it's reasonably comfortable in here.'

'I can't argue with you on that point.' Hope took a seat and a drink, too. She looked at the label again, this time with pleasant surprise. 'As you know, I'm not usually much of a beer drinker, but this stuff is pretty good.'

Megan nodded in agreement. 'That's the same thing I told

Daniel. He explained to me at considerable length that it's due to the origin of the hops.'

'And you feigned fascination throughout?'

'Indubitably,' she repeated, grinning once more.

'So when did you meet Daniel, co-owner of the Green Goat and ostensible expert on hops, because I'm quite sure that you didn't mention him yesterday?'

Checking her watch, Megan replied, 'About an hour ago.'

Hope burst out laughing.

Megan took another long drink and began her story. 'As Amethyst's official representative at the festival, I was the unfortunate person tasked with telling Morris and the rest of the committee that the booth was finished for the weekend on account of the ant infestation. Morris said that we could use another booth as a substitute – which I hastily declined, of course. Because Amethyst is one of the larger sponsors of the festival, I think Morris was worried that upper management would be upset about not having a designated spot for advertising purposes, so he suggested that we use a portion of this tent instead. I declined again, but he was adamant about showing me all of the available options. Sean joined us. You should see the welts on his arm, by the way, after the ants were done attacking him. Stanley Palmer, whom Morris had asked to help set up the space if I changed my mind, came along also. Then Stanley's wife, Amelia, dropped by to offer me her decorating assistance.'

Hope smiled, remembering how, at her and Summer's booth, Amelia had been credited with having an excellent eye for lighting and decor, but Stanley was the one who had been required to install it.

'Shortly thereafter,' Megan continued, 'the next rotation of staff from Amethyst showed up in search of me, since nobody at the hotel or spa had bothered to pass on my message that they were no longer required to be at the festival. And before we knew it, there were nearly a dozen people in here, all just standing around and talking, with nothing in particular to do. Morris said that if we were going to have a social gathering, then we might as well have something to eat and drink. So he contacted Olivia, and Olivia – being the outstanding organizer that she is – promptly contacted the Green Goat, which is evidently another one of the festival sponsors. Daniel arrived from the restaurant's smaller tent in the row opposite this one with the tubs of ice and beer, and we hit it off right away.'

Hope's smile grew. Megan was both exceedingly picky and fickle when it came to men, so she was greatly looking forward to meeting Daniel Drexler and seeing how long he could hold on to Megan's attention.

'And the group has been growing ever since,' Megan concluded, 'as word is slowly spreading through the people working at the festival and more booths close for the day.'

'Booths are closing already?' Hope said in surprise. She glanced toward the flap doors of the tent and saw that the sun was lower along the horizon than she had imagined. Somehow the afternoon had become the evening.

Megan seemed surprised in turn. 'Isn't that why you and Summer are here? Isn't your booth closed for the day?'

'It is,' Hope confirmed, 'although not through our choice. Detective Nate came by earlier and shut us down. He had a lot of questions about Davis and the scarf and the carousel. He indicated that he also has questions for you. And Sean, as well.'

At the mention of Sean, Hope had expected Megan to express even more surprise, but she didn't. Instead, Megan's face grew suddenly serious. Her voice lowered, and she leaned forward in her folding chair.

'It makes sense that the police would have questions for Sean. You remember how I told you before that he's in an excellent mood?'

Hope nodded.

'Well, that's an understatement. I wouldn't go so far as to say that Sean is celebrating Davis Scott's death, but he certainly isn't mourning the man.'

They looked over at Sean. He and Summer were sitting together, laughing and drinking, neither one acting the least bit funereal.

'You mean Sean and Davis were acquainted?' Hope asked, keen to learn the answer to one of her own questions.

'Not only were they acquainted, but Davis is the reason

Sean came to the festival today. He wasn't scheduled for another shift at Amethyst's booth this weekend.' Megan paused and lowered her voice further. 'I'm fond of Sean. He's a good guy, and, as you know, we've helped each other out in the past at work.'

Hope nodded again.

'So what I tell you now is in confidence. I have no desire to be the tattletale who lands Sean in hot water. Unless we end up having some moral obligation from on high, I don't want to share this information with the police.'

'Agreed. Nate won't hear it from me.'

After checking around to make sure that no one was close enough to be able to listen in to their conversation, Megan said, 'When I was at Amethyst's booth earlier, trying to figure out whether there was any way to control the insect incursion without resorting to fire or flood, Sean appeared. He was as chipper as could be, practically walking on air. I wasn't quite as perky in response, so he teased me about having had a late night. I started to explain what had happened on the carousel, but, to my astonishment, he stopped me mid-sentence and said that he already knew all about it.'

Hope was astonished, too. 'He did?'

'Yes. According to Sean, he first learned about Davis's death from some gossipy friend who was working at another booth, and he immediately came to the festival to confirm whether the news was accurate.'

Her astonishment grew. 'Did Sean mention how he knew Davis?'

'That's where it gets mighty interesting.' Megan leaned closer. 'Apparently, Davis was the realtor for Sean's sister a year or two ago. As Sean tells it, Davis talked her into renting a house that she didn't really want but a pal of his owned. After they moved in, the sister's baby – Sean's nephew – began to cough and have breathing troubles. Over the next few months, it got worse and worse, with doctor's visits and medical tests and trips to the emergency room, until the culprit was finally discovered. It turned out that the house was filled with black mold hidden inside the walls. Seriously toxic stuff, by all accounts. Although he doesn't have any legal proof, Sean is convinced that Davis and the owner of the house knew about the mold from the outset, but the owner didn't want to pay to have it remediated, so they just kept foisting the property on unsuspecting victims.'

Hope was appalled. 'That's outrageous! And is the baby all right?'

'To a point, yes. But there's been some permanent lung scarring that makes him more susceptible to bronchitis and pneumonia in the future.'

'How awful! No wonder Sean isn't in deep mourning over Davis. You saw how Summer reacted to his death, and she only had an unsold house to be angry about, not a dangerously ill baby—' Hope broke off abruptly as a startling possibility occurred to her. 'Good god, you don't think Sean was so angry at Davis that he . . .'

She didn't have to finish the sentence, because Megan understood her immediately. 'I hate to say it, but I think there might be a chance. After I got over the initial shock of Sean's story, I started to ask myself the same thing that you are now. In all honesty, I don't believe that Sean would ever *plan* to hurt someone, no matter how terrible a person they were – even Davis Scott. But under the right circumstances, in a weak moment with sufficient provocation, he could be capable of doing something that he would later regret.'

'Based on his present attitude and behavior,' Hope said, 'Sean doesn't appear to be regretting it.'

'No, he doesn't, and I don't know if that helps or hurts his case.'

Hope considered a moment. 'Both Nate and Dylan are of the opinion that Davis's murder wasn't premeditated. If it had been, the killer would have chosen a more dependable and surefire weapon than a silk scarf.'

'Unless,' Megan responded, 'you're as strong as Sean is. The truth of the matter is that the muscles in his hands and arms and upper body are so well developed from his many years of working at the spa, Sean could probably strangle somebody with very little effort at all, regardless of any scarf.'

'That definitely doesn't help his case. It also doesn't help that he switched directions. Nate seems to think that's important.'

Megan frowned. 'Switched directions?'

'It's what you told Rosemarie when you were talking about how a person's eyes could play tricks in the dark. As you were coming to our booth last night, you thought that you saw Sean heading in one direction even though you were certain that he had gone in the opposite direction only a few minutes earlier.'

The frown deepened. 'That's right. I did see Sean switch directions. At least, my eyes imagined that he did.'

'Either way, Nate finds it suspicious. And now that I'm aware of Sean's connection to Davis, I can understand why Nate wants to question him about his movements, especially if the murder wasn't premeditated. Consider this as a possible scenario: After Sean leaves you and Amethyst's booth yesterday evening to head home, he unexpectedly runs into Davis, who we know was wandering around the festival grounds without Rosemarie at that time. The two men go their separate ways, but after a minute, all the bad memories and anger about his sister and nephew come flooding back to Sean. He turns around – switching directions – and confronts Davis. The altercation gets increasingly ugly, and in the heat of the moment, Sean kills Davis.'

Megan sighed. 'That sequence of events fits together well. Too well, unfortunately.'

Sharing the sigh, Hope looked once more at Sean. He and Summer were still sitting together, laughing and drinking, without an apparent care in the world. As Sean reached down to the tub at his side to retrieve a new bottle of beer, Hope caught sight of his arm. As Megan had described, it was covered with countless welts from being stung by the ants. The bright red spots were swollen and irritated. And then Hope noticed the large bandage on Sean's elbow, which was dotted with a darker shade of red. It immediately brought to her mind the blood on the carousel platform.

'Megan, did Sean have that bandage yesterday?'

'Huh?'

'There's a bandage on Sean's elbow,' Hope said. 'Obviously, he hurt himself, but when it happened could be vitally important. Do you remember if he had the bandage yesterday? Or earlier today at the booth? Or was it a result of the ant attack?'

'I don't know about yesterday,' Megan answered slowly, thoughtfully, 'because I didn't see Sean's arms. He had the cape on the entire time, which covered his elbows. When he left and took off the cape, it was too dark for me to notice a bandage. As for earlier today . . .' She hesitated. 'Yes. Sean had the bandage before the ant attack.'

'You're sure?'

'I'm positive. I remember because when the ants were swarming all over his arm and he first tried to brush them off, a lot of them were getting caught under the bandage. And then when Sean poured the water on them to wash them away, he lifted the bandage to rinse off the trapped ones, too.'

It was Hope's turn to be thoughtful. 'Could it have been intentional?'

'What do you mean?'

'If Sean hurt his elbow in the struggle with Davis, is it possible that he intentionally got stung by the ants in an attempt to conceal the wound?'

Megan stared at her.

'From what I've gathered from Nate and Dylan,' Hope explained, 'there was blood on the carousel platform close to Davis's body. So whoever killed the man most likely has an injury of some sort.'

There was a brief, deliberative pause, and then Megan said, 'I can't tell you whether it was inattention or intentional. But I know that Sean could have avoided getting stung. While I was talking to Sorrel at the neighboring booth, I saw him put his hand down smack in the middle of the ants.'

SIXTEEN

For several long minutes, Hope and Megan sat in silence, drinking their beer and pondering what to do next. Did they break their pledge not to tell the police about Sean's connection to Davis? Did they talk to Sean himself about their suspicions? Or did they simply do nothing?

'I don't know,' Hope said at last. 'What if we have it all wrong? We can't accuse an otherwise decent man of murder based on a couple of coincidences, can we?'

'It's more than a couple of coincidences,' Megan corrected her. 'And they're serious ones.'

Hope had no response.

'I wish that we had someone else to ask for an opinion. Not the police, but another person who understands the situation and could give us an impartial assessment—' Megan interrupted herself. 'What about Dylan?'

'What about him?'

'We could talk to him about Sean. Dylan is already familiar with the basic facts of the case. He discovered Davis's body with us, and because of his association with Nate, he probably has a good deal of extra insight that we aren't aware of. You just said a minute ago that you gathered the information about the blood on the carousel platform from him.'

'That's true, but . . .' Hope hesitated.

'Dylan has no prior relationship with Sean, so he won't be unduly swayed by either friendship or enmity. And Dylan doesn't seem like the type who would automatically run and snitch to the authorities. If he promised us his discretion, I think that we could trust him to keep his word.'

'That's true,' Hope agreed again. Still she hesitated.

'Plus, I don't see us having a better option. I can avoid Nate for a while, but sooner or later, he'll succeed in tracking me down, and then I'll be forced to answer at least a portion of his questions. It will be the same for Sean. Obviously, I would prefer that we didn't get into trouble for withholding information from the police if we can work around it.'

Hope nodded. 'Nate is dogged and smart. It's only a matter of time before he figures out that we're keeping potentially valuable evidence from him, and he won't be happy about it. Even without knowing anything about Sean's connection to Davis, Summer said that we should all have our stories straight and get our ducks in a row before Nate comes around with more questions.'

'Exactly! So it's decided. We'll talk to Dylan at the first available opportunity and ask for his advice on Sean.'

'Unfortunately, that might not happen as soon as we would like. When I last saw Dylan this afternoon, he was with Nate.'

'Then we'll have to find a way to separate them.' Megan's lips curled with a hint of a grin. 'That can be your job. I'm sure that Dylan would be more than willing to part from his friend if he believed that he was going to spend some time alone with you.'

Hope rolled her eyes, mildly amused. 'That's your plan? You want me to get Dylan alone under false pretenses, and then we ask him for a favor?'

The grin grew. 'You make it sound so underhanded. There is nothing wrong with a little harmless flirtation for the purpose of potentially solving a murder—' Megan stopped abruptly and gave a short laugh. 'Speak of the devil. Our problem has been solved.'

Not immediately understanding, Hope followed Megan's gaze toward the flap doors of the tent. During the course of their conversation, another twenty or so people had filtered inside, no doubt all in search of a fun and relaxing Saturday evening after spending a long day in a hot booth, smiling ceaselessly at ticketholders. To Hope's surprise, the most recent group of arrivals included Dylan.

'Forget my previous statement. The problem has gotten substantially worse,' Megan amended. 'It appears that the devil has brought the law with him.'

Detective Nate had now also entered the tent. On his heels were Larkin and another woman who was likewise in her mid- to late twenties. Based on the giggles and winks they exchanged, the two women seemed to be friends. The foursome paused just inside the flap doors and began to confer. Larkin leaned against Dylan's arm, while the other woman leaned against Nate's arm.

Hope rolled her eyes again, this time with considerably less amusement and more annoyance.

'The one who's attached herself like a limpet to Dylan looks vaguely familiar,' Megan mused.

'Larkin. She's the new receptionist at Morris's office.'

'Ah, yes. That explains it. I caught a glimpse of her earlier today when I first started to tell Morris about Amethyst's booth being finished for the weekend. Does Larkin not believe in buttoning her blouse?'

It was Hope's turn to give a short laugh, remembering Summer's similar comment on the subject. 'Summer isn't a fan, either. The glittery banner above our booth and the faux crystal ball are both courtesy of Larkin.'

'Hmm.' Megan studied Larkin. 'I wouldn't trust her for a millisecond. Unless I'm grossly mistaken, she intends on getting her talons into Dylan.'

'That was my impression, too.'

'Hmm.' Megan studied her some more. 'Too glib of an air. Smacks of desperation.'

'Perhaps, but none of the men seem to think so. From what I've seen, they all find her delightful. Morris. Dylan. Nate. And now there's this apparent friend of Larkin's who looks to be cut from the same cloth.'

'Another limpet,' Megan remarked, as the other woman leaned even more heavily against Nate's arm.

'I wonder how they heard about this tent,' Hope said.

'It might be that Nate is a truly exceptional detective and managed to ferret out the party from among all the tents and booths on the festival grounds, or – the more probable answer – Larkin learned of it from her employer.'

Hope replied with an irritated sigh. As much as she liked Morris, his lips could be inconveniently loose on occasion.

'In any event,' Megan continued, 'we now find ourselves in a bit of a pickle. Nate and his questions are here. So am I.

And so is Sean. Any brilliant suggestions on how we should proceed?'

'Well, our first order of business has to be getting you and Sean out of this place as quickly and unobtrusively as we can manage.'

As she spoke, Hope glanced over at Sean. He and Summer still hadn't budged from their folding chairs. They were surrounded by a sizable group that included a number of people who were standing rather than sitting, so they weren't immediately visible to Nate. They also didn't seem to have noticed his arrival.

'Hope—'

'It's going to be easier with you than with Sean,' she went on. 'I know you told me before that you didn't want to leave the tent and go back out into the heat, but at this juncture, I believe our best chance lies with—'

'Hope!' Megan interjected again, her voice low but insistent. 'Don't look at the entrance, but I'm pretty sure that we've been spotted.'

Contrary to the warning, her head snapped toward the flap doors. Although Larkin and the other woman were still conferring with Nate, Dylan was no longer focused on them. Instead, he was looking directly at Hope. She winced slightly, expecting to see a considerable amount of ire in his face due to her and Summer's unannounced exit from their booth earlier. But to Hope's relief, Dylan's expression was less resentful and more inquisitive, as though he could discern that she and Megan were discussing something important and he was trying to figure out what it was. To her further relief, it didn't appear as though he had pointed them out to Nate yet.

Taking his silence as a promising sign, Hope met Dylan's gaze straight on, and after a moment, she gave a small shake of her head. He responded with a questioning frown and tilted his own head toward Nate. She shook her head again, and this time, Dylan replied with a nod.

Keeping her eyes cautiously on his, Hope said to Megan, 'I seem to have established an understanding with Dylan. Or maybe it's a détente. I'm not quite certain which. In either case, I think this would be an excellent time for you to leave the tent. Is there any way to get out of here other than that main entrance?'

'Yes!' Megan answered with quiet excitement. 'The perfect opportunity has just presented itself. Two of the guys who work with Daniel and helped bring in the tubs of ice earlier are right now coming through one of the side flaps by the stage with the remainder of the food and drink Daniel promised to supply. I can slip out that way, pretending to be with them. If I turn my back and do it fast, no one – fingers crossed – at the entrance of the tent will take any notice of me.'

Although Hope was tempted to glance over her shoulder at the side flap and the two men, she stopped herself. She didn't want to break Dylan's gaze and risk revealing their plan in advance.

Megan laughed lightly. 'Considering the brevity of our acquaintance, Daniel Drexler is proving himself to be very useful: eye candy, beer, and temporary protection from the long arm of the law.'

Hope couldn't help but laugh, too. Dylan's eyes narrowed slightly, as though he didn't appreciate missing out on the joke.

'You'd better hurry,' Hope cautioned her. 'I'm sensing that Dylan's patience is growing thin.'

'Wish me luck,' Megan said. Then, in one swift movement, she stood up, spun around, and dashed toward the rear of the tent.

Hope didn't look after her, but Dylan did, and she could see that Megan's abrupt departure surprised him. He raised an eyebrow at Hope. She wasn't sure how to interpret it. If he was expecting her to promptly march over to him and provide him with a detailed explanation, then he was going to be disappointed, because her next task now that Megan had succeeded in escaping was to similarly assist Sean. That was going to be substantially more difficult, however, considering that she had to get to Sean without attracting Nate's attention.

Once again, Hope met Dylan's gaze. But this time, she gave him an indication of her intentions. With a subtle wave of her hand, she motioned toward the group in the center of the tent.

Dylan's eyes followed the gesture, and after a minute, he found Summer and Sean on their folding chairs. Looking at the pair, his brow furrowed, and he began to frown. Puzzled by his reaction, Hope looked at the pair, too. They hadn't changed. They were still sitting together, laughing and drinking. And then Hope realized what Dylan was seeing that she hadn't. Summer and Sean looked chummy. Really chummy. *Too* chummy. Their chairs were close. Their smiles were warm. Their conversation was intimate.

There was nothing behind it, of course. Hope knew that instantly. Summer and Sean had not the slightest romantic interest in each other. Both of them were simply relieving stress and enjoying some pleasant company for the evening. But it was easy to understand how the scene could be misinterpreted by an outsider to mean more than it actually did. Hope found herself smiling. It was a shame that she couldn't direct Nate's gaze to Summer and Sean at that moment. If Nate made the same faulty assumption that Dylan did, then it might spark a bit of jealousy in him and finally jolt him into romantic action.

As Hope smiled, Dylan's frown deepened. Larkin frowned also, having apparently at long last realized that the man against whose arm she was leaning wasn't listening to a word she said. She looked around, seeking the cause of Dylan's distraction, and when her eyes landed on Hope, they were cold and unfriendly. Hope could see Larkin hesitate, as though she was debating whether it would be more advantageous for her to point Hope out to the others in a critical fashion or to ignore her existence altogether. But a minute later, it became a moot issue, because Nate discovered Hope of his own accord. Although his eyes were considerably more cordial than Larkin's, they remained on her only briefly before commencing a thorough examination of the tent, no doubt in search of Summer.

While Hope hastily considered how to distract Nate, it occurred to her that even if he located Summer, he might not automatically recognize Sean. Just because Nate wanted to question Sean, it didn't mean that he could identify him by sight. If that was the case, then there was still a possibility that Hope could get Sean out of the tent. But she had to do it quickly, and she had to be the one to reach him and Summer first.

Without further delay or making any attempt to conceal her direction, Hope turned and headed toward the pair on their folding chairs. To her surprise, they were no longer laughing and drinking. Summer and Sean were sitting close enough together that their bodies nearly touched, but rather than looking amorous, they were now engaged in what appeared to be a grave discussion. Both of their expressions were somber, and their conversation was in a low, hushed tone that was clearly not intended to be overheard by others. Was Sean telling Summer about his sister and nephew? At one point, Summer's face grew so grim and her cheeks so ashen that a feeling of dread began to creep through Hope. Could Sean be confessing to Davis Scott's murder?

Then, all of a sudden, the conversation ended. Summer nodded at something Sean said. He nodded in return, rose from his chair, and moved with brisk steps to the side flap by the stage. For a moment, Hope was too astonished to react. Without any endeavor or explanation from her, Sean was leaving the tent the same way Megan had. Did he know that he needed to avoid the police? Had Summer told him about Rosemarie's accusations? Was Sean fleeing out of guilt, or anger, or fear?

For her part, Summer remained seated, and her face remained pale. She was visibly disturbed by whatever she and Sean had discussed. Hope tried to catch her sister's eye, but Summer kept her gaze firmly on the ground. She appeared to be mumbling to herself, with an occasional, frustrated shake of her head. Hope's feet moved faster, but there were now so many people inside the tent that she was continually forced to stop and shift around one boisterous, beer-swilling group after another. Although she was curious whether Nate had spotted Summer or Dylan had noticed Sean's departure, she didn't check on them. It would have required her to stop and turn around, and Hope didn't want to take the chance of losing sight of Summer in the crowd.

Finally, Hope neared her and called out over the din. 'Summer!'

Startled, Summer looked up. The instant she saw her sister, Summer leaped from her chair and rushed toward her. 'Oh, Hope, you were right! Everything you said was right.'

'It was?' Hope responded in confusion. She didn't remember ever telling Summer that she thought Sean might be responsible for Davis's death.

'I didn't want to believe it.' Summer's words tumbled out almost frantically. 'But it's true. Terribly, terribly true!'

'So he confessed to you?' Hope asked her, still somewhat confused. 'Sean admitted to killing Davis?'

'If he has, I'll be the first one to get in line and shake the man's hand,' an unexpected voice said.

SEVENTEEN

The voice belonged to Stanley Palmer, and he was standing beside them, a bottle of beer in one hand and a broad smile on his face. Hope didn't know how long Stanley had been there or where he had come from. She also didn't know how to react to his remark. Based on his smile, it seemed to have been a joke, but considering that it was in relation to a murder, it certainly wasn't a funny one.

As though he could guess the direction of her thoughts, Stanley said, 'No, it wasn't an attempt at humor. I meant it seriously. Davis Scott was a plague on this earth. I apologize to anybody whose sensibilities might be offended, but that's the truth of the matter, and no one will convince me otherwise. Ever since Amelia and I started telling people about the problems we had with the man, we've heard a hundred and one similarly troubled stories in return – and some of them have been much worse than ours.'

Hope remembered Sean's story and silently agreed.

'Amelia realized it from the very beginning,' Stanley went on. 'She warned me that he was a slippery fish.'

Summer gave Hope a nudge with her elbow as if to say, *Ha! I told you Davis was the Palmers' real estate agent.*

'At least there's been a happy ending for us.' Stanley took a swig of his beer. 'Amelia's headaches are gone. The instant she heard about the death, her migraine vanished, and it hasn't shown any sign of returning. But I hate to think of all the people who have suffered lasting problems because of that miserable man.'

Again, Hope's mind went to Sean and his little nephew.

'Amelia is around here somewhere' – Stanley craned his neck to look above the sea of chattering bodies in search of his wife – 'and she'll tell you what a tremendous relief it's been. It's almost hard to believe. Davis has been gone for less than a day, but in that short period of time, it's already been remarkably freeing. Strange, isn't it?'

'It's not strange in the least,' Summer said. 'I understand completely, because I feel the same way.'

'So you had problems with him, too?' Stanley was sympathetic. 'I hope he hasn't caused you any permanent damage.'

'Nothing that a new realtor can't fix.'

'I'm glad to hear it! Amelia and I have adopted a similar attitude. Any new realtor will seem like an angel in comparison. We've even been discussing whether we should change our minds and not sell the house, after all.'

'That isn't an option for me,' Summer told him. 'My house has to sell – the sooner, the better.'

Stanley nodded and took another swig. 'I understand. No doubt there are many others in a similar position. And I must admit to being curious about the fellow you mentioned a minute ago.' He looked from Summer to Hope. 'Did you say his name was Sean? I assume that he also had his share of difficulties with Davis?'

Based on their conversation so far – and Stanley's drinking – Hope had the impression that his lips might be even looser than Morris's. Not wanting Sean's personal details spread about to all and sundry, she deliberately chose a noncommittal answer. 'As you said before, there are a hundred and one troubled stories when it comes to Davis Scott.'

'I'm afraid that's correct.' Stanley nodded again. 'But with this fellow Sean in particular . . .' He spoke haltingly. 'When you talked about him confessing . . . Did he actually admit . . . I mean, if you know something about the death or have any concrete suspicions, you really should talk to the police.'

'Of course. You're absolutely right.' Hope feigned both innocence and ignorance. 'We would definitely talk to the police if we knew something about the death or had any concrete suspicions.'

Her response evidently didn't satisfy Stanley, because he pressed the matter further. 'You need to realize how serious this situation is. Murder is not some trifling matter. If you have relevant information, you must share it with the proper authorities.'

Hope frowned, finding the statement odd. Stanley had made it amply clear that he wasn't spilling tears over Davis's untimely demise. He had even said – joking or not – that he wanted to shake the killer's hand. So why did he care whether she and Summer shared relevant information with the proper authorities?

Taking one last large swallow, Stanley finished off his beer. 'If Morris and Olivia were standing here right now, I'm sure they would agree with me. They would worry and tell you that it was imperative to speak up about this Sean fellow.'

Her frown deepened. Stanley was being strangely insistent. He also seemed to be growing somewhat agitated. It was almost as though he was anxious for them to go to the police and point an accusatory finger at Sean. But maybe she was reading too much into it. It had been another long day for everybody, and Stanley wasn't exactly a spring chicken. When the startling news about Davis was combined with all the booths he had fixed in the intense sun and heat, and then joined with perhaps one bottle of beer too many, it all added up to Stanley saying things that sounded off.

Summer echoed her sister from a moment earlier. 'Of course. You're absolutely right. We don't want to worry Morris and Gram.' Then she blinked at Stanley ingenuously and added, 'Speaking of matters that aren't trifling, I see that you've hurt your knee. It looks like a nasty gash.'

Hope's gaze snapped to Stanley's leg. She had been so surprised by his abrupt arrival and subsequent comments that she hadn't taken any notice of his appearance. Stanley was wearing a mustard-yellow shirt and a slightly stained pair of shorts. His legs were as reed-thin as the rest of him. One knee was wrinkled and boney, while the other knee was wrapped with a thick bandage. It was the type of bandage used to protect wounds, not to provide support, and it had an underlying tinge of pink as though he'd had a difficult time getting the cut to stop bleeding.

'I hope it isn't too painful,' Summer said to him.

Stanley looked down at his knee. 'Oh, no. It stings a little, but nothing unbearable. I've had worse.'

'Is it a recent injury?' Summer pursued, blinking some more. 'I don't remember you having that bandage on yesterday when you so kindly set up the lights and decorations in our booth.'

Although she did an excellent job of concealing it, Hope could tell that her sister's questions were far more than friendly politeness or mere idle curiosity. Did Summer think that it might be Stanley's blood on the carousel platform? Could Stanley have been involved in Davis's death?

Still looking at his knee, Stanley answered, 'It was laziness that got me into trouble this morning. I was on the ladder attaching a cable to hang up a collection of sweetgrass baskets for better showing in one of the booths. I knew that I was in the wrong position, but I didn't want to climb down, adjust the ladder, and then climb back up again, so I foolishly stretched too far and slipped. As I fell, I smashed into the side rail and sliced open my knee. It bled like a gusher. Amelia was so worried that she nearly began hyperventilating. I told her the cut looked much deeper than it actually was, but she didn't believe me. She kept shouting that we needed to go to the hospital for sutures. It took me quite a while to convince her that I was really all right. We were the only ones in the booth at the time, so I think that somehow made her more panicky than she otherwise would have been.'

Hope raised an eyebrow. Stanley and Amelia were the only ones in the booth? That meant there were no witnesses to the accident and no proof as to how and when he had sustained the injury. Stanley gave the impression of being truthful, but should she trust his story? Hope wasn't sure, partly because she was still thinking about his remarks concerning Sean. Could it be that Stanley wanted her and Summer to talk to the police about Sean's possible confession and guilt as a way to shift any potential suspicion from himself? Pushing the blame on to someone else was a good strategy for avoiding a murder charge.

'It wasn't until Amelia had finally calmed down,' Stanley continued, 'that we realized she was hurt, too. She had been holding the ladder while I was on it, and when I tumbled off, I crashed against her. She hit her hand on the opposite side rail and cut open her palm. Let me tell you, those metal edges are sharp! At first, Amelia was bleeding even more than I was, but after applying some pressure, it eventually stopped. She's got her hand wrapped up as though she's about to jump into the ring for a boxing match.'

Both of Hope's eyebrows were now raised. Amelia had a bandage also? Did every person with a connection to Davis Scott have a bloody wound? There was Rosemarie's ankle, Melody's wrist, Sean's elbow, Stanley's knee, and Amelia's palm. Of the group, it was only with Rosemarie and her strappy sandals that Hope knew for certain how and when the injury had occurred. For the rest, it was just their word.

'There she is. I've spotted her. Amelia!' Stanley raised his arm and waved through the multitude. 'Here! We're over here!' He waved once more before returning his attention to Hope and Summer. 'She's seen me and is headed this way. Before I forget, you mentioned the lights in your booth a moment ago. I'm sorry that I haven't fixed the broken strand. Between my knee and Amelia's palm and an infestation of ants in another booth, I simply didn't have the chance to stop by.'

'It's not a problem,' Summer replied. 'In fact, having only one functioning strand might be advantageous. The sweetgrass baskets need extra light to showcase their beauty; for us, a bit of darkness provides atmosphere.'

Although she spoke the words casually, there was a slight stiffness in Summer's tone that made Hope wonder if her sister was also having some doubts about the timing and cause of the Palmers' injuries.

For his part, Stanley didn't seem to notice their misgivings. On the contrary, his broad smile resurfaced. 'I would urge you not to say that in front of Amelia. She takes her decorating skills quite seriously. If she finds out that having one strand of twinkle lights in your booth looks just as good as – or, heaven forbid, even better than – the two strands she arranged, she won't take it well.'

Summer smiled in return. 'Understood. She won't hear it from me.'

'What won't I hear?' Amelia asked.

They turned toward her in surprise. The speed and agility with which Amelia had managed to thread her way through the ever-growing assembly inside the tent were impressive.

Similar to the day before, husband and wife were a matched set, except Amelia's shorts had no stains, and her yellow shirt was a touch faded, making it more lemon than mustard. As Stanley had told them, one of her hands was heavily bandaged. In her free hand, Amelia carried two fresh bottles of beer.

Stanley promptly took a full bottle to replace his empty one. Considering the peculiarity of some of his remarks, Hope wasn't so sure that Stanley needed another beer. She was increasingly glad that she hadn't shared any details about Sean with him.

'What won't I hear?' Amelia asked again.

Having had sufficient time to come up with a believable response, Summer answered, 'You won't hear anything. None of us will hear anything. It's getting so loud and crowded in this place that I'm starting to have trouble hearing myself think.'

'Isn't it wonderful?' Amelia exclaimed. She took a hefty drink from the remaining bottle. 'All the people, all the noise, all the excitement! It's fantastic! Makes me feel thirty years younger!'

'That isn't possible,' Stanley protested. 'If you were thirty years younger, you'd be a babe in arms, and I would get arrested for calling you my wife.'

Amelia burst out laughing – and immediately took another drink. 'What a shameless flatterer you are! May I remind you that we are celebrating our fortieth wedding anniversary next March?'

'You're still as beautiful as the day we were married,' Stanley responded gallantly. And in one slightly clumsy but unhesitating movement, he swept Amelia into his arms and planted a big, wet kiss on her lips.

Both Hope and Summer smiled in amusement at the display of affection. They both also expected it to end with more laughing and drinking from the couple. When the kissing continued instead and grew ever sloppier, the sisters looked at each other.

'Time to exit?' Summer said.

'Time to exit,' Hope agreed.

Turning away from the Palmers and their sustained

smooching, they headed toward the rear of the tent where it was quieter and less congested. The rows of folding chairs in front of the speaker's stage were no longer neat and unoccupied, but the corner of the stage nearest to the side flap was empty. Hope and Summer seated themselves on it, making sure to keep far away from any potential prying ears.

Without preamble, Summer jumped straight to the crux of the matter. 'They've all got injuries.'

'And aside from Rosemarie,' Hope replied, 'they've all got unverifiable accounts of how they obtained those injuries.'

Summer nodded. 'When Stanley was telling us that ladder story, it reminded me of how he almost fell from the ladder in our booth yesterday. Do you remember? You were explaining to Gram that Rosemarie had a new boyfriend, and I said Davis Scott's name. Amelia cried out, and Stanley nearly tumbled to the ground. Even at the time, I thought that it was an awfully strong reaction to the mere mention of the man.'

Hope nodded back at her. 'It could have been a sign of a guilty conscience, except the murder wasn't premeditated.'

'Just because it wasn't premeditated,' Summer countered, 'doesn't mean it wasn't contemplated. One or both of the Palmers could have thought about killing Davis without having put any specific plans into place. Their consciences might have been very guilty, hence their strong reactions to his name.'

'Speaking of strong reactions, I'm glad that Gram can't hear us right now. She wouldn't be happy if she knew that we were discussing the possibility of her good friends Stanley and Amelia being murderers.'

'And her good friend Jocelyn,' Summer added.

'Jocelyn?' Hope said in surprise.

'Jocelyn Frost. Drapery expert and seamstress extraordinaire. She's the one responsible for the burgundy curtains in our booth.'

'Yes, I know who she is. But I don't know why you think that she's connected to any of this.'

'Because she also reacted strongly to Davis's name. It wasn't only Amelia who cried out. Jocelyn did, too.'

Recalling the incident, Hope gave a little gasp. 'And Jocelyn pricked her finger! It was bleeding!'

'Correct,' Summer confirmed. 'Jocelyn claimed that her attention had wandered and the needle had simply slipped, but what are the chances of that happening at the exact moment I mentioned Davis? Plus, Jocelyn was terribly flushed. We assumed that she was overheated from having those heavy layers of velvet in her lap, but looking back on it, I think it was all about Davis Scott.'

'With Jocelyn's finger, we have another bloody wound to add to the list—' Hope stopped and shook her head. 'But there's the premeditation problem again, and it's especially true regarding Jocelyn. She's the one who made the cords for the curtains, and Nate said that with the way they're stitched and the thickness of the fabric, the cords would have been a much better murder weapon than the silk scarf.'

'Except maybe Jocelyn was too clever to use her own cords,' Summer argued. 'Maybe she deliberately chose the scarf so that no one would connect her with the crime.'

'But we aren't even sure if Jocelyn knew Davis.'

'From what we've learned over the past two days, it's pretty clear that *everyone* knew Davis. Or perhaps more accurately, everyone was in some way a victim of Davis.'

Hope sighed. 'So where does that leave us?'

'That leaves us with one dead body and far too many suspects. The upside is that there's no reason to believe anybody else will be killed.'

Hope sighed again. On that point, she wasn't nearly as confident as her sister.

EIGHTEEN

Summer flinched. 'Did you see that?'

'See what?' Hope asked.

They were still sitting on the corner of the stage. Voices and figures moved around them, but Hope had taken little notice, lost in her own thoughts.

'The person,' Summer said.

By Hope's estimation, there were close to fifty people within shouting distance. 'You're going to have to be a bit more specific.'

'Over there.' Summer pointed at the side flap.

The side flap of the tent had been pulled back, leaving a narrow opening. It was presently empty.

'Did you see the person?' Summer pressed her.

Hope shook her head. 'No. Nobody is leaving. The party is too popular.'

'I don't mean inside the tent,' Summer responded impatiently. '*Outside.*'

Shifting her focus, Hope looked through the opening. Night had fallen over the festival grounds. There were a few flickering spots of light in the distance but no discernible people.

'There it is again!' Summer exclaimed.

Hope squinted into the darkness.

'It's only visible for a couple of seconds. The shadow appears. It moves closer. And then it fades away again.'

Although she squinted harder, Hope still didn't see anyone.

'It's him,' Summer declared. 'I'm certain of it.'

'Who?' Hope said.

'Gary, of course!'

Hope turned to her sister in surprise.

'It's Gary,' Summer told her emphatically. 'This is the second time tonight that I've seen him.'

'You have?' Hope asked, even more surprised. 'When was the first time?'

'When I was talking to Sean on the folding chairs. All of a sudden, I had this strange feeling that I was being watched. I looked over at the main entrance to the tent, and there he was! His body was mostly hidden behind the flap doors, but I clearly saw his face. Gary was staring straight at me! It startled me enough that I almost fell from my seat. I must have turned awfully pale, because Sean said he was worried I might faint.'

That explained to Hope why Summer had looked so grim and grave during her conversation with Sean. But Sean had looked grim and grave also, far too much to be due solely to concern over her sister's pallor. Hope was about to ask her about it, but Summer didn't give her the chance.

'This proves that Melody was telling us the truth at her booth. Gary did see me yesterday and this morning, even though I didn't see him. It wasn't a coincidence. Gary has been following me!'

Hope was momentarily silent, remembering how she had seen Gary in a similar manner that afternoon, partially concealed beneath the floppy purple awning at the back of Amethyst's booth. At the time, she had wondered whether it might be an optical illusion. Now she wondered whether it was confirmation that Gary was indeed following Summer. Could there be an innocent explanation?

'I don't understand why he's doing it,' Summer continued. 'It must be what you said before. The divorce proceedings have been dragging on for too long, and that's starting to affect him. It's Gary's own fault, because he was the one who selected Davis and has caused all the delay with the sale of the house. So I can't feel much sympathy for him, especially now that he's decided to creep about and spy on me.'

'Are you sure?' Hope asked her.

Summer scrunched up her nose indignantly. 'Yes, I'm sure! Do you think my eyes are playing tricks like Rosemarie's? I'm imagining that Gary is lurking around corners and skulking in the dark?'

'That isn't what I meant—'

'And I'm not mistaking him for someone else,' Summer

added irritably. 'I lived with the man for enough years to know what he looks like. Just because Gary is concealing himself behind doors doesn't make it so I can't recognize him.'

'That isn't what I meant,' Hope said again. 'Of course I don't think you're imagining it, and of course you can recognize Gary. I was just wondering if maybe he wasn't actually spying on you.'

Her nose remained scrunched. 'Do you have another way to explain his prowling and peering?'

Hope replied with some hesitancy, not wanting to upset her sister further. 'Well, I don't know about the other occasions, but as to earlier this evening, when you saw Gary at the main entrance to the tent, it's possible he wasn't following you at all. He might have come here because he had heard about the party.'

Summer frowned at her.

'Maybe when he arrived, Gary saw you sitting on the folding chairs. He stayed by the flap doors, debating whether to go in, and then decided against it. Did you happen to catch a glimpse of Aaron or Melody? They might have been with him.'

The frown deepened, and Hope figured that it was best to shift the subject.

'Speaking of Melody,' she said, 'we had intended to go back to check that she was all right and hadn't collapsed in a charred heap. But I suppose it's too late for us to do that now. The booths closed a long time ago.'

'I have no doubt that Melody is fine,' Summer responded dryly. 'And even if she ended up a little woozy from too much sun and heat, Aaron can revive her with a cup of mead and some soothing aloe vera lotion. It's the least he can do considering that the teeny-weeny bikini was his idea.'

Hope smiled.

'My sympathy is no greater for Melody than it is for Gary,' Summer went on. 'She knows perfectly well that her husband is a cheat just like mine. That might be acceptable to her, but it's not acceptable to me. I find it infuriating that she keeps talking about my imminent reunion with Gary and the two of us miraculously patching things up. She's probably been saying the same things to him.'

'She probably has,' Hope agreed.

'I wouldn't be surprised if she's even gone so far as to encourage Gary to follow me, telling him that it would promote intimacy, or reconciliation, or some other bunch of nonsense. The more I think about it, the madder I get—' Summer cut herself off abruptly. 'And there he is again!'

Although Hope quickly followed her sister's gaze toward the side flap, she found it as empty as before. The few flickering spots of light in the distance were still visible through the opening, but there was no sign of Gary – or anybody else, for that matter.

'I'm tired of it, and I'm going to bring it to an end,' Summer resolved. 'Once and for all. There's no sense in prolonging the agony, either for him or me.'

'But what if—' Hope began.

Summer paid no attention, brushing aside any question or doubt. She sprang up from her seat on the stage, gave her sister a distracted nod in parting, and marched with determined steps out of the tent.

Unsure how to react, Hope watched her leave. Summer didn't appear to encounter anyone immediately upon her exit. After a few feet, she turned left and disappeared into the night. Hope debated for a moment whether she should go after her. But then she decided that it was a situation Summer was better off handling alone. Hope wasn't convinced that Gary was even out there.

She remained on the stage for another minute or two. The party held no interest for her, and now that so many people had come inside, the tent was beginning to feel rather stuffy and warm. With less urgency than her sister, Hope stood up and headed toward the side flap. While not truly cool, the air outside was fresher and less humid than it had been during the day. There was a hint of a breeze, which – when combined with the lack of blazing sun – made for a much more pleasant evening than Asheville had experienced in quite a while.

Heading to the spot where Summer had turned left, Hope found a slim alley that ran alongside the tent up toward a row of booths. The passage was filled with various pieces of equipment that presumably had some purpose in relation to the festival but were mostly unidentifiable in the dim light. Neither Summer nor anyone else was there. Hope started to weave her way through the gear in the direction of the booths. When she came to a large wooden packing crate, she halted and leaned against it, taking advantage of the momentary peace and quiet. Voices and laughter could be heard from inside the tent, but they were no more than a background hum. She looked up at the sky. Only one edge of the crescent moon and a smattering of stars were observable tonight. The remainder had been blotted out by the leading edge of a long line of encroaching clouds. She wondered if the weather might at long last be changing. Could the storm that Summer had been wishing for, with its thunder and lightning and torrential downpour, finally be in the offing?

Realizing that she was still holding a half-empty bottle of beer dating back to when she had been sitting in the tent with Megan, Hope took a sip from it. She grimaced at the taste. The liquid was warm and flat.

'So this is where you've decided to hide,' said a voice suddenly.

Hope jumped in surprise and nearly dropped the bottle.

'Didn't your grandmother ever teach you that it's a bad idea to drink alone in back alleyways in the dark of night?'

'Good lord, Dylan.' Hope took a deep breath to steady herself. 'Don't sneak up on someone like that. You nearly made my heart stop.'

'It serves you right. You shouldn't be out here by yourself.'

'I was enjoying the serenity of solitude,' she replied dryly.

'May I enjoy it with you?'

Not waiting for her answer, Dylan walked over to the packing crate and leaned against it next to her. This time, instead of almost stopping, Hope's heart responded with a slight flutter.

After a moment, Dylan said, 'Your grandmother should have also taught you that it isn't polite to issue an invitation and then rescind it without informing the person.'

'I have no idea what you're talking about.'

'The Green Goat. You and Summer invited Nate and me to join you at the Green Goat this evening.'

'Oh, yes. I had forgotten about that. The plan sort of fell by the wayside. You can blame it on Megan.'

'Megan doesn't like the Green Goat?' Dylan asked.

'She likes it too much. Or more accurately, she likes its owner – whom she met this afternoon – too much.' Hope smiled, remembering Megan's comments regarding Daniel Drexler. 'According to her, the man is eye candy, and instead of going to the Green Goat tonight, she wanted to stay here and further her acquaintance with him.' She didn't add that Megan was also using Daniel to avoid being questioned by Nate.

'So it's the eye candy's fault that I've lost out on my complimentary cocktail?'

Hope's smile grew. 'The complimentary cocktail was for Nate, not you,' she corrected him.

'That isn't how I recall it.'

'Then your memory is faulty. But if you feel that strongly about it, you can have this.' She offered him the half-empty bottle of warm beer in her hand.

He made no move to take it. 'Your generosity is over-whelming, but I prefer my beverages chilled.'

'I can't argue with you on that.' Hope set down the rejected bottle behind her on the packing crate. 'Dinner and an icy cocktail in an air-conditioned restaurant would have been nice.'

'It's still an option,' Dylan proposed. 'A late dinner is much better than no dinner.'

'Again, I can't argue with you. But I'm afraid that Summer's evening is fully booked. She went to confront her shifty husband. Gary has taken up following her around the festival grounds. At least, it's possible that he has,' Hope amended. 'I'm not really certain.'

'Nate will be disappointed about the Green Goat. He was looking forward to it.'

'Was he? I'll tell Summer. It will offer her some much-needed encouragement.'

'I was looking forward to it, too,' Dylan added.

His voice held enough meaning that Hope's heart responded with another slight flutter.

'There are always other evenings,' she said, offering her

own encouragement. 'Where is Nate, by the way? I hope he wasn't required to go back to work at this hour.'

'No. He's inside the tent with Larkin and Janice.'

This time there was no fluttering or encouragement. Hope's reply was crisp. 'Then you and Nate can still go to the Green Goat tonight. I'm sure that Larkin and her friend would love to accompany you.'

'They've hinted at it. Repeatedly.'

Although she continued to lean against the crate, Hope shifted away from Dylan. 'If that's the case, I'm surprised you came out here. From what I saw earlier, the four of you looked pretty cozy together.'

'And from what I saw earlier,' he rejoined, 'your sister looked pretty cozy with that guy she was sitting next to.'

Hope was tempted to ask if Nate had seen the pair also and whether their seeming intimacy had appeared to spark any jealousy in him, but then it occurred to her that if Dylan didn't recognize who Summer had been sitting next to, then in all likelihood neither did Nate. That meant she had guessed correctly in the tent. Although Nate wanted to question Sean, he couldn't identify him by sight.

'How well does Summer know that guy?' Dylan went on. 'Because the way that he sprinted out of the tent seemed a little off.'

She hesitated, debating whether she should still talk to Dylan about Sean as she and Megan had planned. Hope almost laughed, remembering how Megan had suggested that she manipulate Dylan to get him alone. It turned out that no manipulation was necessary, just the night air.

'The man at issue,' Hope answered after a moment, 'is actually a closer friend to Megan than to Summer. And I'm glad that you brought him up, because Megan and I wanted to ask your opinion regarding him.'

'I'm flattered,' Dylan said.

'But we need you to be discreet. We're not eager to accuse Sean of something that he may not have done.'

'So the guy who was sitting next to Summer and then bolted was Sean? The same Sean who Rosemarie believes was an accessory to Davis's murder?'

'The same Sean,' Hope confirmed.

'And you and Megan are beginning to think that Rosemarie might be right?'

'Honestly, we're not sure what to think. That's why we wanted your opinion . . .'

Hope proceeded to share with him all that she and Megan had learned about Sean's connection to Davis, his movements during the previous evening, and the injury to his elbow. Dylan listened without interruption. When she had finished, he was silent for a long minute, digesting the information.

'Based on what you've told me,' Dylan said at length, 'there are some reasonably strong indicators pointing to Sean's involvement in the death. For starters, he had a compelling motive due to what happened with his sister and nephew.'

Hope nodded.

'Also, he had the opportunity. Sean was on the festival grounds last night after the booths had closed and Davis had gone missing.'

She nodded again.

'And finally, he had the means. Considering his occupation and what I saw of his build when we were inside the tent, it's clear that Sean wouldn't have had any difficulty overpowering Davis on the carousel. In fact, that could be turned around as an argument in his defense. With Sean's physical strength, he wouldn't have needed – or bothered – to use the scarf. His bare hands would probably have been more than sufficient to strangle the man.'

'Megan said the same thing.' Hope was thoughtful. 'Setting Sean aside for a moment, wouldn't the murderer have to have been stronger than Davis in any event? It didn't occur to me before, but that rules out smaller and weaker suspects, doesn't it?'

Dylan shook his head. 'Not necessarily. The killer couldn't have been someone who was deemed medically frail, but any moderately able-bodied person would have been up to the task given the right conditions. If they took Davis by surprise, if they got the scarf around his neck at the proper angle, if they stunned him with a blow before he was able to fully defend himself. Those are all factors that could allow for a smaller or weaker person – especially someone with sufficient grit and determination – to successfully overpower an opponent who was taller or stronger. There was a contusion on Davis's head. Based on its location and presentation, it's difficult to determine when exactly it occurred: whether it was the first step in the attack on him or a result of his fall on to the platform, or an incidental injury while he struggled to free himself. The medical examiner might be able to tell us more, but it's unlikely to be determinative. At this point, I wouldn't rule out any suspects based solely on their physical size.'

Hope made a mental note that she needed to commend Megan on her prescience. Megan had said that Dylan probably had a good deal of extra insight regarding the case that they weren't aware of, and she had been proven correct.

In pursuit of even more information, Hope said, 'Speaking of incidental injuries, it's interesting how many people with a connection to Davis presently have a wound. Have the police made any progress with the blood you found on the carousel platform?'

Dylan's lips twitched with a hint of amusement. 'I will compliment you on how smoothly you inserted that question into the conversation, but I have no intention of answering it.'

'Why not?' she demanded.

'Because Nate asked me not to discuss that piece of evidence with you. He doesn't want you or your sister involved – and frankly, I agree with him.'

'But we are already involved,' Hope argued. 'I discovered the body, and Davis was Summer's realtor. Plus, as far as I'm aware, all the current suspects are friends and acquaintances of ours. Not to mention, according to Rosemarie, we're suspects, too.'

'Precisely. That's another reason you and Summer shouldn't have any further involvement.'

Hope wavered, wondering if a little sweetness and cajolery might manage to loosen his tongue. Then she saw that Dylan's jaw was firmly set, and she knew that no amount of coaxing would budge him an inch.

'Fine. If that's the way you want it,' she said crossly. 'But you and Nate had better not come around later and expect us to tell you which of the suspects have wounds and how they claim to have gotten those injuries.'

'You have just validated our concerns,' Dylan responded, 'by admitting that you've been questioning suspects in a murder case about the cause of their injuries. Has it ever occurred to you how dangerous that might be?'

'Summer and I aren't in any danger,' Hope scoffed.

'Famous last words.'

She shook her head. 'It's all but certain that Davis Scott was killed because of one – or more – of the many egregious acts he committed as part of his profession. Aside from Summer's house, we had no connection to the man or his profession, so there's no reason to think that anybody would blame us for his bad deeds.'

'That may be true, but irrespective of any original blame, the murderer may decide to blame you now for nosing around and asking questions and potentially getting them caught by the authorities.'

'We aren't nosing around. And we've barely asked any questions—'

'I look forward to explaining that to your grandmother,' Dylan cut her off. 'Although I knew what you were doing and did nothing to stop you, the fact that you and your sister only asked a couple of questions from a few suspects will no doubt absolve me from all responsibility in Olivia's eyes when something goes wrong.'

His tone was so wry that Hope couldn't help smiling. 'Nothing will go wrong. And even if it did, Gram is well aware that Summer and I make our own decisions. She wouldn't hold you responsible.'

'Famous last words,' he said again.

The smile continued. 'I appreciate your concern over our well-being and your many helpful suggestions, which I'll be sure to pass along to Summer.'

'But you're not going to do a single thing differently, are you?'

'Well, no.'

Dylan threw up his hands. 'You are the most exasperating woman I have ever met!'

Hope choked back a laugh.

'You don't listen to a word anyone says. It's the same with your sister; Nate has complained about it, too. Summer pretends to agree with him but promptly proceeds to do whatever is the exact opposite. And then there are your disappearing acts—'

'Disappearing acts?'

'When you simply vanish. One minute you're there, and the next minute you're gone. As in your booth, earlier this afternoon. Or in the tent this evening. I glance away for half a second, and when I look back again, you've evaporated into the ether.'

Still struggling to suppress her laugh, Hope said, 'You shouldn't take it personally. I don't leave because of you.'

'No?'

'No, it was—'

Hope caught herself just in time. With regard to their booth that afternoon, she and Summer had departed partly because of Larkin's simpering behavior and partly to warn Megan and Sean about Rosemarie's accusations and Nate's questions. Except neither reason was one that she wanted to share with Dylan. The exit from the tent that evening, however, could be more easily accounted for.

'I told you already that Summer went to confront Gary. As for me,' Hope explained, 'I was tired of the noise and so many people inside the tent. It's much nicer out here, wouldn't you agree?'

'I would.'

Dylan shifted somewhat closer to her on the packing crate. Hope didn't move away.

'Can I try again?' he asked, after a brief pause.

She looked at him, not understanding. 'Try what again?'

'You said before that I nearly made your heart stop. I'd like to try again.'

Before she could offer any reply, Dylan's hand went under her chin, tilting it toward him, and his lips met hers.

It began as a light kiss, questioning and searching, and when Hope responded, it deepened, Dylan's mouth taking full possession of hers. Hope's mind whirled with a flurry of sensations. The sultry warmth of the August air, her pulse racing through her limbs, the increasing darkness as the clouds obscured more of the stars. And in the next moment, it all faded away. She no longer felt her heart pounding inside her chest or the trace of a breeze cooling her cheek. There was only Dylan. His fingers on her skin, his lips moving over her throat, his body pressed against hers.

'Dylan?'

It was a murmur in the distance, and neither Hope nor Dylan paid any attention to it.

'Dylan?'

The murmur became a voice.

'Dylan, are you out here?'

The voice was now too loud and close to ignore. Recognizing it as Larkin's, Hope tensed, and she immediately pulled back from Dylan.

'Hope . . .' Dylan began unevenly.

She looked at him. As though reflecting a last remaining star in the sky, his eyes glittered silver at her.

'Hello?' Larkin called, having evidently spotted their movement. 'I'm trying to find someone. Have you seen . . . Oh, Dylan, it's you!'

Dylan didn't answer her. His gaze remained on Hope.

'I've been searching for you *everywhere*!' Larkin exclaimed. 'What on earth are you doing in this alley?'

Larkin started to walk toward them. It didn't appear as though she had noticed Hope, who was on the far side of Dylan and further concealed in the shadows.

'We're having such a good time.' Larkin gave a happy laugh. 'Why don't you come back inside? Nate suggested that we . . .'

Hope didn't hear the remainder of the sentence. As Dylan turned to speak with Larkin, she slipped silently into the night.

NINETEEN

It began with a slow, steady hammering. *Thump, thump, thump.* The tempo was even, almost rhythmic. *Thump, thump, thump.* At first, Hope thought that it might be part of a dream, but as the haze of sleep gradually faded away, she realized that the noise was coming from outside her bedroom rather than inside her head. The construction company had evidently already commenced working on the brownstone next door. Wasn't there some city ordinance that prohibited them from starting at such an ungodly hour?

Thump, thump, thump. Hope opened a groggy eye. Pale pink light filtered through one pane of the window, telling her that dawn had broken but only a short while ago. She frowned. The contractor and his crew were never there this early. Not to mention that it was Sunday. And then it occurred to her that she also didn't normally hear them above the ground floor. The whir of a drill or clunk of a shovel reverberated occasionally through the boutique, but it had never traveled beyond that, which made sense considering that the work was taking place in the neighbors' cellar to remedy water seepage along the foundation.

The hammering continued. *Thump, thump, thump.* If it wasn't going away, then there was no possibility of Hope going back to sleep. With a sigh, she pushed off the blanket and rose from the bed. Seeing her clothes from the prior evening in a jumble on the floor, she sighed again, this time with frustration. She wasn't sure if she was more frustrated with Larkin, Dylan, or herself. In any case, the night hadn't ended well. Even though she hadn't intended it, she had once more pulled a disappearing act. Perhaps Dylan hadn't minded her abrupt departure. Perhaps he had been only too glad to return to the party in the tent with Larkin. Except it had been an awfully good kiss . . .

Leaving the clothes where they lay, Hope pulled on her silk

summer robe and opened the bedroom door. When she was halfway down the hall, the hammering stopped, and she exhaled with relief. Her nerves weren't prepared for that much pounding, especially before coffee.

'Morning.' Summer greeted her at the bottom of the staircase holding a pair of steaming mugs. 'I assume that it woke you, too?'

Hope gratefully accepted one of the mugs. 'Unfortunately, yes.'

Summer turned and padded in her own bathrobe and bare feet in the direction of the kitchen. Hope followed her.

'I was right, wasn't I?' Summer said.

'You usually are,' her sister agreed amiably, feeling better with the first sip of caffeine, 'but I'm not sure about what on this particular occasion.'

'I predicted from the outset that yesterday was going to be an unholy mess. And it was! The whole thing was terrible from beginning to end.'

'Well, maybe not every single minute of the day' – Hope thought once more of the kiss that she had shared with Dylan – 'but for the most part, you are correct.'

'And this day hasn't started off any better—'

The words were barely out of Summer's mouth when the hammering began again. *Thump, thump, thump.*

'Aargh!' she exclaimed. 'If this keeps up, we're going to have to talk to Miranda and Paul. I understand that they need to fix the leakage in their cellar, but construction work on Sunday morning just after dawn can't become a regular occurrence.'

Hope nodded. 'Let's try to ignore it and keep our fingers crossed that it stops again soon, permanently.'

Summer grumbled in reply.

Leaning against the side of the kitchen island, Hope took another sip from her mug. 'So, moving on to an equally irksome topic, how did it go with Gary last night?'

The grumble repeated itself.

'That bad?' Hope asked.

'It wasn't bad or good. I never caught up with him.'

'Oh.'

'I know you think that Gary wasn't actually outside the tent last night,' Summer said, a touch heatedly, 'but he was! I'm certain that he's been following me!'

Hope was saved from having to respond by the hammering, which chose that moment to increase both in speed and volume. *Thump, thump. Thump, thump. Thump, thump.*

Summer let out an agitated squawk. 'I can't endure that for the entire day!'

'You won't have to. We'll be at the booth,' Hope reminded her. 'And by the time the festival closes this evening . . .' She paused, reflecting.

'Nate won't try to keep our booth closed today, will he? He'll get an earful from me if he does! Morris and the committee need the ticket sales, and we need every opportunity to promote the boutique . . .' It was Summer's turn to pause, watching her sister's brow furrow. 'What's wrong?'

'Listen,' Hope said.

'Listen? I can't hear anything but that horrendous hammering.'

'Yes, but follow the direction of the sound. I didn't realize it until a second ago. The hammering isn't coming from the brownstone next door. That's the wrong way. I think it's coming from the boutique.'

Summer now listened also. 'You're right. It does sound as though it's coming from the boutique.' Her hazel eyes suddenly widened. 'Good lord, better from the boutique than from the attic.'

'Small blessings,' Hope agreed.

Together, they listened for another minute, both trying to determine what the noise might be.

'I can't figure it out,' Hope said at last. 'But whatever it is, we need to put a stop to it – and fast. Otherwise, Miranda and Paul will soon be complaining to us instead of the other way around.'

They promptly headed from the kitchen through the hall to the back entrance of the boutique.

'If it were winter,' Hope mused, 'the noise could be air clanking through the pipes from the boiler.'

'The pipes never clank that long or uniformly,' Summer countered.

'And if it were later in the day . . .'

The sentence was left unfinished as the hammering stopped once more. After a moment, Hope and Summer stepped into the boutique. The interior was dusky and still. Slowly, their eyes circled, searching for the source of the noise. They found nothing. The shop looked just the same as it had on the previous morning before they had gone to the festival.

'I don't understand.' Hope shook her head. 'Shouldn't we be able to see something amiss?'

Summer drew a shaky breath. 'Maybe it is the attic, after all.'

'Except we haven't given it any reason – or at least not any new reason – to be troublesome or upset. And the attic is usually the least active between dawn and noon. Creating that sort of a disturbance takes a lot of energy.'

'That's true. But if it's not the attic, then—'

Thump, thump, thump.

In unison, their heads snapped toward the front of the shop. There was someone standing outside, directly behind the shade covering the door, so they couldn't immediately identify them. But they could identify the cause of the hammering. The person was holding a long, thick umbrella and was banging the heavy wooden handle against the frame of the window that faced the street.

Thump, thump, thump.

'For criminy sake,' Summer muttered. 'How can an umbrella make that much noise?'

'It's hitting the metal trim, so it's echoing.'

'But why on earth are they doing it at all! The boutique is appointment-only on Sundays. And even if it weren't, this is not anywhere close to normal business hours.'

Hope flipped on the main light switch, and the shop brightened. The hammering instantly ceased.

'Hello!' came a yodel.

This time, their heads snapped toward each other.

'Is that Rosemarie?' Hope said in astonishment.

Summer responded with an affirmative snort. 'This is exactly what I told Nate would happen. Now that Rosemarie's had a chance to calm down and properly think things through, she's realized how ridiculous her accusations against us were. She didn't really mean any of it, and she wants to apologize and make amends. Granted, I had assumed that it would take longer than a day for her to come to the boutique, but I guess either her feet are fast healers or she is *really* eager for a reading from you.' There was another snort. 'Maybe she has questions about whether there's a new beau in her future.'

Hope wasn't as amused as her sister. 'On the other hand, maybe Rosemarie isn't interested in a reading or forgiveness. Maybe she hasn't changed her mind in the slightest and still believes that you're a murderess. Maybe Rosemarie has come for revenge.'

Summer stared at her.

The yodel repeated itself. 'Hello!' It was followed by one sharp thump against the window frame.

Not wanting Rosemarie to start hammering again, Hope hastily headed toward the front door.

'Wait!' Summer called. 'What if she really is seeking revenge and has a weapon with her?'

'I'm confident that we can defend ourselves against an umbrella.'

A third yodel was just beginning to take shape when Hope turned the lock and unlatched the door. Rosemarie didn't rush inside with her typical gusto. Instead, she stood hesitantly on the threshold of the boutique, as though she wasn't quite sure whether to enter at all. Also different was the pattern of her billowy dress. The usual garish flowers had been replaced by sedate fern fronds.

Hope offered her a welcoming smile. 'Good morning, Rosemarie. You – and your umbrella – are out and about early today.'

'I've come prepared,' she answered earnestly, waving the umbrella in the air. 'It's going to rain.'

'Do you think so?' Hope looked through the doorway and up at the sky. Not one cloud from the prior evening remained. The cerulean blue was unblemished.

'It may be sunny now, but just wait until this afternoon.' Rosemarie waved the umbrella again as though to emphasize the point. 'The weather was already beginning to change yesterday evening. Percy could feel it in his little bones and was whining half the night.'

Hope's gaze went to Rosemarie's feet. The strappy sandals had been supplanted by white tennis sneakers. Percy was nowhere to be seen.

'Where is Percy?' she asked in surprise.

Rosemarie seemed surprised in turn. 'He's at home asleep, of course. I would never wake him at this hour. Percy needs his beauty rest.'

There was a grumpy harrumph from Summer. Hope was inclined to agree with her sister. It was rather annoying to be dragged out of bed by the hammering of an umbrella when pug Percy was allowed to remain peaceably snoozing.

'I also didn't want to take the chance that he might encounter a sudden shower,' Rosemarie continued. 'Percy catches cold easily.'

Although it was difficult to imagine any rain shower being cold in the current temperatures, Hope nodded politely.

Rosemarie nodded back at her. 'As for me, I'm from sturdy stock. With my umbrella, I can handle any sort of weather. And it came in extra handy this morning for knocking on your window.'

'You're fortunate that the neighbors didn't call the police to complain about the noise,' Summer remarked peevishly.

'Oh, gosh, they wouldn't have done that, would they? I did try knocking regularly on the door at first, but then I realized that you would never hear me if you were upstairs or in the garden. So I switched to tapping on the frame.'

Tapping on the frame was a considerable understatement, but Hope knew that there was nothing to be gained from belaboring the point, so she replied mildly, 'Well, we've heard you now. Why don't you come inside and have a cup of coffee with us?'

'That would be nice. You're both so nice. And I'm not nice at all . . .' Rosemarie let out an anguished wail and abruptly burst into tears.

Hope turned and exchanged a glance with her sister. That settled the matter: the purpose of Rosemarie's visit was forgiveness and not revenge.

A second wail almost immediately followed the first. It was at such a pitch and volume that Hope honestly began to worry about the neighbors calling the police. She took a quick step forward and wrapped her arm around Rosemarie's shoulders.

'There's no need to be upset,' she said as soothingly as she could. 'Everything is fine.'

'Everything is *not* fine,' Rosemarie protested. 'I told the police detective horrible things yesterday. Horrible, horrible things!'

Hope was nearly deafened by a third wail, and she hurriedly guided Rosemarie through the doorway into the boutique. With any luck, Miranda and Paul had good insulation and were sound sleepers.

'I'm so embarrassed!' Rosemarie cried. 'And Percy was so embarrassed for me that he barely touched his dinner!'

The sisters exchanged another glance, and this time, they restrained a smile. It was highly unlikely that the pug's hearty appetite had been impeded by any concern over Rosemarie's chagrin.

'The words from yesterday have been forgotten today,' Hope told her.

'Entirely forgotten,' Summer agreed. She handed Rosemarie a tissue.

Rosemarie blew her nose vigorously and dabbed at her eyes.

'Everything is fine,' Hope reiterated.

'It's behind us, and we're all good friends,' Summer added graciously. 'Now why don't we sit down and have that cup of coffee?'

'That's wonderfully kind of you. And ordinarily, I would very much enjoy a cup, but . . .' Rosemarie hesitated.

'But?' Hope asked her.

'But the reason I came here so early this morning . . . I need to talk to you about . . .' Again she hesitated.

Hope restrained another smile. So that was what had prompted Rosemarie's speedy contrition. Summer's guess had been spot on: Rosemarie wanted a reading.

'What kind of a reading would you prefer?' Hope started to walk toward her palm-reading table. 'We could draw a Tarot card or—'

'Oh, no,' Rosemarie interjected. 'I've already had a reading.'

Hope halted in surprise. 'You have?'

'Well, yes,' she admitted.

For a moment, Hope was at a loss how to respond.

'You've gone to someone else?' Summer's tone held a mixture of incredulity and indignation, as though Rosemarie had been shockingly unfaithful.

Rosemarie flushed. 'I know that I shouldn't have, but I had such a bad feeling yesterday evening. It was just like the feeling I had the day before, when Davis . . .' She swallowed hard, and tears once more welled up in her eyes.

'We understand,' Hope said gently. 'You should talk to whoever helps you to feel better. That's the most important thing.'

'But it didn't help me to feel better!' Rosemarie exclaimed. 'It frightened me terribly! She said . . . she said . . .' The words came out in such a frenzy that she couldn't continue.

Exasperation overtaking sympathy, Summer frowned at her.

Hope tried to be patient. 'Who said?'

Rosemarie drew a great gasping breath. 'Madam Gina. She said that there had been another death!'

TWENTY

'Madam Gina?' Summer mouthed silently to Hope. Hope could only shake her head. She had never heard of Madam Gina, either.

'Don't you understand?' Rosemarie was aghast at their lack of reaction. 'This is an emergency! That's why I've come before breakfast. That's the reason we don't have time to sit down for coffee. There's a poor soul who has departed!'

'Yes, well . . .' Hope searched for a soft, roundabout response.

Summer took the direct route. 'I don't wish to sound callous, Rosemarie, but there are always deaths. Every day. From old age and illness and accidents—'

'That isn't at all what I'm talking about,' Rosemarie interjected. 'That isn't what Madam Gina meant.'

'And who, pray tell, is Madam Gina?' Summer said.

Hope couldn't fail to catch the sarcasm in her sister's tone. She knew what Summer was thinking: *Madam Gina* had the same unfortunate brothel connotation as *Madam Bailey*. Thankfully, Rosemarie didn't seem to notice.

'You don't know Madam Gina?' Rosemarie replied in surprise.

'Nope. Not even a little bit.'

'That's odd. Because Madam Gina certainly knows you.'

It was Hope's turn to express surprise. 'She does? Are you sure?'

'Oh, yes.' Rosemarie nodded. 'She told me that everyone with the gift knows each other.'

Hope and Summer exchanged an amused look.

'And what sort of gift does Madam Gina purport to have?' Summer inquired.

'She can summon spirits.'

Hope and Summer looked at each other again, this time with uneasiness.

'What kind of spirits?' Hope asked Rosemarie.

'Any kind you want. She gave me the impression that people are mostly interested in their deceased friends and relatives.' Rosemarie's expression grew melancholy. 'I would love to see my dear Bruno again.'

'Bruno?' Summer echoed. 'I knew that you had been divorced twice, Rosemarie, but I didn't realize that you were also widowed.'

'Goodness, no.' Rosemarie smiled wistfully. 'Bruno was my cocker spaniel. He was with me for fourteen years before Percy came into my life. I have some photos . . .' She started to reach into her handbag but then stopped herself. 'I'll show them to you later. We can't allow ourselves to be distracted. Madam Gina told me that there had been another death, and we must take immediate action.'

Hope chose her words carefully. Madam Gina was in all likelihood a classic charlatan. But if she wasn't, then she had the potential to be extremely dangerous. 'Did Madam Gina give you any indication of where this death had taken place, or what the person—'

'Here!' Rosemarie exclaimed. 'The death was here at the boutique!'

'Here at the boutique?' Hope frowned at her. 'That isn't possible.'

'Have you checked?' Rosemarie asked.

'I think that between the three of us,' Summer responded dryly, 'we would have noticed a corpse lying on the floor.'

Rosemarie considered a moment. 'Madam Gina wasn't specific about the room. So the death could have occurred in an extension of the boutique. The kitchen or the hallway, for example.'

'Even if we include the entire brownstone,' Hope said, 'only Summer and I are here. And we're both still alive.'

Summer gave a little chuckle in confirmation.

'What about Olivia?' Rosemarie pursued. 'Heaven knows that I don't wish her any ill, but it's important that everyone is accounted for.'

'Gram spent the night at Morris's house. So any prognostication in relation to the boutique or the brownstone wouldn't apply to her.' As she spoke, Hope glanced at the clock on the wall. The investigation into the hammering and the revelation of Madam Gina had taken a good deal of time. She and Summer should be getting dressed and preparing for their day at the festival.

'I don't understand it.' Rosemarie seemed genuinely perplexed. 'Madam Gina was absolutely certain that there had been a death. She said that she had a vision.'

'Thankfully, the vision was in error.' Again, Hope was careful in choosing her words. She didn't know whether Rosemarie would run back to Madam Gina with a full report of their conversation. 'Don't forget that we're in an old building in the middle of the city's historic district. Over the years, there have probably been a considerable number of deaths in this area, both natural and unnatural. Maybe Madam Gina's vision was connected to one of those. It's easy to confuse the present with the past. Regardless of how skilled or gifted Madam Gina might be, divination is not an exact science.'

'I guess that makes sense.' Rosemarie didn't appear entirely convinced. 'And it's better not to have a dead body, I suppose.'

There was another little chuckle from Summer. 'Yes, it's always better not to have a dead body.'

'How did you meet Madam Gina?' Hope asked Rosemarie.

'She has a chair at the farmers' market.'

'A chair? Not a stall or a table like everyone else?'

'No, just a chair. She sits on the side of the main aisle and watches as people walk by. If she sees a spirit with someone, trying to communicate, she tells them.'

Summer raised an eyebrow. 'After cash has exchanged hands, I presume?'

'Well, she does request a small fee to compensate for her time.'

The eyebrow remained elevated. 'And without an official stall or table, she doesn't have to share a portion of that fee with the market for its upkeep and maintenance.'

Rosemarie frowned. 'That never occurred to me.'

'But I'm sure that it's occurred to her,' Summer remarked.

Hope returned the focus to the more pressing matter before them. 'You said that you met Madam Gina at the farmers' market, Rosemarie, but you also said earlier that she told you about the death yesterday evening. The market isn't open Saturday evening.'

'I called Madam Gina last night when I had the bad feeling, and she generously invited me to visit her at her house,' Rosemarie clarified. 'She had given me her number one of the times that we chatted at the market.'

'And did any of those chats happen to include a mention of Summer, or me, or the boutique?'

'Of course! I told her that Percy and I love coming to your shop – and how good you are at palmistry and reading the Tarot, and all about Summer's tinctures and teas, and that you've given talks on crystals and semi-precious stones . . .' Rosemarie might have continued, but in her zeal, she ran out of breath.

Hope was thoughtful. That explained how Madam Gina knew about them. She had listened closely to Rosemarie's stories and then recited them back to her, pretending to have known all along. It was a rudimentary deceptive practice. But that didn't explain why the woman had claimed to have a vision of a death at the boutique. Perhaps she was trying to make herself important through her ostensible prophecies. Or maybe she was hoping to convince Rosemarie of the extent of her supposed gifts so that Rosemarie would write her a large check to summon the spirit of dear departed Bruno, possibly multiple times with multiple checks. Hope was about to give Rosemarie a warning to be cautious before engaging too many of Madam Gina's services, but she was interrupted by the singing of the wind chimes above the front door of the shop, signaling a new arrival.

'Hello?' The door, which had been left ajar after Rosemarie's entrance, opened further. 'Is anybody here?'

'Sorrel!' Summer exclaimed in surprise.

Sorrel Packard of Sorrel's Sachets stepped from the sidewalk into the doorway. She was dressed in the same eclectic fashion as when they had met her the day before: a multicolored patchwork skirt, zebra-print smock top, and a jaunty mocha beret set on top of her ginger hair. A bulging canvas tote bag was slung over each shoulder.

She waved at them in greeting. 'I hope it's all right that I popped in without giving you any advance notice of my coming. I was on my way to the festival, and your store was only a short detour.'

'Pop in any time. No notice required,' Summer replied cheerfully. 'But isn't it a while before the festival opens?'

'I want to get there early,' Sorrel explained. 'I left the booth in somewhat of a mess yesterday evening. And I need to check on the little beasts next door to make sure that they haven't finished off Amethyst's chocolate bowls and decided to march over to me looking for their next meal.'

Not understanding the reference, Rosemarie's brow furrowed. 'The little beasts next door?'

'An invasion of ants, at the booth next to mine.' Sorrel was apparently perceptive enough to realize that she had walked into the middle of a conversation that went far beyond ordinary neighborhood gossip, because she added, 'I'm sorry if I've come at a bad moment. I didn't mean to interrupt.'

'You aren't interrupting at all,' Hope told her. On the contrary, she welcomed the diversion. The discussion of Madam Gina had not only run its course, but it was turning increasingly awkward, particularly since it wasn't clear whether Rosemarie continued to believe in the woman's alleged vision of a dead body at the boutique. Sorrel's arrival was the perfect excuse to move off the topic permanently. 'But you have reminded Summer and me that we need to begin getting ready for the festival ourselves.'

Summer caught her sister's hint and took it a step further by gently encouraging Rosemarie's departure. 'If you go to the festival today, Rosemarie, you have to stop by our booth. And you must bring Percy along! We'll be sure to have plenty of his favorite treats on hand.'

Sorrel responded to the prompt before Rosemarie.

'I won't keep you,' she said. 'But I will give you this before I leave.' Reaching into one of her tote bags, she pulled out a small plastic pot. It held fresh black dirt and a short green stalk with two diminutive leaves.

'The pineapple sage!' Summer exclaimed, eagerly taking the pot from Sorrel. 'Oh, it looks wonderfully healthy.'

'I clipped a nice fresh shoot from a sturdy specimen this morning. I don't see why it wouldn't grow for you, but as you've undoubtedly experienced with your own garden, these things are never certain. Mother Nature always makes the final decision, often for reasons known only to herself. If the cutting wilts unexpectedly, just let me know. I'd be happy to give you another one.'

'Thank you, thank you!' Summer was so enthusiastic about her new little plant that she hugged the pot in her arms. 'Speaking of gardens, you must come and see ours. It's through here . . .' She started to turn toward the back of the shop.

'But, Summer . . .' Hope interjected swiftly, trying to stop her sister. If Sorrel stayed for a tour of the garden, then in all likelihood so would Rosemarie. And at some point, the subject of Madam Gina and the hypothetical dead body would inevitably resurface, possibly even in front of Sorrel.

Sorrel must have sensed Hope's hesitation, because she replied, 'I don't want to make you late for the festival.'

'No worries. We have plenty of time. We'll just take a quick look.' Summer once again turned toward the back of the shop.

Hope sighed to herself. Summer was not going to be deterred from showing off her beautiful garden to a fellow lover of plants. She glanced at Rosemarie to see what direction she planned on heading. As expected, Rosemarie showed every indication of participating in the tour. All Hope could do was stick close by her side and try to keep the conversation light and focused on vegetation rather than corpses.

Together, the group walked from the boutique into the brownstone and down the hallway that led to the green space at the rear of the property. Summer and Sorrel debated the efficacy of various slug and snail deterrents, while

Rosemarie told Hope about Percy's new orthopedic bed that helped to relieve the pressure on his joints. When they collectively stepped outside on to the patio, Sorrel paused and inhaled deeply.

'Do you smell that?' She turned toward Rosemarie. 'You were smart to bring along an umbrella today. It's going to rain. Although it may be sunny now, just wait until later this afternoon.'

Rosemarie beamed at the validation. 'I said the very same thing!'

Sorrel inhaled again. 'It's the moisture in the air. You can smell its approach. And then there was the color at dawn.'

'It did have a touch of pink,' Hope agreed, remembering the light through her bedroom window.

'Red sky at morning, sailors take warning.'

'Percy loves the ocean,' Rosemarie contributed.

Hope smiled. When she saw Sorrel look at Rosemarie questioningly, it occurred to her that the two hadn't been properly introduced, and she remedied the oversight. As Sorrel and Rosemarie engaged in a friendly dialogue – which mostly consisted of Rosemarie sharing stories of Percy – Summer and Hope moved slightly to one side.

'Sometime next week,' Summer said, keeping her voice low so that the others couldn't hear her, 'we must visit the farmers' market. We'll pick up some fresh peaches and check on this Madam Gina.'

'My thoughts exactly.'

'I don't like to see Rosemarie taken advantage of. And she's especially vulnerable now, after what happened to Davis.'

Hope nodded. 'If we run into Gram later today at the festival, let's ask her about it, too. She and Morris regularly go to the market. She might have seen the woman on her chair and be able to tell us more.'

Summer nodded back at her. 'Good idea.'

Watching Sorrel and Rosemarie wander off the patio toward the garden, Hope said, 'It would be better if you and Sorrel continued your tour on another day when Rosemarie isn't here. We don't want to have to explain prophecies of dead bodies to Sorrel, and you know that it's only a matter of time before the subject comes up again with Rosemarie—'

An ear-splitting scream shattered the peace of the morning.

'She was right!' Rosemarie cried. 'Madam Gina was right! There has been another death!'

TWENTY-ONE

Hope's initial reaction was one of stunned disbelief. There had been another death? Madam Gina's prophecy was correct? Granted, the patio and garden weren't the boutique. But in relation to a dead body, they were disturbingly close.

'He's over there!' Rosemarie pointed toward the far back corner bordering the alley, and she immediately set off in that direction.

They all raced after her, weaving their way through the labyrinth of greenery, past the raised beds, and around the towering trellises. At the end of the winding path of flagstones lay the wrought-iron gate that separated the rear of the property from the alley.

'My god!' Sorrel exclaimed, reaching the spot first. 'It's the man from the booth. Amethyst's booth. He's the one who wore the cape and the crown the other night.'

'Good lord, that's him!' Rosemarie confirmed, coming up next to her, panting.

Hope and Summer arrived last.

'Sean!' Summer gasped.

It was indeed Sean. He was inside the garden, slumped in a seated position with his back supported by the gate. He looked as though he was sleeping. Sean's eyes were closed. His chin tilted down toward his chest. His arms lay in a relaxed position at his sides, with one hand resting, palm up, in his lap. The only thing that wasn't natural about Sean was his neck. It was pulled backward toward the gate, held firmly against the wrought iron by what at first glance appeared to be a dark-colored piece of cloth.

Summer gasped again. 'Hope, it's a cord!'

Hope didn't have to ask her sister what she meant, because she recognized it, too. There was no mistaking the heavy burgundy fabric. The cloth wrapped around Sean's neck was one of the cords that had fastened up the curtains in their booth. Their cord had been used to strangle him.

'It was me!' Rosemarie cried. 'I'm guilty!'

They turned to her in astonishment.

'Now I understand why I had the bad feeling yesterday evening. Deep down inside, I realized what was happening, and I knew that I was responsible. It's my fault!'

Summer's mouth opened, but no sound emerged. Hope was likewise rendered momentarily speechless. Sorrel looked utterly bewildered.

'It's my fault!' Rosemarie cried again. 'It's because of all those horrible, horrible things I told the police detective. I accused this poor man of being involved in Davis's death, and now see what he's done. I'm to blame!'

'No—' Hope began.

'Yes!' Rosemarie's voice rose to a fevered pitch. 'I'm to blame! I drove him to suicide. He took his own life, and I'm his killer!'

'You are not—'

'But look at what I've caused! Look at—'

In her hysteria, Rosemarie stumbled over the corner of a flagstone. Her arms flailed as she tried to regain her balance, and the end of her umbrella inadvertently struck Sean's knee. His leg twitched, and Sean gave a slight moan.

There was an instant of stunned silence, then they burst into action.

'I'll call for an ambulance!' Sorrel shouted, pulling her phone from one of the tote bags still slung over her shoulder.

Hope dropped down on the ground next to Sean. She touched his arm. His skin was cool but not cold, and the arm was limp rather than stiff. Leaning closer, she heard him breathe. It was shallow and irregular, which was not a good sign, but at least he was alive. That was the most important thing. There hadn't been another death. Madam Gina's prophecy wasn't correct, after all.

'Sean?' Hope said, touching his arm again.

'Sean, can you hear us?' Summer asked anxiously.

He didn't respond. Neither the twitch nor the moan repeated itself. He was clearly unconscious.

Shifting her position to examine his neck, Hope drew her own uneven breath. There had been no confusion in their initial shock and panic. The length of cloth used to strangle Sean was definitely one of the cords that had fastened up the curtains in their booth. She shivered. It turned out that Nate had been prescient in his remarks. Dreadfully prescient. He had said that with the way the cords were stitched and the thickness of the fabric, they would have been a much better murder weapon than the silk scarf. Thank heaven Summer had insisted on showing off the garden to Sorrel. Unlike Davis, they had found Sean in time.

Hope hesitated. Did she try to loosen the cord now, or should she wait until the ambulance arrived? She didn't want to destroy any important evidence. There might be fingerprints, hair, or other fibers present that should be preserved for the police. There could also be something significant in how the cord had been wrapped or knotted. She listened to Sean's breathing. It was ragged and only intermittent. He wasn't getting sufficient oxygen. In all likelihood, he hadn't had sufficient oxygen in quite some time. Hope glanced at Sorrel. She was talking to the emergency services and providing information about their location and situation, but there was no indication as to when someone might reach them.

Once more, Hope leaned forward to examine Sean's neck. His skin was red and swollen, and the cord was visibly tearing into his throat. She couldn't wait for help. It was better to destroy potential evidence than let Sean suffer further injury – or worse. The cord was tied outside the gate, at the back of his neck. Hope stretched her hands through the narrow gaps in the wrought iron. Her fingers touched the knot and felt the overlap of the fabric, but she couldn't get a grip on it.

She turned to Summer, who was partly watching her and partly trying to console Rosemarie.

'Sean isn't getting enough air,' Hope said. 'Sometimes he doesn't seem to be breathing at all. We need to untie the cord as soon as possible, but I can't reach the knot from this side of the gate—'

Summer didn't require any further explanation. 'I'll go! I'll do it!'

The gate was too tall to jump over, and it didn't have the necessary horizontal supports to allow for easy climbing. The only way to quickly reach the other side was from the alley. Summer sprinted back through the garden and into the brownstone.

As she waited for Summer to reappear, Hope looked at Rosemarie. She was huddled on the bench that sat beneath the star magnolia. Streams of tears were running down her cheeks, and her eyes were filled with abject misery.

'You aren't to blame,' Hope told her. 'This isn't your fault.'

'I know that you're trying to make me feel better,' Rosemarie sniffled, 'but what you're saying simply isn't true. It's a blessing from above that he didn't succeed, but he still attempted to take his own life – because of *me!*'

'It is *not* because of you,' Hope replied wearily. Rosemarie's uncontrolled bursts of emotion were beginning to strain her patience. 'For starters, I'm not sure if Sean was even aware that you had accused him of anything. And second, he didn't attempt to take his own life. He was attacked. Somebody strangled him intending to kill him.'

Rosemarie stared at her.

'If you have any further doubt, here's the irrefutable proof.' Hope gestured toward the cord around Sean's neck. 'How could he possibly have tied that himself?'

Rosemarie's astounded gaze moved to the cord.

'I'm coming! I'm coming!' Summer called.

Her feet pounded along the alley. A moment later, she skidded to a halt in front of the gate.

'There might be a little extra pressure on your throat,' Hope explained to Sean. 'Summer is going to undo the cord now.' She didn't know if he could hear her or had any comprehension of her words, but if he did feel something, she wanted him to know that it was from a friend, not a foe.

Summer knelt behind Sean, studied the knot briefly, and then began working at it. 'Hell's bells,' she mumbled, 'this thing is tight.'

Putting her hand on the upturned palm in Sean's lap, Hope gave it a gentle squeeze. His fingers didn't respond.

'I can't get it,' Summer reported with frustration. 'It's only a simple knot, but it's stuck. Really stuck.'

Hope offered as much encouragement as she could. 'Somebody tied it, so I have faith that you can untie it.'

'But they meant to hurt him, and I don't want to hurt him. Every time I pull at the knot, the cord chokes him more.'

Although Hope could see the increased tension at Sean's throat, and she could tell that it was further restricting his breathing, the cord had to come off. Every minute that it remained on might be increasingly deleterious to his health and even survival.

'Just remove it, Summer. Do whatever it takes to remove it.'

Summer nodded and struggled furiously with the knot.

'You're fine.' Hope squeezed Sean's palm again. 'It will all be fine. She'll have it done in a jiffy, and then everything will be good.'

There were a few choice words muttered by Summer regarding the cord, the knot, and whatever foul person had tied it.

Having finally succeeded in composing herself, Rosemarie rose from the bench. 'I could get a pair of scissors,' she suggested, 'or a knife, or—'

'It's loosening,' Summer exclaimed. 'I can feel it loosening!'

As the knot released slightly, Sean's weight also shifted slightly. The movement caused Hope to realize that although the cord was holding him against the gate now, as soon as it was removed, his body would in all likelihood fall forward. She wasn't sure if she had enough strength to hold him on her own.

'I need your help, Rosemarie,' she said quickly. 'When Summer gets him free, Sean will probably tumble toward us. Can you catch him with me? I don't want him to drop to the ground and hit his head on the flagstone.'

Rosemarie joined her without hesitation. Hope glanced over at her. The tears were dried, and Rosemarie's expression was composed and focused on the task at hand.

'Get ready,' Summer warned them. 'I've almost got it . . . I've almost got it . . . And there it is!'

The instant that the knot came undone, Summer pulled the cord away, and as predicted, Sean tumbled forward. Hope hastily grabbed one of his shoulders, while Rosemarie grabbed the other.

'Mercy me, he's a big man, isn't he?' Rosemarie wheezed, laboring with her half of the weight.

'He is indeed,' Hope agreed, also struggling.

Now that she was dealing directly with Sean's substantial size, it made Hope wonder how someone had managed to strangle him in the first place. But then she remembered what Dylan had told her the night before as they were leaning against the packing crate outside the tent. Under the right conditions, a smaller or weaker person could successfully overpower an opponent who was taller or stronger – if they took him by surprise, if they got the cord around his neck at the proper angle, if they stunned him with a blow before he was able to fully defend himself. She looked at Sean's head. There were two large purple welts forming, one on his crown and another at the back. She didn't know if they had been caused as part of the initial attack on him or in the subsequent struggle. In either case, it demonstrated that even Sean's prodigious muscles were no guarantee of protection against someone who intended him harm.

'How is he doing?' Summer asked with concern from the alley. Even though Sean was no longer held to the gate, his body was still blocking it, and Summer couldn't get through to the garden.

'His breathing seems to have improved,' Hope told her, 'but he's not responding at all. There's been no movement in his limbs, and as far as I've seen, his eyelids have remained shut, without so much as a flicker. But I don't honestly know what I should be looking for or what I should be doing to help him.'

'That goes double for me,' Rosemarie added regretfully.

Hope sighed. 'I wish Dylan were here right now. We could really use his medical expertise. And I wish those paramedics would hurry.'

'I'll go out to the front of the brownstone and watch for them. Then when they arrive, I can at least get them to Sean without any further delay.' Summer turned and, with rapid steps, headed up the alley toward the street.

'Speaking of needing more medical expertise,' Sorrel said, having at last finished the phone call with emergency services, 'they asked me a hundred questions that I couldn't begin to answer. About his height and weight, his pulse, and the dilation of his pupils. How long he had been here, to what degree his oxygen might have been restricted, and if there had been any damage to his spinal column . . .'

There was another sigh from Hope. 'Thank you for talking to them. Summer and I really appreciate it. I'm sure that none of this was included in your plans for the morning.'

Sorrel replied with a small shrug. 'There are days that take unexpected turns. But unless you need me for something more, I'd like to leave. The festival is opening soon, and I don't have any help with my booth.'

'Oh, feel free to go. We've got things covered, haven't we, Rosemarie?'

'All good on this end,' Rosemarie responded cheerfully, while at the same time huffing and puffing to support her half of Sean.

'Thanks again,' Hope said to Sorrel.

'Do you want me to call anybody else before I go? You mentioned someone named Dylan?'

Hope considered briefly, then declined. There was no point in contacting Dylan when the ambulance was already on its way. Nate needed to be informed of what had happened to Sean, of course, but it would be much better if they did that themselves. He would also have a hundred questions that Sorrel couldn't begin to answer.

Sorrel departed, politely wishing Sean a full and speedy recovery. Just as she was entering the brownstone, Summer and the paramedics came rushing out of it. The paramedics took immediate control of the situation. They worked briskly and efficiently, and in a few short minutes, Sean was safely removed from the garden and loaded into the ambulance. Although the paramedics tried to discourage her, Rosemarie insisted on accompanying Sean to the hospital, not wanting him to wake up alone and confused. The paramedics warned her that he might not wake up for some time, but Rosemarie wasn't deterred. Climbing into the ambulance, she waved goodbye to Hope and Summer and promised to supply them with regular updates on Sean's condition.

As the ambulance drove off with its lights flashing and siren blaring, the sisters were left standing on the sidewalk in front of the boutique, still wearing their robes, watching the vehicle maneuver through the narrow street.

'Is it too early in the day,' Summer said after a long moment, 'for me to pour us a couple of stiff drinks?'

TWENTY-TWO

Half an hour later, Hope and Summer were once again in their garden, but with neither coffee mugs nor liquor glasses in their hands. They had barely finished dressing before Detective Nate and a team of sundry investigators had arrived at the brownstone. It turned out that Nate had received news of the attack on Sean through the emergency services, and he was more than a little displeased that he had not been informed by the sisters directly.

'Were you ever planning on reporting the incident to me?' Nate asked them in a stiff tone.

Hope and Summer were sitting on one of the rattan settees on the patio while the detective stood in front of them, the toe of his scuffed shoe tapping impatiently against the equally scuffed leg of the resin coffee table.

'Of course we were,' Summer said. 'Everything just happened so quickly. Wouldn't you like to sit down?' she added, gesturing toward the neighboring settee while offering Nate a conciliatory smile.

She had apparently used that smile with him once too often, because he responded with a harrumph rather than a smile of his own.

Summer's tone stiffened in kind. 'There was no delay on our part. Sorrel called for an ambulance immediately.'

'Who is Sorrel? What was she doing here? And how is she connected to Sean and/or Davis Scott?'

At the litany of questions, Summer folded her arms across her chest. 'She is Sorrel Packard of Sorrel's Sachets. While on her way to the festival this morning, she dropped off a cutting from a plant that she had promised me. And as far as we're aware, she has no connection to either Sean or Davis.'

Nate harrumphed again. 'How certain are you of that last fact?'

'Are you suggesting—' Summer began sharply.

In an effort to keep things amicable, Hope interjected, 'In the short time that we've been acquainted with Sorrel, she has never once mentioned Davis or alluded to the events on the carousel. With regard to Sean, when we initially discovered him in the garden, Sorrel didn't even know his name. She only recognized him as having been at Amethyst's booth because it's located next to her booth.'

Hope expected Nate to pull out his notepad and start scribbling in it, but he continued to tap his shoe against the coffee table instead.

'And Rosemarie?' he inquired. 'When did she arrive?'

'Before Sorrel,' Summer answered. 'Rosemarie—'

She was interrupted this time by a shout from a member of the investigatory team at the gate. They beckoned to Nate, and with a gruff instruction to the sisters to stay where they were, he headed down the flagstone path.

As soon as he was out of earshot, Hope said, 'It's probably best if we don't tell Nate about Madam Gina.'

'Agreed. It will only confuse him and the whole situation further. Her prophecy was wrong, anyway. There hasn't been another death – thankfully – and certainly not at the boutique.' Summer frowned. 'I don't understand why she would pretend to have a vision like that. A dead body in a specific location can so easily be proven false. Why didn't she predict something hazier and less precise? That would have been a lot more convincing if her goal is to talk Rosemarie into paying for a doggie séance.'

Hope nodded. 'I've been wondering the same thing. It's pretty clear that Madam Gina got her information about us and the boutique from Rosemarie's exuberant chattiness. No doubt Rosemarie also told her about what happened to Davis on the carousel, which then gave her the idea of a second body turning up elsewhere. Even so, throwing around revelations of a fictitious corpse is a bit excessive.'

Summer considered a moment. 'Unless being excessive is precisely the point.'

'What do you mean?'

'Well, it could be that we're looking at it wrong. Maybe it has nothing to do with Rosemarie and her wallet, or that's only a secondary goal. Maybe the primary goal is *us* – to get our attention.'

'But why?'

'I have no idea. But I think that we definitely need to visit the farmers' market next week as we planned to learn more about the woman. After all, forewarned is forearmed. That applies equally to charlatans and the spiritual world.'

'You're right about that!' Seeing that Nate had started back toward them after concluding his discussion with the team at the gate, Hope added quickly, 'Don't be too hard on him, Summer. Dylan told me that Nate was really disappointed about the Green Goat last night. Apparently, he had been looking forward to it.'

'The Green Goat?' Summer's brow furrowed. 'I have to confess that with everything going on yesterday evening, I forgot all about it.'

'I did, too. I gave Dylan a vague explanation and excuse, and I suggested that we try again another time.' Hope didn't add that Dylan and Nate had possibly gone to the Green Goat with Larkin and Janice instead.

Summer's brow remained furrowed. 'When did you see Dylan last night?'

Hope hesitated, unsure whether to tell her sister about the cozy foursome that had entered the tent while she had been talking to Sean on the folding chairs, but Nate returned before she could say anything more.

'Any helpful clues?' Summer asked him, both her expression and her tone brightening perceptibly.

'We'll address that in a moment,' Nate responded, his own expression contemplative. 'First, I'd like to go back to Rosemarie. You said that she arrived before Sorrel. Why was Rosemarie here?'

'It was exactly what I told you would happen yesterday,' Summer explained. 'After Rosemarie had a chance to calm down and wrap her mind around things, she realized how absurd her accusations against us had been. She came to the boutique to apologize and make amends.'

'But so early in the day?' Nate questioned.

Summer spread her hands and gave a little shrug. 'If

someone comes to our door upset and crying, Hope and I don't send them away simply because we haven't yet finished our morning cup of coffee.'

Hope restrained a smile. Not only did Summer succeed in completely avoiding the topic of Madam Gina, but she also made herself sound remarkably kind and warm-hearted at the same time.

Nate must have thought so, too, because when Summer once more motioned toward the neighboring settee and invited him to sit down, he readily accepted. Summer caught her sister's eye and inclined her head in the direction of the potting stand beside the patio door. They used the potting stand as a makeshift bar. It was crowded with whiskey, bourbon, and a host of assorted liquor bottles. Hope restrained another smile, knowing what her sister was thinking: Nate could have probably used a stiff drink, as well.

'We're going to need your fingerprints for elimination purposes with regard to the gate,' he said after a minute.

They nodded.

'And we're also going to need a list of everyone who may have recently been in contact with the gate, the back of the garden, and the alleyway.'

'But the alleyway isn't restricted,' Summer told him. 'Anybody can access it. All the neighbors and whoever decides to wander down from the adjacent street, regardless of the hour of the day.'

Nate's harrumph returned. 'You should get a lock for your gate.'

'We have a lock,' she replied. 'Unfortunately, it's a wee bit broken at the present moment.'

'Due to Sean entering your property without permission?'

'Oh, no, the lock has been broken for a while.'

The harrumph repeated itself. 'Then I suppose later today I'll be installing a new lock for you.'

Summer didn't express any surprise at the offer, nor did she decline it. Instead, she gave the detective a demure smile and thanked him in a soft voice.

'We would greatly appreciate that, wouldn't we, Hope?' She didn't wait for her sister's answer. 'If you come by after the festival closes, we can open up a bottle of wine, relax out here on the patio, watch the sunset . . .'

There was not the slightest hesitation from Nate. 'I would very much enjoy that.'

Hope choked back a laugh. Forget the Green Goat on some indeterminate day in the future. Summer had managed to wrangle herself a date for that evening. Whatever time Nate had spent with Janice the previous night had clearly not dampened his interest in Summer even a little.

'If it's all right with you,' Nate said, 'I'll invite Dylan to join us. I installed a lock on my aunt's gate a few weeks ago, and it required four hands.'

'Then we'll open up two bottles of wine,' Summer responded smoothly.

'Let's hope the weather holds for us,' he added. 'A few clouds are beginning to roll in, and some of the team were saying that rain is expected later.'

'That does seem to be the popular opinion. Rosemarie brought along an umbrella this morning, too. But if it should decide to rain this evening, we'll simply take the wine inside,' Summer remarked with the same smoothness as before.

Nate nodded, apparently well satisfied with the plan. Summer nodded back at him. The two shared a warm look. Hope sighed, wondering whether Dylan would feel any warmth toward the invitation now that he had spent more time with Larkin.

A voice carried to them from the group at the gate. Although it wasn't directed toward Nate, it returned his focus to the more pressing matter at hand.

He cleared his throat. 'Going back to an earlier point, did Sean have permission to enter your property?'

'We didn't specifically allow him to enter,' Summer replied, 'but we also didn't prohibit him in any way.'

'So, then, what was he doing in the back of your garden?'

For the first time since Nate's arrival at the brownstone, Summer wavered. She glanced at Hope, but Hope couldn't help her. She didn't know what Sean had been doing in the back of the garden, either.

'It's possible,' Summer answered slowly, 'that Sean was looking for me.'

'Looking for you?' Nate echoed. 'In the middle of the night?'

Summer shifted awkwardly on the settee. 'Well, yesterday evening I was talking to Sean in the main tent at the festival.'

Hope listened with increased interest. She had been waiting for a further explanation as to what the pair had discussed so gravely on the folding chairs.

'Sean was telling me a very sad story about his sister and young nephew. And I was telling him about—' Summer stopped and shifted again.

This time, Hope knew why her sister was reluctant to continue. Summer had been telling Sean about Gary possibly following her, and she didn't want to share that piece of information with Nate, understandably enough.

'You were telling Sean about what?' Nate prompted her after a moment.

Summer shook her head. 'It's not relevant. What's more important is that Sean abruptly cut the conversation short and said there was a person in the tent whom he recognized from the night before. I remembered what Megan had told us about seeing Sean switch directions after the booths had closed for the evening and Davis had disappeared, so I asked him about it. Sean confirmed Megan's story and started to explain that he had turned around because he had been curious about where this particular person was going. I never found out who the person was or where they went, because Sean said the person was now leaving the tent. Then he jumped up from his chair and raced out of the side flap. That was the last I saw of him until the gate this morning.'

There was a brief silence.

'It sounds,' Nate mused, 'as though Sean spotted something two nights ago that he wasn't supposed to, but he didn't understand what it meant at the time. Then, when he recognized the person in the tent yesterday, he must have realized that what he had witnessed was connected to Davis's death.'

Summer drew a shaky breath. 'So Sean knows who the murderer is.'

'In all probability, yes. He must have confronted the person after leaving the tent, or, at a minimum, given them a reason to worry that they were going to be exposed. It would explain why Sean was attacked last night and very nearly silenced for good.'

'But why did Sean come here looking for you?' Hope asked her sister.

'My guess,' Summer answered, 'is that he was trying to warn me. Sean was awfully distracted while we were talking, so he easily could have imagined that he told me more than he had. Or he planned on telling me afterward, because I already knew part of the story. What I can't figure out is why he went to the garden and not the front door. Maybe he thought it would be faster or safer somehow.'

'There's a good chance that going to the garden saved his life,' Nate remarked.

Both Hope and Summer looked at him in surprise.

'While in the process of strangling Sean, the assailant must have gotten spooked before being able to finish the job. A dog barked nearby, a light turned on in one of the neighboring brownstones, or a car drove down the adjacent street. Sean was already unconscious, which caused the perpetrator to believe – or at least strongly hope – that he was dead, and they decided to get away before somebody appeared. A less robust person might have succumbed more quickly, but Sean was strong enough to make it through the night until you found him this morning. It also helped,' Nate added, 'that we're in the middle of the summer and not the winter. Being exposed to freezing temperatures for so many hours in his condition would have made survival much less likely.'

'Then we're grateful for a steamy August,' Hope said.

Summer nodded in agreement. 'And we're grateful that Sean will wake up to tell us who did this to him – and who killed Davis.'

'You shouldn't count on that happening immediately,' Nate replied. 'From the preliminary report I received on my way here, Sean is expected to make a full recovery, but he might not regain sufficient consciousness to be interviewed for a day or two. And even then, he could have some memory problems in the short term. In my experience, that's not uncommon with his type of injury. While we're waiting on Sean to provide us with more information, you're going to have to be vigilant.'

Summer frowned. 'Vigilant?'

'*Vigilant*,' Nate repeated with emphasis. 'Someone – presumably Davis's murderer – almost succeeded in murdering Sean last night, using your gate, in your garden, at your home. Which means that the person knows who you are and obviously where you live. So you must remain alert and be vigilant.'

Hope and Summer exchanged an apprehensive glance. Neither one had thought of it quite like that.

'And while we're on the subject of your gate, your garden, and your home,' Nate continued, 'I would like you to identify the attempted murder weapon.'

The sisters exchanged another glance and this time also a sigh.

'It's one of the cords from our booth,' Hope said.

'You're sure?' Nate asked.

'Positive. We recognized it almost as soon as we found Sean.' Summer cocked her head at him questioningly. 'You've been in our booth and looked at the cords. You must have recognized it, too.'

'I did, but I needed confirmation from you. And I also need you to tell me who could have taken the cord from your booth.'

Summer responded with a weary shrug. 'Anybody.'

'Can you be more specific?' Nate pressed her.

'No. We left our booth yesterday afternoon – after you closed it – and we haven't been there since. During that time, anybody could have walked in and taken one of the cords. The cords at the back curtains would have been especially easy to grab, because there aren't any booths facing us to the rear.'

Nate was thoughtful. 'Where did the cords originally come from?'

'Jocelyn Frost. She made them – along with the accompanying curtains – specifically for the festival.'

'Would Jocelyn Frost have had any reason to make an extra cord that wasn't used with the curtains?' Nate inquired.

'I can't imagine why—' Summer stopped abruptly and looked at Hope. 'But Jocelyn did have a bloody finger.'

'That is an excellent point, one which I had completely forgotten about.' Hope turned to Nate. 'Did they discover any blood at the gate? Is that why they called you down there before? And now that we've broached the topic, what results have there been concerning the blood found on the carousel platform?'

There was no immediate reply from Nate.

'Yes, yes,' Hope said impatiently. 'Dylan told me that you didn't want to discuss that piece of evidence with Summer and me because you were trying to keep us from becoming any further involved. But that ship has sailed, the train has left the station, and the horse is out of the barn. After what happened to Sean here last night, we couldn't be any more involved unless somebody tried to strangle us, too.'

Nate raised an unamused eyebrow at her.

'Just a minute ago, you warned us to be vigilant,' Summer reminded him. 'How can Hope and I be adequately vigilant when we're missing crucial details in the case? If you don't give us all the facts, we'll be forced to find them out for ourselves. Who knows what kind of trouble we could land in then?'

The eyebrow remained raised. 'That sounds remarkably close to extortion.'

Summer blinked at him innocently – and appealingly.

Nate sighed. 'Fine. You win. The blood from the carousel platform is being tested, but at this juncture, it's only circumstantial at best. Hundreds of people rode the carousel on the day of the murder, and the blood could have come from any one of them. In the same vein, traces of blood were found at your gate a short while ago—'

Summer's gaze widened with interest.

'But as you stated yourself,' Nate went on, 'access to the alleyway isn't restricted, so, again, the blood could have come from anyone who passed by. More promising is the blood on the cord. Although the majority of it belongs to Sean as a result of the abrasions to his throat, early indications show that a small amount might have come from a secondary source. If that's the case, and we can eventually match the blood to a specific person – plus, ideally, to one of the other sites – then we'll finally have some concrete evidence to work with. All of that will take time, however.'

A shout came from the team at the gate. Nate looked over in their direction, and they once again waved at him to join them.

Rising from the settee, Nate said sternly, 'I'll keep you informed of any future developments, so there's no need for you to do your own investigating. And in the meantime, *vigilance*. Do we understand each other?'

'We understand each other,' Summer responded.

'No investigating,' Hope confirmed.

Nate nodded in a manner that indicated he considered the matter closed, but on his way down the flagstone path toward the gate, he glanced back at the sisters still sitting on the patio. His expression was doubtful, as though he wasn't entirely convinced that he should take them at their word.

TWENTY-THREE

Hope and Summer's agreement with Nate lasted only as long as the sunshine, which began to fade by the time they reached the festival grounds. The early clouds observed from the patio had doubled and then tripled in number until, eventually, the sky was more puffy white than dappled blue. To the west, the clouds were thickening and taking on a gray tint. The chance of rain seemed to be increasing. A considerable number of festival attendees must have been in accord with Rosemarie and Sorrel's weather prognostication, because there were plenty of umbrellas sticking out of bags and tucked under arms.

The first thing the sisters did when they arrived at their booth was to inspect the curtains. Summer's guess turned out to be correct. The cord used to strangle Sean had been taken from the back curtains, specifically the curtain on the left side. The cord had been neatly detached, not torn or haphazardly cut away. Its removal was so clean, in fact, that if Hope and Summer hadn't known to look at the cords, they might not have even noticed that one was missing until they tried to fasten up the curtains to let in the freshening breeze.

'So whoever attacked Sean must have been familiar with both the booth and the arrangement of the curtains,' Summer mused. 'Does that narrow down the list of suspects in any way?'

Hope shook her head. 'Not really. We've had countless people march through here over the last couple of days. Who knows which of them took particular notice of the cords? Ironically, the one person who probably didn't know anything about either the booth or the curtains was Sean.'

Summer sighed. 'I almost can't believe I'm saying this, but I'm glad that Sean has Rosemarie with him at the hospital. If there is anybody who would make absolutely certain that a person was receiving the best possible care and attention, it's

Rosemarie. By now, she's no doubt introduced herself to every doctor, nurse, and miscellaneous staff member in the building.'

'She might have even gotten Percy temporarily certified as a therapy dog so that he can visit Sean with her.'

'I wouldn't put it past her!' Summer concurred with a smile.

Although Hope smiled, too, it quickly waned. 'While we're on the subject of narrowing down the list of suspects, I don't suppose that you can shrink the possibilities of who Sean might have seen last night in the tent?'

'I've been trying, but it's impossible.' Summer sighed again. 'There must have been nearly a hundred people gathered in the tent by then. I'm not even sure what direction Sean was looking toward at the time. And I don't know whether he was referring to someone who had just entered the tent or who had been inside for a while already.'

'So that isn't going to help us at all.'

'Sadly, no.' Summer was thoughtful. 'I keep wondering if Nate has more information about the blood than he's letting on. He seems unduly secretive about it, even with what he told us this morning. Or maybe it's only my imagination.'

Hope's smile resurfaced. 'Well, you can find out for certain this evening while on the patio with one of those bottles of wine. All you have to do is slide closer to Nate on the settee and whisper sweet queries of blood in his ear.'

Summer laughed. 'You don't mind that Dylan is joining us tonight, do you?' she asked after a moment.

'We don't know whether he actually is joining us,' Hope replied, avoiding a direct answer. 'Dylan might have other plans. And right now, *we* have other plans. We're already late opening the booth today. We shouldn't make it much later.'

'That's true. Yesterday was cut short, too. When it comes to the final ticket tally, we are going to be woefully short.'

'I'm afraid so. Which means that we need to get some more tickets now. If the weather turns sour later, everybody will leave the festival.'

While Hope was speaking, the tent darkened dramatically. She glanced outside. The sun had disappeared permanently behind a dense wall of clouds. At the same time, the breeze picked up, swirling the curtains.

'At least our booth is covered, so a few drops of rain won't be a problem for us.' The curtains blew again, and Summer added, 'That feels wonderful compared to yesterday when there was no air at all.'

Hope responded with an inattentive nod.

'What are you looking at?' Summer followed her sister's gaze down to the ground where the crystal ball lay in the same spot as it had the day before, still partially covered by the surplus piece of velvet. 'You aren't seriously considering pulling out that ludicrous thing!'

'Of course not. My mind just wandered for a second.' Hope didn't explain that seeing the crystal ball had made her think of Larkin, which, in turn, had made her think of Dylan. She wondered if Nate had contacted Dylan and told him about the attack on Sean – along with the proposed plan for wine and a new lock on their gate that evening.

'Aren't you going to interpret hand shapes again?' Summer asked her. 'Those abridged palm readings were a big hit yesterday.'

'No, today it's going to be party Tarot.'

Summer gave a shout of approval and clapped her hands. 'Brilliant! Everybody loves party Tarot! They'll only draw one card?'

'They'll only draw one card,' Hope confirmed. 'I brought the grungy old deck that anybody can touch, so I don't have to worry about negative energy transferring to a good deck. And just as when I do it at parties, I've removed a few of the bleaker cards to keep things light. No Death or the Devil or their kin to upset people.'

'Brilliant,' Summer said again. 'When word spreads that you're reading the Tarot today, the line will be huge. People won't care what happens with the weather. They'll be too eager to draw a card.'

It took the sisters only a short minute to finish the necessary preparations for opening the booth. Summer once more picked up the gold-wrapped ticket box. Hope sat down at the table draped with the velvet cloth. And then the Tarot readings began, with the sequence of events similar each time: Hope shuffled the slightly reduced deck, the ticketholder drew a card, and Hope interpreted the card. It was easy and fun for everyone. Summer was correct in her prediction about the line for their booth and the worsening weather. The number of visitors didn't diminish even when the sky turned an ominous green hue. Thunder could be heard rumbling in the distance. The sole working strand of twinkle lights flickered precariously above their heads as though it might lose power at any moment. And the formerly refreshing breeze became mighty gusts. One squall was so strong that it grabbed the ticket box out of Summer's hands and blew half of the Tarot deck from the table.

'Let's take off the other cords,' Summer suggested, as they collected the stray cards before admitting the next ticketholder. 'That will close the curtains and block the heavier gusts somewhat.' She shivered. 'I'm almost a little cold.'

'Me, too. I was actually wishing that I had a sweater.'

There was a sudden swoosh as the remaining cord from the back curtains was removed and the curtain on the right side swung loose to match the one on the left. Both Hope and Summer jumped at the unexpected movement and whirled around. To their astonishment, they found Dylan standing inside the booth, holding the cord in his hand.

'You said that you were cold and wanted the curtains closed.' He tossed the cord on the ground.

'Good lord, Dylan.' Hope's startled heart hammered against her lungs, and she put a hand on the table to steady herself. 'Why must you continually appear without warning?'

'Why must you continually disappear without warning?' he rejoined.

She looked at him.

His lips curled with a rakish grin. 'It's particularly upsetting when you vanish while we're in the middle of something so pleasurable.'

No chilling wind could keep Hope's cheeks from growing warm. Dylan was talking about their kiss the night before.

'How long have you been standing back there?' Summer demanded.

The grin remained. 'Long enough to listen to some of your sister's purported Tarot readings. That last one was especially entertaining. The man's card was the Chariot – whatever that supposedly means – but Hope didn't tell him a single thing about it. Instead, the man spent ten solid minutes reminiscing with great nostalgia about his marvelous weekends forty years ago at his uncle's farm helping to change the oil in an old truck. He left your booth thinking that Hope had amazing otherworldly insight, and all she had done was smile and nod at him a couple of times.'

'Has it ever occurred to you that Hope does have amazing otherworldly insight?' Summer countered.

Dylan responded with an amused snort.

'Why don't you draw a card?' Summer challenged him. 'I dare you.'

There was another snort.

'Or better yet,' Summer amended, 'Hope can do a full reading for you this evening with a complete deck.'

'Summer—' Hope began to object.

Not letting her finish, Summer continued to Dylan, 'Are you coming to the brownstone tonight? Did Nate talk to you?'

'Yes, and yes,' he answered. 'That's the reason I'm here. Nate sent me to keep an eye on the two of you. He doesn't trust you to be careful. And for that matter, neither do I.'

'Nonsense,' Summer scoffed. 'Of course Hope and I are being careful. And even if we weren't, what could possibly happen to us here at the festival? It's the middle of the day with people swarming everywhere. Nobody is going to be able to sneak up on us without our noticing.'

'I was able to sneak up on you only a few minutes ago,' Dylan reminded her dryly. 'And you didn't notice a thing.'

'That's different. Hope and I were distracted by the wind and—'

Summer was interrupted by a flash of lightning, followed by a loud boom nearby. The remaining strand of twinkle lights popped and went dark. There was a momentary silence as everyone's eyes adjusted to the sudden gloom. Mimicking the color of the sky, the interior of the booth took on its own ominous green hue.

'Gram said from the outset that the booth should have a spooky atmosphere,' Hope remarked.

Summer chuckled. 'Even she would probably find this a bit too spooky. We need to fasten up the curtains again, although it won't block the wind as much. But it will let in some extra light. Otherwise—'

She was stopped by another flash of lightning and a rolling band of thunder. Large, heavy drops began to fall on the top of the booth.

'It sounds as though we're about to lose our customers to the rain,' Summer said. 'I'll check if anybody is waiting outside, or if they've all sprinted for the exit.'

Before she had taken more than a step forward, the curtains at the front of the booth started to move. There was a powerful gust of wind, and Morris Henshaw was propelled inside, the folds of velvet flapping wildly around him.

'Dang and blast!' Morris exclaimed at his contorted umbrella. 'That's the third time in three booths that you've turned inside out.'

He shook the umbrella, trying to flip it back to its normal shape, but he only succeeded in spraying the rest of them with water.

'I'll fix it,' Dylan volunteered.

'That's much appreciated.' Morris handed the dripping umbrella to his son. 'I didn't expect to find you here, Dylan. But I'm very glad to see you. The entire festival committee is presently running from booth to booth. We could use your assistance – and considerably younger legs.'

'What kind of assistance?' Dylan asked him. He gave the umbrella a sharp jerk, and it snapped back to its correct position.

Morris cast the umbrella an admonishing look as Dylan returned it to him. 'The National Weather Service has issued a severe storm warning for our area. We have been advised to shut down the festival immediately. Anybody who hasn't already left the grounds should collect their belongings and head to the main tent without delay. While not ideal from a protective standpoint, it's by far the sturdiest structure in the vicinity.'

'And you want me to help spread the word?' Dylan said.

'Yes—'

Morris was cut short by a howling wind that rushed through the booth, accompanied by a sideways shower of cold rain. One of the chairs at the table tipped over, and the oscillating fan tumbled backward with a crash.

Dylan turned to Hope and Summer, who were hastily laying down the other chairs to keep them from flying. 'Let's go.'

Hope shook her head. 'We'll secure what we can here first. We don't want things to blow away and cause damage or hurt anybody.'

'She's right,' Morris agreed. 'While they finish doing that, we need to warn the rest of the booths in this row.'

Dylan hesitated, his eyes on Hope. 'You'll come to the tent as soon as you're done? No dawdling or disappearing?'

Before she could answer, another blast of wind and sideways shower of rain whipped through the booth.

'We must hurry, Dylan.' Using his umbrella, Morris steered his son in the direction of the front curtains. 'The radar indicated only a small cluster of storms, but they're dangerously strong. We have to make sure that everyone is aware of the situation.'

The pair were about to leave when Morris abruptly turned back.

'I almost forgot,' he said. 'I ran into Randall White a short time ago.'

Summer and Hope stopped packing up the booth and looked at Morris in surprise. Randall White was Summer's lawyer for the divorce. He had come highly recommended by Morris.

'Randall said that you need to go to his office tomorrow,' Morris told Summer.

'I do?' She had shown no evidence of nervousness at the storm, but now her voice quavered. 'Is something wrong?'

'Apparently, Gary called Randall repeatedly this weekend and left at least half a dozen messages for him. I don't quite understand what it's about, and I don't think that Randall does entirely, either. Something to do with Gary not wanting to choose a new real estate agent, and he isn't going to sell the house, after all.'

'But he has to choose a new real estate agent!' Summer exclaimed. 'That's part of our agreement. And the house must be sold for the divorce!'

'Oh.' Morris frowned. 'Maybe I got hold of the wrong end of the stick. It was all very rushed. The wind and the rain were starting. I was racing in one direction while Randall and his family were racing in another. No doubt it will clear itself up tomorrow.'

With a swift nod in parting, Morris and his umbrella exited the booth, pushing Dylan out ahead of him.

'This is exactly what I feared would happen,' Summer moaned. 'Even though Gary is required to pick a new realtor, he won't do it. Instead, he'll drag his feet for as long as possible so that he can keep on living and partying in the house. Maybe Melody even encouraged him to act this way as part of her bizarre reconciliation scheme.'

Hope shook her head. 'I don't think Melody has anything to do with it. And also I don't think that you should worry too much about it at this point. You heard Morris. He didn't fully understand what Randall White told him. It's probably a mistake, and the message got muddled somewhere along the way. Morris might have even gotten it backward. Maybe Gary *has* picked a new realtor, and the sale of the house *is* proceeding.'

Summer responded by knotting her hands together fretfully.

'Don't worry,' Hope repeated, trying to be as positive as she could. 'You'll go to the lawyer's office in the morning, and it will all get straightened out. Right now, however, we really should head to the main tent.'

The storm intensified, shaking the booth violently. Water began to leak through every crack and seam. A fury of wind tore off a portion of the back curtain on the left side, leaving a gaping hole that was promptly filled by a torrent of rain. To avoid getting soaked, Hope and Summer dashed to the opposite corner.

'Forget the main tent,' Hope amended. 'We'll stay where we are. It must be safer than going out in the middle of—'

The sentence was left unfinished as the back curtain on the right side blew sharply upward. To Hope's astonishment, a figure seemed to be standing beneath it.

'Are my eyes playing tricks,' Summer said, apparently seeing the figure also, 'or is that a person over there?'

Hope squinted at the figure, but it was difficult to discern much more than an outline. Rain was sheeting down, making everything blurry, and the surrounding area was nearly as dark as night.

'Is it Dylan?' Summer asked.

'It must be him. He and Morris have alerted the other booths in the row, and Dylan came back to check that we went to the tent.' Hope shouted to him, 'We're not leaving! We're hunkering here. Hurry up and come inside before you get hit by some flying debris.'

The figure stepped through the remnants of the curtains and into the booth. A bright ribbon of lightning snaked across the charcoal sky, illuminating the person's face. In unison, Hope and Summer gasped. It wasn't Dylan.

TWENTY-FOUR

He was drenched from the rain. His hair was flattened against his head, his clothes were saturated, and there was so much water dripping from his face that his eyes appeared to be streaming tears. But he wasn't crying. There was no mistake about that. Gary Fletcher's expression was unambiguously cold and hard.

Outside the booth, the storm continued to rage. Jagged bolts of lightning were met by booming thunder. The wind roared, and the rain pounded on the earth. But inside the booth, there was an eerie silence. No one spoke. Gary didn't move or make any attempt to dry himself. His gaze was fixed on Summer with such intensity that Hope shifted uncomfortably. Any lingering doubts were gone. It hadn't been a mirage beneath the awning at Amethyst's booth or an optical illusion behind the flap doors of the tent. There could be no more strained excuses and tenuous explanations. Gary had been following Summer.

'Hello, Gary,' Summer said after a long, tense moment. 'What are you doing here?'

Her voice held a forced friendliness. Gary's tone was not as cordial.

'Morris Henshaw should mind his own business,' he growled.

Summer cast her sister an apprehensive look. If Gary had heard the conversation with Morris, then he had also heard Summer's subsequent remarks accusing him of dragging his feet on choosing a new realtor so that he could keep living and partying in the house.

'You don't need to go to Randall White's office tomorrow,' Gary informed her. 'You can call and tell him that his services are no longer required.'

'But why,' Summer began in confusion, 'would his services no longer be—'

Gary cut her short. 'We are not selling the house.'

There was a pause, then Summer's words came slowly as though she was choosing them carefully. 'If you'd like to stay in the house for a while longer – or even permanently – I'm sure that we can work something out. The lawyer could come up with an arrangement that would allow you to—'

Again Gary stopped her. 'I don't need "an arrangement" to be allowed to live in my own home. And I have every intention of staying there permanently – with *you*.'

Stunned, Summer stared at him.

Hope wasn't nearly so startled. She had previously wondered whether Gary might be using the house as a way to hold on to Summer and prevent their divorce from being finalized. But she was quite certain that a violent thunderstorm was not the best time to commence a debate over Gary's marital infidelity and Summer's resultant lack of interest in continuing their relationship. Plus, there was a strange look in Gary's eyes that was beginning to make her nervous. The wind chose that moment to abruptly switch directions, and Hope used it as an opportunity to try to move off the subject.

'No doubt the two of you have plenty to discuss,' she said, 'but the booth isn't a good place for it, considering that the whole thing might be swept away at any second. It would be much better to wait until—'

'Stay out of this, Hope,' Gary snapped.

She responded with an acquiescent nod. His behavior didn't seem to be entirely rational, and she didn't want to provoke him further. On the contrary, Hope had the distinct feeling that she and Summer should get away from Gary as soon as possible, even though that required leaving the booth during the middle of the storm.

'Of course, you and Summer need to make your decisions together, without influence from me or anyone else. But right now, you're soaked to the bone, and Summer and I are getting pretty wet ourselves from the blowing rain.' Hope nudged her sister with her elbow, trying to give her a hint to play along. 'We really should go somewhere dry and warm before we all end up with pneumonia.'

Summer must have understood the plan, because she wasted

no time in adding, 'You're shivering, Gary. I can see it. That isn't healthy. You've always been susceptible to sore throats and coughs.'

'I'm fine,' he replied brusquely. 'And you're fine, too. Nobody will end up with pneumonia or any other ailment – not unless you make me mad.'

Hope and Summer exchanged a glance. What did that mean?

'We are *not* selling the house,' Gary repeated with emphasis.

'All right,' Summer answered quickly. 'We won't sell the house. Problem solved.'

'Davis Scott wanted to sell it. He said I had to move out.'

'Yes, well' – Summer used her mildest, most appeasing tone – 'you don't have to move out anymore.'

'Damn right I don't have to move out! I told Davis I wasn't leaving, and he told me I had signed the listing contract requiring me to follow through. Except that wasn't our agreement! The listing contract wasn't supposed to be real, and the house wasn't supposed to sell. But Davis had gone to your shop with that dippy girlfriend of his. He saw the brownstone, and that altered everything.'

Hope and Summer exchanged another glance. Davis's interest in the brownstone had been a problem from the very first moment that he had mentioned its potential sale and the attic had expressed its displeasure.

Gary began pacing back and forth in front of them, clenching and unclenching his fists. 'Davis thought that if he could sell the house, then afterward he could convince you to sell the brownstone. The brownstone was the big prize for him. But I didn't care about the brownstone. All I cared about was the house! I explained that to him again and again. He just laughed and said I should be smarter and less sentimental. I was here, by the booth, when Davis came out in a huff the other night. His girlfriend ran after him, but she was limping and couldn't catch up to him. While she was hobbling around looking for him, her dog's bandana got snagged on the edge of a post and came off. After she turned around to go back to your booth, I went over and picked it up.'

An icy shiver crawled down Hope's spine. Had she heard him correctly? If Gary was the one who had picked up Percy's missing bandana – or, more accurately, Percy's missing scarf – then that meant Gary was the one who had . . .

Summer must have come to the same ghastly realization, because all the blood drained from her face. 'My god, Gary,' she whispered. 'What have you done?'

'I didn't mean to do it!' he cried. 'I followed Davis to give him the bandana for his girlfriend and explain once more that I didn't want to sell the house. But he was in a foul mood and wouldn't listen to anything I said. He started cursing and told me I should quit being stupid. He was sitting on the edge of the carousel, leaning against one of the horses and smirking at me. No matter what I did, he wouldn't stop smirking! I got so mad. We argued and fought. I don't know how it happened. Suddenly, he was dead.'

Hope shuddered. Summer drew a ragged breath.

'I didn't mean to do it!' Gary cried again.

His words had a pleading quality, as though he was a child seeking forgiveness after having accidentally damaged the neighbor's fence with a ball or trampled the prized tulip border with his bicycle. The difference was that the fence could be mended and the tulips would regrow the following spring. Davis Scott could not be brought back to life.

Gary continued pacing in such an agitated manner that he didn't notice the cord that Dylan had removed from the back curtain and left lying on the ground. His foot stumbled over it, and he stopped to look down at it. Hope and Summer looked at the cord also, and it instantly brought to mind the matching cord that they had discovered so horribly wrapped around Sean's neck that morning.

'And Sean?' It was Summer's turn to plead, asking Gary to deny it, not wanting him to be responsible for the attempt on Sean's life, too. 'Why go after him?'

'Because he saw me,' Gary admitted bluntly. 'Sean saw me follow Davis to the carousel.'

Reaching down, Gary picked up the cord and whipped one end of it against the side of the booth in frustration. The motion was so sharp that the cord snapped back against his arm, slicing open the skin. Bright red blood rushed to the surface of the cut. And then Hope saw the cut on Gary's other arm.

Unlike Melody's wrist, Sean's elbow, Stanley's knee, Amelia's palm, and even Jocelyn's finger, there was no bandage covering it. Although the blood on the old cut had clotted, the wound was raw and visibly irritated, indicating that the spot had been injured more than once over the past few days. There could be no doubt. That cut was the source of the blood on the carousel platform, and the gate in the garden, and the cord that had been used to strangle Sean.

Gary whipped the cord against the side of the booth again, this time with considerably more anger than frustration. His demeanor began to change, too. The child-like angst and beseeching for forgiveness vanished. Gary's expression became just as cold and hard as when he had first entered the booth. He pushed the damp hair back from his forehead and turned to face Summer.

'This is your fault,' he said.

Summer's mouth instinctively opened to argue, but she caught herself.

'Without you, I never would have known what Sean saw. Without you' – Gary's voice rose – 'Sean wouldn't have realized it himself. But then you decided to tell him that I was following you. And Sean – like Morris Henshaw and Randall White and all the others – couldn't mind his own business. He told me to stop. He told me that I should leave you alone. And I told him that he should keep his filthy hands off you.'

A slight protest now emerged from Summer's lips.

'Don't pretend that it didn't happen,' Gary spat. 'That was something *I* saw. You and Sean looked awfully cozy sitting together in the tent, laughing and drinking and flirting. You seem to have forgotten that you are *my* wife!'

Gary took a heated step toward Summer, and Hope hastily took her own step forward in an attempt to calm the situation.

'It was the same with Dylan,' she said quickly. 'Dylan misinterpreted what he saw in the tent, too. But Summer and Sean weren't flirting. There was nothing romantic about it at all. Sean was sharing a sad story about his sister and nephew—'

'I told you to stay out of this, Hope,' Gary barked.

'Yes. I just wanted to explain—'

'I don't need you to explain anything regarding me or my wife. I've tried to be patient. I know how fond Summer is of you, so I've restrained myself up to this point. But no more! I've warned you, and I won't warn you again. I warned Sean, too. And he didn't listen. He had to go running to Summer. He wanted to tell her what I had said and what he had seen. I couldn't allow that. When I caught him creeping into the garden at the brownstone last night, it made me mad. *Don't make me mad!*'

His eyes bulged with fury, and his face was almost as red as the blood dripping freely from his arm. Hope didn't dare to utter a syllable or even draw a breath. The storm was gradually moving away. The rain had slowed, and the thunder had dimmed to a distant rumble. But one peril had been replaced by another. Instead of a flood or a lightning strike, there was Gary.

He snarled at her for a moment longer, then his focus returned to Summer. 'I don't want to hear any more about Sean!' he commanded her.

Summer was wise enough to nod without dispute.

'And tomorrow you're moving back to our house.'

She nodded again.

'There will be no divorce. There will also be no further complaining about . . .'

As Gary began a list of decrees, Hope tried to figure out how she and Summer could get away from him. The first option was to run. She looked around. The walls of the booth were tilting on every side, and the back portion of the makeshift ceiling was in the process of collapsing. The twinkle lights and curtains were tangled together. Chairs and debris were strewn around. The booth was an obstacle course, and it seemed unlikely that they could navigate it successfully before Gary realized what they were doing.

The second option was to sit tight. Sooner or later, someone would come to the booth to check on them. But Hope didn't know when that would be, especially considering that she had no idea how the conditions were on the rest of the festival grounds. Gary was already dangerously unstable. It wouldn't take much more for him to completely lose control. She and

Summer couldn't simply bide their time and wait for an eventual rescue. They had to act to protect themselves now.

She looked around again, searching for a potential weapon. Nothing of use was immediately visible. The table was too heavy. The chairs were all still in one piece. The curtains were too soft. And Gary was in possession of the loose cord. There was a soggy cardboard box in the corner that had the possibility of containing something helpful. Hope took a slow, cautious step toward it, assuming that Gary would remain concentrated on Summer. She was in error. He instantly interpreted her movement as interference.

'How many times do I have to tell you to stay the hell out of this!' he bellowed at her.

Before Hope could respond, Gary charged forward and flung her to the ground. She slid across the wet grass and slammed head first against a leg of the table.

'Hope!' Summer cried.

'Don't worry about her!' Gary shouted, spinning back toward his wife. 'Worry about yourself . . .'

Hope didn't hear the rest. She was too dazed. Her head hurt, and her vision was blurred. There was a warm oozing on her brow. Lifting her hand to touch it, she felt something sticky. When she looked at her fingers, they were covered with crimson. She tried to stand up, but her limbs didn't seem to comprehend her brain. She half sat, half leaned against the table leg, dizzy and unstable.

Gary was yelling ferociously, and Summer was replying in a quiet, fraught manner. All the words sounded garbled to Hope. But she understood their import. There was no longer any way to placate Gary. Summer was going to feel his full wrath.

Her hazy mind struggled to think. She blinked hard, trying to clear her foggy gaze. And then she saw it. The crystal ball. Although its velvet cover had blown away during the storm, the crystal ball hadn't budged an inch from where she had deposited it on the ground the day before. It wasn't far from her. She might be able to reach it.

Gary was approaching Summer, the cord grasped tightly in his fists. Summer was backing away from him, her hands raised defensively. Gary was going to strangle Summer the same way that he had strangled Sean and Davis Scott.

Hope stretched out her arm. With crimson fingers, she took hold of the crystal ball. She knew that she only had one chance. If she threw it and missed, Gary's rage would be deadly. With supreme effort, Hope struggled to her knees. She lifted the crystal ball, directed her aim as well as she could, and hurled the missile with all of her might.

The crystal ball struck Gary on his left temple. His head snapped toward her, venom in his eyes. He started to turn, tottered, and, a moment later, crashed to the ground. For a few horrible seconds, Hope thought that she might have killed him. With immense relief, she watched Gary's chest rise and fall. He was insensible but still alive.

Summer collapsed in a tearful, exhausted heap. Hope sank back down against the supportive leg of the table. The sun broke through the last remaining clouds. A songbird twittered high up on a wire. Steam rose all around them as the cold rain evaporated from the warm grass.

Hope didn't know how long they sat there. And then, suddenly, they were no longer alone. Dylan was beside her, examining her head and asking her a flurry of questions. Somebody – was it Nate? – was talking to Summer. Other people seemed to be scurrying around. One of them called to Dylan, seeking his assistance with Gary. Dylan declined, but the person pressed him.

Dylan looked at Hope questioningly. 'You'll be all right? I'll only be gone for a minute.'

'I'm fine. Check on Gary.'

'You're sure? You won't—' Dylan hesitated.

Hope smiled. 'I won't disappear,' she promised him.

M

11-22

EMMA S. CLARK MEMORIAL LIBRARY
SETAUKET, NEW YORK 11733
To view your account,
renew or request an item,
visit www.emmaclark.org